S'MORE THAN A FEELING

Blueball Band of Brothers # 2

MARIKA RAY

S'more Than a Feeling

Copyright © 2023 by Marika Ray

This book is a work of fiction. Names, characters, places, and incidents are products of the author's imagination or are used fictitiously. Any resemblance to actual events, locales, or persons, living or dead, is entirely coincidental.

First Edition: August 24, 2023
Cover Model: Travis
Photographer: Lindee Robinson
Cover Artist: Jennifer Olson

Ebook ISBN: 978-1-950141-62-3
Original Paperback: 978-1-950141-63-0
Special Edition Paperback ISBN: 978-1-950141-64-7

I think I just slept with Mr. Perfect. Too bad he turned out to be my brother's best friend.

The tattooed stranger rode a motorcycle while helping me collect stray cats. My boots gave me blisters and he carried me on his back. I needed help and he didn't ask questions before assisting me. Could there be a more perfect man? It just made sense to lick him and claim him as mine right then and there.

I probably should have asked him more questions before we slept together.

Like, what's your last name? Where've you been living before moving here to my hometown? Is my older brother your best friend?

You know. Those kinds of questions.

But sadly, I didn't. And now I'm staring at two pink lines and Mr. Perfect is nowhere to be found, leaving me brokenhearted and on my own. Even though I love my son with every fiber of my being, he's also a daily reminder that I've made the worst mistake of my life.

It's only years later when Mr. Perfect shows up in town again that I begin to see that I was never in love with him back then.

But I might be now.

CHAPTER ONE

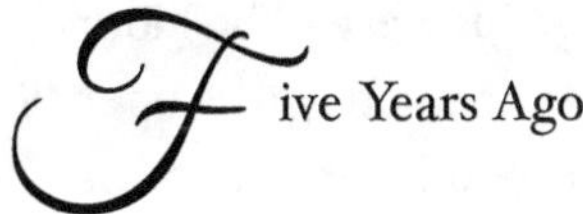ive Years Ago

Keva

"OH MY GOODNESS, Miss Lucy is going to kill me!"

I didn't have much time to make things right. Despite the tough-as-nails narrative men had been screaming from the cave-top since the dawn of mankind, their damn swimmers were fragile little fuckers. One degree north or south for a minute too long and they went belly up.

I held the little plastic cup in a nondescript bag as far from my person as I could manage while hustling down the road in my brand-new boots. They'd looked as cute as an Instagram influencer when I tried them on, but unbroken leather, plus a bit more than a kitten heel, and I was liable to pitch face-first into a ditch before I got to Main Street and found someone to hitch a ride with.

"Damn car. I swear that piece of shit is going to be the death of me." The scrub oak tree off to the left didn't answer, but I could have sworn she nodded those branches in agreement. She'd been witness to no less than four breakdowns on this road either coming or going from my job at Coastal Fertility Clinic.

I'd been trying to do something nice by insisting Lucy go home early to her precious kiddos and hot-ass husband. Transferring this sperm sample to the larger bank in San Jose for further testing that we didn't have the equipment for was on my way to the fancy restaurant my single friends and I wanted to try out tonight. Friday night in the city, baby. The perfect way to find a man. A man *not* from Auburn Freaking Hill, aka Hell. I may live here now, but my heart still felt at home in the big city.

The echo of a door slamming had me jumping, the newly formed blisters on my heels groaning in protest. The door to Yedda's National Cat Protection Society gaped wide open, a sight that would terrify anyone from around here. Cats of all sizes and colors streamed out the doorway, their noses in the air, smelling the natural odor of freedom.

And then the odor of freedom hit my own nose. "Oh dear God!" My lip snarled up so violently, my eye started twitching. Holy rotten eggs. That had to be a stink bomb. Nothing else could make that nasty of a smell.

"Get back here, my darlings!" Yedda exited the building and waved her spindly arms in the air, spinning left and right, probably uncertain of which direction to go. The cats had scattered far and wide, all one hundred of them choosing a different path to freedom.

"Need some help?" I called out across the street, forgetting about my own situation. I could tell, even from a distance, her thoughts were frantic with worry over her cats. I didn't go around bragging about it, but I had a highly accurate telepathy. Came in handy with tricky relationship situations when I could read the other person's mind. Not so great when I got the real scoop on what someone thought of my new pants. Guess they did make my butt look fat.

Yedda's head whipped over and she smiled that famous smile of hers. Even in the midst of chaos, she could spare a smile for someone else. "Oh, hi there, Keva. I seem to be having some problems here."

I walked across the street after looking both ways. Kinda silly since there wasn't much traffic along Brinestone Way late on a Friday afternoon. Yedda squinted her eyes and watched the last of her precious cats run all the way down the street to the famous roundabout. Hopefully they could navigate it better than Peggy Sue, the old lady who frequently found herself going round and round until her steering fluid ran dry.

"I see that. What happened?" It was fairly common for a cat or two to escape, but all of them at once? That was a new one. I fluttered my hand in front of my face. The stench was stronger on this side of the road.

Yedda's brightly colored lips opened and closed a few times before she started talking. "Well, I thought Poppy was delivering the mail. The little flipper-flapper thing on the front door flapped and in popped a little package. I went over to investigate, but then tripped over Frankie and ended up stepping on the package. The damn thing popped and out came a stench that seared off my eyelashes. I stumbled and grabbed the doorknob to keep from going down, but I guess the door opened and my poor kitties shot right out while my eyes were stinging. They didn't care for the stench either."

My head bobbed in sympathy. Her thoughts were scattered, but she kept coming back to one thought fragment that left me puzzled. But hey, "no judgies" was my motto when it came to mind reading. "Well, don't you worry, Yedda. I'll help you collect the cats and get you back to that porno you intended to watch this evening."

Yedda's head swiveled so quickly, I thought it might just twist right off. "Well now, I hadn't thought about that, but maybe that could spice up my Friday night plans after poker night with the girls." She patted my cheek. "Such a thoughtful young lady."

I smiled warmly at her, feeling better now that I'd laid her worries to rest. I gave her a confident thumbs-up and hightailed it out of there. I had cats to wrangle and sperm to deliver. Several yards away from the Society, the air cleared and I could take a full breath again. Okay, new plan. I'd put the sperm back in the temperature-controlled chamber at the fertility clinic and collect cats. Then I'd go back and get the sperm and get it over to San Jose. If I hurried and the cats somehow came willingly, I could still make it before closing time.

I put the sample back and texted Lucy to let her know what had happened with the cats. I'd just locked up the fertility clinic again when a guy with a black helmet peeked around the corner of the building, looking in the direction of the Society.

"Can I help you?" I demanded, hands on hips to look intimidating.

Probably would have been more effective if I'd been taller than five foot two.

The man startled and nearly tipped over. His denim-clad legs straddled a tiny banana-yellow scooter, the windshield of which did not come up high enough to protect his face. His bright blue eyes went wide underneath the black helmet.

"Uh. Yeah. I'm new in town. I was looking for Main Street?"

Oh, heavens. That voice flowed over me like warm butterscotch. Based on the thoughts running through his head, he most definitely didn't find my ass too big in these jeans. His thoughts were practically indecent, but maybe that was just me thinking a little too hard about the tattoos covering his forearms or the way his T-shirt spread across his thick chest. I wanted to be straddled like that miniature scooter.

"Ma'am?"

I blinked hard and tried to corral my thoughts. "Oh, yes. Well, this is Brinestone Way. Classic mistake, really. That roundabout sucks people in and spits them out in all kinds of directions. Main Street is that way." I pointed to the right, trying to be helpful. I pushed out my chest, shamelessly trying to get a ride. "Any chance you can give me a lift to Main Street? I need to rally the troops to collect those cats and then hitch a ride to San Jose."

He gave me the once-over, and if I wasn't completely insane, his eyes heated a few degrees. He nodded once and I walked over, my boots no longer even touching the ground. As I came up along the scooter, I realized the ride-along idea might not be suited for this vehicle.

"Um, is there room?"

The man looked down, like he'd forgotten his own stead. "Oh, shit. Yeah. Sorry. My Harley is in the shop. This was their only loner."

He swiveled and joined me in eyeing the tiny patch of black vinyl behind his own seat. That little cushion was definitely telling me my ass was too fat. "Uh, maybe I'll just call a friend instead."

"Nah. We can fit. It's only a couple miles, right?" He patted the cushion and smiled.

It was the smile that did it.

I was a sucker for a good smile, and boy did this stranger have a smile that could melt panties right off. If I was wearing any. Shh. That was my little secret. They said wearing sexy underwear made you feel more confident, but I found going commando was the real way to feel like you could kick some ass. At least I saved time and embarrassment from having to dig the cute thongs out from between my cheeks.

I lifted one heavy leather-booted foot and straddled the baby beast. The tilt of the seat meant I slid right into the man, my crotch now glued to his impressive backside, sending off a fireworks display of tingles in my nether regions.

"Oh!" I exclaimed on impact, wrapping my arms around his waist before I could talk myself out of it. Oh no. The man had abs. Hard ridges of muscles that lay just below my hands.

He chuckled, more of a vibration than a sound. But Lordy, did it do wonders between my legs. How the hell did I end up on the back of a scooter, smacked up against some tatted-up biker dude who hadn't even given me his name? My brain scrambled and I said the only thing I could think of.

"Does this mean I'm your ol' lady now or is that not applicable for scooters?" In my defense, it was the only biker slang I knew.

He chuckled again, harder this time. I rode out the vibration by squeezing my eyes shut and trying to focus on the cats that needed rescuing. He revved the engine to life and off we went. The poor little scooter couldn't go very fast, and I could have sworn the added weight of my person was causing the back end to ride a bit low. We nearly bottomed out when we went around the roundabout and hit a pothole.

"Oof!" I hollered in his ear by accident. Damn. My butt would be sore for days when I got off this thing. "Over there!" I pointed to the right, where Main Street branched off from the roundabout.

Our scooter cut across the other lane, earning us a honk from Clyde the tow truck driver I would be calling later, who'd just entered the roundabout and was in no danger of hitting us. Damn guy just liked to honk at people. I risked a glance around the broad shoulders of my stranger and saw a cluster of people forming in the middle of the street.

"Stop!" I shouted, seeing that the cavalry had already arrived.

The stranger pulled over and shut off the scooter. He got off, standing impressively tall, extending his hand to help me off. His palm held calluses on top of calluses. Clearly, he worked with his hands. I only tripped once getting off, those strong tatted arms supporting me and giving me butterflies at the same time.

"I see my boss, Lucy, over there with her husband, the prison warden. They'll get the crew together and we'll round up the cats. Thanks so much for your help." I smiled up at him, my lashes doing a bit of a dance. What could I say? My lashes liked to flirt a little.

"I'll come with you. I know Bain."

Again, with that voice. Did he practice talking like he drank whiskey all day long? Maybe he did commercial voiceovers in his spare time? He could sell me anything, anytime with that voice. If I'd had panties, they would have been wet with longing.

I stuck my hand out, nearly jabbing him in his washboard abs. "I'm Keva, by the way."

He paused, his eyes crinkling at the corners before he took my hand in his. "Linc."

"Oh!" Even his name was sexy. All that lash flirting and all I could come up with was a lame response.

"Keva?" Lucy called my name, interrupting the deep staring going on between me and my new obsession, Linc.

I spun and walked over to the group, seeing that Lucy had gathered up her whole crew of friends. Lenora held baby Star, who fussed for her favorite blankie, zero interest in the cats running around down below. Jayden juggled Red in his arms, a full-grown toddler so big he only needed one well-placed kick and he'd be set down to run amok with the cats. Bain stood there glowering with Roxy on his right and Heston on his left, both clinging to his hands and trying to tug him in the direction of a darting cat. A very pregnant Amelia was already running across the street, chasing a cat who'd dared rub against her black leggings and left a swath of hair behind. Titus had three cats in his arms, running after Amelia, telling her to be careful. Charlie sat cross-legged in the middle of Main Street with his arms wide open, charming the cats to come sit with him. Crazy enough, it was working. At least twenty cats sat on their haunches, mesmerized by their new guru.

"Thanks for letting us know about the cat dilemma. We should have them wrangled shortly. Finnie has a whole load already in the back of her truck. She's heading over to the Society now to drop them off with Yedda. I've got some catnip in the back of Bain's truck." She paused and her gaze went over my left shoulder. "Hey, Lincoln. Welcome to Auburn Hill and all our craziness!"

Linc and Lucy hugged. I'd never been so jealous of a hug.

"Hey, man, did you do it?" Bain's voice rose over the cacophony of toddlers whining.

Linc brushed a hand over his chin, obscuring the smile I'd come to obsess over. There was dirt under his short nails, and normally that would turn me off, but something about Linc getting messy with his hands made my insides ignite and melt.

"Maybe," he hedged.

Bain tossed his head back and roared with laughter, clearly in on a joke the rest of us weren't. "That's awesome. Mission accomplished, bro. Now let's clean up this mess."

Lucy and I looked at each other with raised eyebrows. Sounded like Bain was up to one of his stupid dares. Lucy finally shrugged and tossed the keys to Bain's truck at me. Linc snatched them out of the air.

"I've got this. Hop in, Keva."

Didn't have to tell me twice. I sprang into action so fast my boots creaked at the sudden change in direction. I hopped into the passenger side of the truck and directed Linc around town as we found cats and put them in the back of the truck. We were at max capacity and heading back to the Society to drop the critters off when I saw one last kitty roaming the side of the road, just barely out of the flow of traffic in the roundabout.

"Over there!" I shouted, pointing.

Linc yanked the wheel and cut off Poppy in her mail truck in the inside lane. She stuck her hand out the window and gave me a rude gesture I won't describe. Linc hit the brakes and Poppy veered around us, barely missing clipping our back bumper. She pulled to a stop while I hopped down from the truck, gaze laser focused on the poor kitty shaking on the curb. Although on further inspection, the cat looked surprisingly pink and not very catlike.

"What in Sam Hill is going on around here?" Poppy demanded from behind me.

I ignored her and crouched down to croon to the cat that probably wasn't a cat. "Hey, pretty little thing. Are you lost?"

The lump of pink with black spots shivered and then let out a mighty snort. She lifted her head and I saw a snout. "Oh my God! It's a baby pig!"

Poppy leaned over my shoulder and almost made me squish the pig. "First there are cats all over the place, and now this. This town is going to hell, I tell you!"

I reached out and let the pig sniff my hand. She didn't shy away, so I attempted to pick her up. She came willingly and even quit shaking as I held her to my chest. Poppy's hands went to her hips, her eyebrows drawn together like she hated pigs. How could anyone hate an adorable mini pig?

"I shall name you Spunky," I declared. Spunky let out a pig squeal and her thoughts smoothed over me like liquid love.

"Is that thing from the Cat Society too?" Linc asked, arms crossed over his chest, the sun sinking into the background behind him, lighting him up like a dark angel sent to earth to lure women with his good looks and charm. Good Lord, that man was a fine specimen.

"Well, hello there, Mr. Handsome. I'm Poppy Strauss. Mail carrier by day... Well, I can't tell you what I get up to at night." Poppy winked lasciviously at Linc.

Poppy was flirting. With my man. Well, not my man, but more my man than hers.

The mini pig gently snorted, and I couldn't have agreed more. The sight was highly disturbing. Linc smirked. I had to hand it to him for not cringing or outright laughing. I mean, Poppy wasn't a day younger than sixty and poor Linc here was probably only mid-twenties. She was barking up the wrong tree, though I kind of understood. That kind of prime man candy made a woman go a little batty.

Linc unfolded his arms in slow motion and reached out, wrapping his arm around my shoulders. He gave me a yank and suddenly the mini pig was pressed between our two chests, bleating out a warning signal at the change in cabin pressure. Linc's head tilted down and blotted out the sunset. His lips hit mine and I forgot to breathe. There was nothing shy about the way he plunged his tongue into my mouth, eating me up before I even realized what was going on. My head spun up to the skies and I began to shake at the sensations pinging through my extremities. He was warm and tasted like that peanut butter whiskey I'd recently discovered.

"Got room for a third?" Poppy's loud voice interrupted my best kiss ever.

Damn, that woman was bold.

And also, ew.

I swallowed hard as Linc reluctantly looked up from my face, his lips wet. "We got the pig and three's all we can handle. Sorry."

And then he was on me again, his teeth nipping at my lips, his hand dipping down to grab my ass. The squished mini pig's snout came up to bop me under my chin, but still, I didn't lean away from that kiss. The whole town of Hell could go up in stink bombs and I'd be right here, fusing my lips to this dark stranger with the banana-yellow scooter and the abs I could count through his T-shirt. I shifted as close as I could get without climbing inside his skin, catching a faint whiff of rotten eggs. I had a sneaking suspicion Linc caused the cat kerfuffle, which I normally would have protested, but he had helped clean up the mess.

And the resulting escaped cats and a spoiling sperm sample had brought us together.

"That's okay. I have plenty of toys from the Hardware Store."

Linc broke the kiss looking confused. I grimaced, knowing exactly what Poppy was referring to and, quite frankly, I didn't need to know about Poppy's sex toy hobbies. Linc's warm hands let me go, leaving both me and mini pig whimpering. Poppy cleared out and we hustled back to the Society before all the cats finished with the catnip in the back of the truck and realized we were delivering them back to Yedda.

The whole gang stood there when we pulled up. Yedda was counting each of her babies and Hazel made sure they got extra wet food tonight as a reward for coming back home. We stood in a circle, chatting, the warm presence of Linc right behind me more distracting than the way Yedda knew each cat's name without looking at the collars. Linc breathed on my neck and I couldn't help the goose bumps. He brushed his hand against my hip, and I begged the universe to make everyone disappear.

"Dude, what happened to your bike?" Bain asked Linc, clearly done with the cat business.

"In the shop." Linc shrugged and I could feel it since he was standing so close.

Bain chuckled. "Aren't you a mechanic?"

Linc straightened and my ears perked up. Yeah, what did Linc do for a living? And why was he in town? And was he dating anyone? The kiss said no, but then again, that might have just been to get Poppy off his tail.

"I work on planes, not motorcycles, man. Minor repairs I can do, but not the big stuff. Some asshole hit me on the road last week and I was lucky to walk away with both nuts intact."

Nuts. Sperm. Oh shit!

"Lucy!" I called to her across the parking lot where she was trying to get Roxy to put down the cat she was hugging like she intended to take it home. Her head popped up as I checked my watch. "I forgot to come back and take that sample to San Jose. They close in like twenty minutes."

Lucy grimaced and I felt awful. I told her I'd take care of it and now I'd let her down. Oh no, she was already thinking of firing me, I could just tell.

A warm hand hit my back and the shiver told me who it was. "I can take you."

I looked over my shoulder to see Linc's disheveled brown hair and concerned blue eyes. "Yeah?"

He smirked and dipped his head. "Yeah. Hop on." His hand swept over to his yellow scooter with the helmet hanging off the handlebar. Apparently, the gang had brought it back for him.

"Um, not to look a gift horse in the mouth, but will that thing get us there?" I wanted nothing more than to be pressed up against Linc's fine body for the next twenty minutes, but not if it meant dragging ass all the way to San Jose. My self-esteem couldn't handle it.

He frowned at the scooter. "It's a fifty-fifty chance."

I paused and then shrugged. "Good enough for me!" I ran toward the clinic next door, careful not to jostle Spunky more than necessary. "Let me just get the sperm!"

"The what?!" Linc yelled back at me.

Oops. Probably should have told him we'd be transporting some poor guy's sperm along with Spunky. Hey, if Linc couldn't handle a little spunk and a mini pig named Spunky, he should just bail now.

I came back out of the clinic holding both, wondering if Linc would have hightailed it out of there.

Instead, he was standing next to his scooter, the black helmet extended out to me, a leather jacket making him look even tougher than before. He rolled his eyes, but the smirk was there.

"Everyone told me things might get crazy if I moved to Hell, but I hadn't expected crazy to be a hot girl with a pig and some sperm."

"That's how we roll!" Amelia hollered at the top of her lungs. Everyone else hooted and hollered, and if the cats weren't traumatized before, they were now. Damn, I loved my town.

I bit my lip and climbed on the scooter.

Linc called me hot and liked my crazy.

And if I got really lucky, maybe he'd find out later tonight that I didn't wear underwear...

incoln

BAIN HAD WARNED me moving to Auburn Hill, aka Hell, might be a culture shock, but I'd welcomed it with open arms. Lord only knew I needed something very different from what I'd experienced for the past eight years. If I spent one more day in the damn desert, living on base with a bunch of assholes who I loved and fought with like brothers, while trying to keep my cool in combat situations no human should have to see, I'd do something crazy just to get myself dishonorably discharged. Thankfully, I'd kept my shit long enough to leave at the end of my second tour with my honor still intact. Settling in a small town like Auburn Hill sounded like paradise.

Of course, my buddy Bain, a guy I'd grown up with but lost touch with when he went to college and later I went into the military, hadn't made things easy. He'd insisted that the only way to be accepted by the other guys in town was to pull a prank on my first day. I knew all about friendly hazing from my first year in the Army, and I wasn't about to let some pussy prison warden get the better of me. 'Course, I didn't realize until it was too late that I was pulling a fast—and stinky—one on an old lady. That didn't seem so honorable to me, but then again, I hadn't lived as a civilian in a while.

"Make a left here," came the feminine shout in my ear.

I blamed that whole "not a civilian" thing on how I already had a hot girl on the back of my bike on day one in Hell. She could have been a serial killer for all I knew, but something about the way she'd cradled the mini pig to her gorgeous breasts made me think the closest she got to a serial killer was watching a detective show on Netflix while she squeezed her eyes shut with dread. She'd flashed those blue eyes at me and suddenly I'd found myself offering to drive her all over the damn state with a fucking pig tucked into my leather jacket.

I made the left into a parking lot, the ridiculous scooter I'd been loaned making a groan that spelled future disaster if I didn't give it a break soon. The stamp of Keva's breasts, which had been plastered to my back for a solid twenty minutes now, left me feeling cold as she unwound herself from me and hopped off the bike.

Without a word, she ran to the building, intercepting a man leaving out the front door and trying to lock it. She jumped up and down, a wince with every movement. Normally, I wouldn't have noticed, but I found myself studying her intensely, trying to figure out what it was about her that had me giving a shit about her job instead of worrying about my own ass. The guy's shoulders dropped, but he let her back into the building where she was gone for a few minutes. I checked the gas gauge and thought we might have enough to make it back to Hell. If I had to, I'd get her home while carrying her on my back. Anything to keep her plastered against me.

Damn, I really needed to get laid.

How long had it been? I searched the night sky, jumping at every little noise, and there were a lot of them here in the city. Another reason Auburn Hill had sounded like paradise. Quiet. I needed a place to call home and the little town, set right along the ocean, seemed like just the right therapy for a guy like me. A guy I'd served with for the last few years, and also my best friend, would be joining me next week on his quick leave. Figured I'd scope out the town and create a homebase for whenever he was discharged too. We hadn't said it out loud, but I think we were both looking to use the other as a crutch, afraid we wouldn't blend back into civilian life. At least if we crashed and burned, the other person would be there to clean up the mess.

"I can't thank you enough for hauling me all the way out here." Keva stood to my right, startling me.

I hadn't even heard her approach, which was highly unlike me. Horns and chatter a street away had distracted me.

"No problem." The words tumbled out, both of us knowing it *had* been a problem. First the cat roundup and then the drive completely out of my way on the lamest transportation I'd ever had the unfortunate luck to drive.

Keva's lips curled into a small smile. I liked how she'd painted them red before she'd come back out of the fertility clinic and climbed on my bike. Almost like she'd taken a moment to spruce herself up before riding with me. Like she wanted to impress me. Consider me impressed.

"I was planning to meet some friends here..." She trailed off, biting that bottom lip I'd already gotten a taste of.

Fuck. What was it about this young woman that made my gut clench? I should let her go and drive straight to the new house I'd rented. My focus needed to be on building my new life, not trying to get in the pants of the first girl I saw. Although her pants did look mighty fine on her ass.

She frowned. "You don't like animals?"

I tilted my head, wondering where that came from. I had her damn pig stuffed in my jacket at this very minute. "Uh, no, actually. Animals are fine."

Her face cleared instantly. "Oh, sorry. Sometimes my mind

reading is off when I'm distracted."

There was a lot to unpack there. I'd start with the obvious. "You can read minds?"

She blushed, looking down at the toe of her boots before looking back at me, defiance straightening her spine. "Some people think I'm crazy, but I really can read minds."

I'd seen some crazy-ass shit in my time, along with learning to trust my gut more than a multimillion-dollar piece of equipment. If my gut said run, I ran. That sixth sense had saved my life on more than one occasion. Who was I to judge this woman's intuition, even if she called it mind reading?

"I don't think you're crazy," I said simply. She grinned so wide, I thought of what else I could say to get her to flash me another one. "Now what's got you distracted?"

She shrugged and it made her breasts bounce. I was a bastard for noticing, but cut me some slack. I hadn't seen breasts on the regular for eight years. I was basically the sexual maturity level of a teen boy. Her grin turned positively flirty, pushing her wide grin out of first place in the list of best grins on the planet.

"I was distracted by you and this whole macho-man-in-a-leather-jacket thing you got going on," she practically purred.

My chest puffed up with pride under her lustful gaze. The pig must not have liked that as it stuck its head out above the zipper and snorted. Fucking mood killer.

"I'm glad you see beyond the banana-yellow scooter and the mini pig carrier."

She did a little eyebrow waggle. "Just adds to your charm."

Instinct told me to go for it. "Wanna grab a bite to eat and head to my place?"

Keva didn't even answer me. She just swung her leg over the scooter and wrapped herself to my backside, her hands danger-ously close to discovering that I was packing more than a pig underneath these clothes. I had a raging hard-on that seemed outrageously out of place when the pig let out another snort and stomped her back foot right on the goods.

The tiny engine firing to life drowned out my groan. The mini pig was trying to cockblock me from her new mama, but she didn't know who she was messing with. Staff Sergeant Lincoln Angelo didn't stand down at the first sign of adversity.

However, the second sign of adversity came much quicker than I thought when the little-scooter-that-couldn't up and died right in the middle of the road a mile or two outside of Auburn Hill city limits.

"Oh no!" Keva climbed off, pulling the helmet off her head, hair flying everywhere. I wanted to smooth it down and then wrap it around my fist and drag her to my house. "Linc?"

Her gaze flew to me, trust shining there that I would know what to do about this turn of events. I climbed off too, kicking the yellow bastard for good measure. It let out a groan, then a puff of gray smoke from the tiny engine before tilting in slow motion and eventually settling on the gravel to the side of the road.

No use trying to get that thing to come back to life. I trusted my own two feet more than that heap of metal. I made sure the pig was secure in my jacket and turned my back to Keva, crouching down. "Hop on."

"What?" Her startled response had me wondering what type of men she'd been hanging out with here in this little town.

It was beyond obvious her feet hurt in those stupid boots that hid her calves. The leather was new and the wince with each step was a dead giveaway. I thought I could live to a hundred and still not understand why women wore ridiculous shoes they couldn't walk in.

"You want to walk the whole way in those boots?" I asked over my shoulder.

Her cheeks went pink, but I had to give her credit for not arguing and postponing the inevitable any longer. She hopped on my back and I settled her legs around my waist before I took off down the road at a fast clip.

"You're going to carry me all the way home?" Her lips

brushed my ear as she spoke, the intimate contact causing a need to swell up in me so fiercely I briefly considered pulling off into the trees and having my way with her right then and there. I gritted my teeth and trudged on, picking up my pace.

"I've carried heavier rucksacks for days on end in the desert. Pretty sure I can handle a mile with you and the pig."

"Hmm," she rumbled. The heat of her on my back made me break out in a sweat. Not from exertion, but from the sheer willpower of not spinning her around to my front so I could taste those lips again, pig be damned. "Does that mean you're in the military?"

"Was," I bit out, not wanting to get into that right now. No offense to the pretty girl on my back, but the spark of attraction I felt for her was just that. A spark that would flare hot tonight and then burn out by morning. Talking about my time in the military was not part of the deal when I suggested dinner at my place.

Keva remained blessedly silent the rest of the way to the little house I'd rented. Once inside, I put her down and handed over the pig who'd somehow fallen asleep while I walked.

"Be right back." I left her in my living room without even a chair to sit in. Several cardboard boxes kept her company while I headed to the kitchen to pick up the phone and dial for pizza takeout from the only pizza place that showed up on the map on my phone. Half meat lovers, half cheese in case she was some crazy-ass vegetarian. I pulled open the fridge, happy it worked and even happier to see a six-pack of beer in there. Bain would be getting my thanks later.

"You really are new in town, aren't you?" Keva's voice came from the living room the minute I hung up the phone.

I found her spinning around, taking in the house I'd rented, sight unseen. Bain had checked it out for me and given it his stamp of approval. That was good enough for me.

"Yeah. Moved here today, in fact."

Keva spun back to me, her painted mouth making the cutest

little "o" as she stared at me. "You moved here today, and you just spent four hours helping me round up cats, save a mini pig, and give me a ride to the city?"

I shrugged like it was no big deal and it wasn't. I didn't have a job lined up yet, so why not spend the day with a pretty girl? Keva's eyes darkened and she didn't take them off me as she set the pig down on the ground. She bit her bright red bottom lip and that thread of lust that had been there all afternoon exploded into an inferno.

"Keva," I warned as she sauntered around me in a full circle, her finger tracing along my chest, my arm, my back, and around to my chest again.

She went up on tiptoes and whispered in my ear, "We have twenty minutes until the pizza is here. What can you do to me in twenty minutes, Linc?"

All the blood in every vein and artery in my body converged in my dick the very moment she took her lips away from my ear. I didn't wait a single second to outline what I could do. I'd bet a hundred dollars I could get at least one orgasm out of her in twenty minutes. Failure was not an option.

Bending down, I picked her up and threw her over my shoulder in a fireman's carry, hustling out of the living room and into my bedroom. Fortunately, I'd thought ahead to have a mattress delivered and it was waiting for us on the floor. No sheets or a headboard, but at least her back would be against something soft when I pounded into her. She squeaked when she landed on the mattress, the noise turning into a giggle. I tugged on her boots hard, sliding them both off at the same time and tossing them over my shoulders. Next up were the jeans practically painted onto her gorgeous body. She lifted her hips to help me while sitting up to whip her sweater over her head. She lay back in a black bra, which wasn't lacy or racy in any way, but even so, I didn't think I'd ever seen anything prettier in this whole wide world.

"Fuck, Keva," I grumbled out loud, taking her in and

wondering how the hell I got so lucky on my first day in town. Looked like things were finally turning around for me.

"Yes, please!" she said enthusiastically and then giggled some more.

Remembering the time constraints, I grabbed my shirt behind my head and pulled it off. The jeans and boots could wait. Fuck, she was pretty just lying there, wiggling on the bed. I sniffed, smelling her perfume and the faint trace of her arousal that permeated the air. The growl that crept up my chest and out of my throat was unavoidable, born from years of pent-up frustration. I shoved her knees apart far rougher than I should have, and I could have wept at seeing her bared before me. Fuck, I loved pussy.

Kneeling between her legs, I dove in, swiping up her slit and tasting her like a starved man. She gasped and squirmed, but I couldn't stop or ease her into it. I buried my face between her thighs and lapped at her, using my chin, my thumbs, and my tongue to make her moan. I was ravenous. Two seconds after I focused on her clit, she let out a shriek. I settled a hand on her stomach to keep her from vibrating right off the mattress, not stopping for even a breath as she rode out her first orgasm.

"That's one," I rasped.

"Ohh."

I smiled smugly and crawled up her body, reaching around to unclasp her bra while she tried to catch her breath. When her eyes fluttered open, she smiled at me and I just knew I could get another from her before the doorbell rang.

Ignoring the pain that came from behind my zipper as I plowed ahead with providing her so much pleasure she'd scream my name, I cupped Keva's cheek and kissed her. She tasted like caramel apples and magical unicorns, which meant she tasted like nothing I'd tasted before. She exuded happiness and joy, even in her kiss. When her tongue darted out to tease mine, I slipped my hand between her legs and caught her gasp in my mouth. I smiled against her lips, feeling like the most powerful man in the world for making her writhe and gasp and sigh beneath me.

Two fingers slid inside her tight, wet body. Her breasts rose up into the air in invitation as her back bowed off the mattress. I latched on to her left nipple, giving it all my attention as I slid back out of her and then back in, setting a fast pace I knew she could handle. Her hands tried to grab my hair but it was cut too short for her to find purchase. Instead, she cupped the back of my head and held me against her. As if I had any intention of leaving these breasts anytime soon. A third finger joined the first two and Keva began to chant.

"Linc, oh, Linc," she gasped.

That was it. Just a little more and she'd be screaming it. I moved my head to her other breast, gently biting, sucking, and flicking her nipple with my tongue. My thumb found her swollen nub and worked her over in rhythm with my fingers. Her mouth opened and closed, her eyes squeezed shut tight. A couple strands of dark hair lay across her face, stuck to the fine sheen of moisture she'd worked up. I thrummed across her clit one more time and she did it.

"Linc!" she screamed, nearly dislodging my hand between her legs as she rammed her thighs closed.

Fuck, yeah. Still got it.

She grabbed my face and pulled me to her in a messy kiss. Her legs trembled, and I felt her tighten around my fingers. She groaned again, this time into my mouth. The doorbell rang out, making her pause before relaxing bonelessly back onto the mattress.

"Oh my God, Linc," she whispered, staring up at me like a sex god. I could get used to that look aimed in my direction.

I smiled, even as I had to grab my dick through my jeans and tell him to settle down. We had pizza to eat, and then maybe, if the lady indulged me, she'd let me sink into her heat all night long.

"Stay there." I pressed a quick kiss to her mouth and reluctantly left her, hoping I could get the beast to stay down long enough to answer the damn door without embarrassing myself.

I swung the door open, with a twenty-dollar bill thrust forward. "Thanks, man..."

I trailed off, seeing a familiar woman standing on my doorstep. A rather large, retirement-aged woman. In a U.S. Postal Service uniform. Holding my pizza. And eye-fucking me.

Whoa. That tamed the beast all right.

"Looks like you got started without me!" she trilled.

"Poppy, right?" I put two and two together, remembering the way I'd kissed Keva just to avoid this woman earlier today. Maybe my luck wasn't turning around after all.

"I was finishing up delivering mail when I saw the pizza guy roll up." She wiggled her eyebrows and it did not do the same thing to my insides as when Keva did it.

I leaned against the doorjamb and smirked. "You always deliver pizza in your off hours?"

She thrust the box at me, which had my mail stacked on top, and snatched the twenty out of my hand. "Only when I get a half-naked man answering the door and new gossip to spread. Welcome to Hell, Lincoln Angelo."

With that, she twirled around and two-stepped back to her mail truck to some country song in her head. She was an odd thing. Then again, Bain had warned me about this town.

"Linc?" Keva called from inside.

I shut the door and headed back into the bedroom, not wanting to waste a minute while I had Keva's scent all over me and her waiting in my bed. Maybe she'd let me eat the pizza off her bare stomach just so I could ogle her boobs while I ate. There she was, sitting up on the mattress with paper towels spread out for our dinner and clad only in her birthday suit. She smiled up at me sweetly despite being completely naked. Fuck. I could marry this girl.

Sitting across from her, I placed the box down in the middle of the bed and moved the mail onto the floor. "Meat or cheese?"

Her smile turned devilish. "Give me all the meat," she practically growled.

My stomach clenched, and even though I'd been hungry an hour ago, I didn't particularly care if I ate a damn thing tonight. Keva bit into a slice of pizza and gave a little moan of appreciation.

"Stop it."

She stopped chewing. "Excuse me?" she said around a bite of food.

I wolfed down a half a slice of pizza. If we had to eat, I'd do it quickly so I could get back to the good stuff. "You can't moan like that or I'll throw this pizza out and slide inside of you before you can swallow your bite."

Her eyes widened and her breasts began to heave as her breath sped up.

I shoved the rest of the slice in my mouth and threw the box on the floor. She squealed as I lunged for her, holding her slice above her head out of harm's way. I caged her in with my arms and legs, crawling up her body, kissing and tasting along the way, making sure I paid equal attention to every square inch of her. When I got to her breasts, I cupped them in my hands and squished them together so I could taste them, one right after the other. Mmm...pizza and hot woman.

"Lose the pants, Linc," Keva whispered hotly.

About fuckin' time. I climbed off of her again and stood. "Lose the pizza," I responded, hand hesitating on the button of my jeans. Keva's eyes dropped to my hand. Then she tossed the piece of pizza over her shoulder, letting it splat somewhere on the floor behind the mattress. Okay, then. I'd have to clean that up later.

I popped the button and unzipped my jeans, pulling my boxers down with them and kicking them off my feet. Keva licked her lips and kept her gaze trained on my cock. I dropped to a knee and grabbed a condom out of my wallet in the back pocket of my jeans. They were from my last two-week furlough in the States about a year ago. I'd only gone through two of them in those two weeks, which was a crying shame. I rolled it on and braced myself over Keva. She spread her legs and let my hips nestle there.

"I don't know how gentle I can be, sweetheart," I managed to say. I wanted to be honest with her because she lived up to the nickname. I also wanted to see her again, despite my initial thoughts of just one night together.

Her eyes went soft and she cupped my face. "I won't break."

My hips had a mind of their own, like some sort of heat-seeking missile, plunging forward and lodging my cock inside of her before she'd even quit speaking. My blood pressure soared at the intense pleasure, the way her pussy seemed to suck me in and hold me there. To my embarrassment, my arms began to shake. I pulled almost all the way out and thrust back in, the mattress moving an inch across the floor.

"Yes, Linc, give it to me." Keva kept her hands on my face, her eyes widening with each thrust and her mouth dropping open. She didn't let me go and I didn't want to be anywhere but staring right down into her pretty face as I fucked her into stunned silence. She felt like heaven, if the place was a constant orgy with no end in sight. I could die right here on top of Keva's body and have zero regrets.

My pace increased to the point I knew it couldn't be pleasurable for her. I couldn't seem to stop myself. My body needed to fuck the dark past out of my system and Keva was the unfortunate willing party. She gasped over and over and I got off on each little puff of air until a wave of pain and pleasure hit my balls so hard I couldn't breathe. I shuddered and thrust, my seed spilling from me like a geyser that had been bottled up for centuries. In the back of my brain, I knew I should have somehow pulled back and waited for the lady to come first.

"Linc!" Keva screamed in my ear, her teeth biting down where my neck met my shoulder. Her hands left my neck to scrabble across my back, clutching and scraping my skin.

I kept thrusting in a desperate attempt to make it good for her, though my rhythm was now scattered to the wind. I felt no pain, only utter bliss as wave after wave of primal pleasure flooded my body and left me speechless. My hips froze as they ran out of gas and ground to a halt. Fuck. I dropped my forehead on the mattress beside her head, completely spent. I'd never come that hard before.

Sweat built up between our two bodies as we tried to catch our breaths. The second I felt like I could muster something passing for coordination, I pushed back up onto my elbows and gazed down at her. Her cheeks were stained red and more dark strands of hair stuck to her sweaty face. Her eyes were still closed, but her mouth was curved up into a dreamy smile. I felt ten feet tall knowing I'd been the one to put it there.

Already formulating a way to see her again with what little brain power I had left, I pulled out and rolled next to her. Her eyes popped open and I braced for the regret to surface on her face.

"I could so use some pizza right about now," she said, then turned her head to wink one pretty blue eye at me. She sat up and scooted over to the side of the mattress, stealing my Army T-shirt and putting it on.

I took a little longer to recover. Maybe because it had been so long for me since I'd felt the warmth of a woman who giggled and smelled good and made my eyes roll back in my head. Even watching her eat pizza in my T-shirt was turning me on. I gave her a few minutes before reaching for her again, needing a second piece of her before I could think about food, but the doorbell rang out.

I groaned and swiped a hand across my face. "I'll get it."

Rolling off the mattress, I got to my feet and grabbed my jeans off the floor. A slap echoed through the empty room and then my ass cheek lit on fire. Keva had fucking slapped my ass. She gave me an impish grin and kept right on eating. Instinct had me wanting to tackle her and doubly repay the slap on her gorgeous ass cheeks, but the doorbell rang again.

I growled instead and headed out of the room to get rid of whoever was interrupting my first night with a woman in ages. Ripping open the door, I already had my mouth open to tell them I wasn't buying anything and to get the hell off my property. But then I saw who it was.

"Tank? What the hell are you doing here, man?" I stood frozen, my brain scrambling to figure out why my best friend was already here when he wasn't due until next week.

His face split into a smile I'd seen a million times right before he did something reckless that had me scrambling to save his ass. "They started my leave early, so I drove all day to get here."

He stuck his hand out, and after I blinked myself out of my fog, I reached out to grab it, going through our special handshake.

"Today's a good day to mess some shit up," he said on a wink, repeating the line we'd said almost every day we were deployed together. Nothing like a little pep talk with your boys to chase away the nightmares.

"Fuck, yeah," I said, pulling him inside the house and slapping him on the back.

"Boston?" came Keva's voice from behind me.

I spun around, my hand still wrapped around Tank's. She had on my T-shirt, looking better in it than I did and leaving her curvy legs bare, which I appreciated. Her hair lay down her back, tangled like she'd gotten good and fucked recently. Even her red lipstick, now fuzzy around the edges, seemed to scream sex.

"Annabel?" Tank asked, tensing beside me.

"Who's Annabel?" I asked, feeling like I was missing something.

"What are you doing here with Lincoln?" Tank asked, ignoring me.

He pulled his hand from mine and a sliver of unease shot up

my spine. Something wasn't right. How did Tank know Keva? And why was he calling her Annabel? The only Annabel I knew of was Tank's kid sister.

Oh. Fuck.

My gut clenched tight, and I blew out a strained breath. There were some lines you never crossed with your brothers, and I was pretty sure I'd just trampled right over the very thickest of lines with my dick out. Shit, shit, shit.

Tank's gaze took in Keva from head to toe before swinging back to me with thunder and lightning and clear understanding streaking across his face. His meaty hands balled into fists, and I knew they itched to pound my face.

I pointed at Keva, making sure to step away from Tank. "You said your name was Keva."

She put one bare foot on top of the other and folded her arms across her chest, which was a good idea considering her nipples were poking through the thin cotton. "My name *is* Keva. Keva Annabel Mooney. And this is my brother, Boston. How do you two know each other?"

Tank took a step toward me and I didn't back away this time. I'd slept with his baby sister my first day in town. He and I both knew you fucked the first willing girl on leave and never thought about her again. No amount of telling him how much I liked Keva and wanted to keep seeing her would change his mind.

I deserved whatever I had coming.

"He's my staff sergeant and best friend," Tank ground out between his clenched jaw.

"Oh, shit," Keva whispered, finally grasping the gravity of the situation.

Oh, shit was right.

Tank's arm cocked back and I winced, refusing to even block him.

Keva screamed and then pain bloomed across my face.

CHAPTER THREE

eva

"Look. I don't want to talk about him anymore. I just want to forget about him. He doesn't exist in my world. Okay, Jenika?"

I shoved my cell phone between my ear and my shoulder as I ran around my tiny apartment above Coffee on Main Street. I'd lucked out getting to rent this place when I came here two years ago at the tender age of eighteen. I think the owner took pity on me and gave me the place just because I was so pathetic with my story of woe. Dead parents, a nasty uncle who had custody of me for exactly eight months before I aged out, and a big brother off in the military. I'd made the seven hundred square feet a home though and Miss Lucy had given me a job at the fertility clinic I'd come to love.

"I thought you said he ruined all men for you after your one day together," Jenika reminded me, doing what friends do: call you on your shit.

I snorted, pulling on a pair of black pants that looked mostly clean. "He did ruin me for all men, just not in the way I thought."

Jenika snickered and then shouted at me to hold on while a train went by. I took the twenty seconds to toss the phone on my bed and pull a blouse over my head. A quick dash of lipstick and I was ready to head out the door. Oh wait. Shoes. I grabbed the phone, shoved my feet in my favorite black flats, blew a kiss to Spunky in his play pen, and headed out the door in the hopes of grabbing a cup of coffee before walking to work now that my car had died for the last time.

"Okay, I'm back," Jenika said.

I rolled my eyes and trampled down the stairs. "You really need to move out of that place. A train every hour on the hour? Just move here already. I promise you'll fit right in with these weirdos."

"Hey!" Dante, the hot guy my age running the cash register downstairs in the coffee shop, handed me a steaming cup of coffee just the way I liked it. I lifted on tiptoes and kissed his cheek. He winked and I knew he wasn't mad about my weirdo comment. Hell citizens thrived on being weird. They wore it like a badge of honor.

"Actually, I was thinking of moving once my lease is up next month."

I squealed at that news and then darted behind the corner of the diner when I saw a familiar head of hair getting out of a parked truck. My heart raced and I held my breath.

"Hello?" came Jenika's voice in my ear.

"Hold on," I whispered, daring to dart a look around the corner a moment later and letting out a sigh when Linc wasn't anywhere to be found. I wasn't sure if I was relieved or sad. What was he doing waltzing around my town when he should have been headed to my place to make things right between us? "Okay, I'm back."

I put my head down and rushed down the sidewalk, intent on

reaching the clinic without seeing that asshole. I just wanted to be someone's priority. Was that so much to ask?

"Were you just doing your ninja thing to avoid him again?" Jenika asked on a sigh. "You know, with all the darting around you'll have to do in that small town to avoid him, maybe you should move back here."

"Nah, I love my job and it's really not that hard to avoid him. It's been two days and I haven't bumped into him once," I stated proudly, always the optimist.

"Yeah, but you haven't even talked things out with your brother and you have to slink around like a thief. Seems to me like maybe you should either smooth things over or think about moving out of town just for some peace."

Jenika was always the voice of reason in our friendship, which made it even harder to be two hours away from her. I reached the clinic and put my key in the door to open up the place before the first client arrived.

"You might be right about moving, but I was here first," I whined.

"Okay, then smooth things over with him."

I dropped my bag on the front desk and hit the power button on my computer. "Yeah, no. Boston beat the shit out of him and he just took it." The skin on my arms broke out in goose bumps just thinking about it. "You should have seen it, Jenika. Linc just let Boston hit him until blood flew and splattered the shirt of his I was wearing. I've never seen something so horrible and all my fault on top of it. There's no way I can smooth things over, trust me. It's best I just pretend Linc and I don't know each other."

Jenika huffed, but left it alone. She was thinking of the entire forty-eight hours I'd spent crying in my tiny apartment, sniffling into the phone when she tried to talk me through it and refusing to let her take time off of work to come console me. Even Spunky hadn't been able to cheer me up. Jenika had assured me it wasn't my fault, but I'm pretty sure no guy deserved to have the crap beat out of him simply for sleeping with me. I was an adult for crap's sake, and that's exactly what I'd told Boston when he'd tried to talk to me with his knuckles all scraped up from Linc's gorgeous face. I was officially no longer speaking to Boston, which sucked because he would be going back to his base in just a few days and I wouldn't see him again for who knew how long.

Linc, on the other hand, didn't even try to talk to me again. Either to apologize for ending our night together in that manner or to beg me to take him back. Okay, that last part was just what I dreamed about when it was late at night and I couldn't sleep. But he hadn't even tried to talk to me. Sure, it wasn't even a full day together, but I thought we'd gotten along so well. I thought there'd been a spark there before my brother drove his fist into Linc's eye and Boston threw me in his truck to drive me home. However, Linc must not have thought so because his absence screamed that he was unfazed by the whole thing. He even had my clothes delivered to my doorstep the next morning without a note. Granted, he'd cleaned them, but no note was just rude.

Out of the corner of my eye I saw Lucy drive into the parking lot in her mom van. "I gotta go, Jen. Boss is here."

"All right. Call me later."

We hung up and I got busy opening up the calendar book for today to see what rooms I needed to get ready. Lucy swung the front door open with the bicep strength of a mom who'd carted little ones on her hip for a decade straight.

"Good morning, Keva!" she trilled with her normal enthusiasm, dumping a box on my desk and carrying another back to her office. "Will you stock the pregnancy tests for me?"

"Sure thing!" I hopped up and gave her a smile. Grabbing the box, I made my way to the bathrooms in the back of the clinic. As I bent down to put the tests in the proper bin in the cabinet, Lucy answered her cell phone loudly.

"What do you mean he left?"

I lifted my head and inched out into the hallway where Lucy

had her phone jammed between her shoulder and her ear as she dug through her huge purse.

"I thought he rented that house out on Sailview?"

My heart leaped into my throat. Linc had taken me to his house two nights ago. On Sailview Drive.

"Well, that's just rude. You went out of your way to find him a place and he just ditches everything after two days?" Lucy sighed. "I know. Civilian life isn't easy to adjust to, I just thought he'd try a little longer than two days."

I squeezed my eyes shut and ran out the back door of the clinic into the little patio area Lucy had built as an outdoor break room of sorts. Bending at the waist, I held myself with my hands on my knees, struggling to breathe. I couldn't feel the blisters on the back of my heels any longer. I couldn't even feel the anger about Linc not reaching out to me.

He was gone.

Just like that. As if I meant nothing to him.

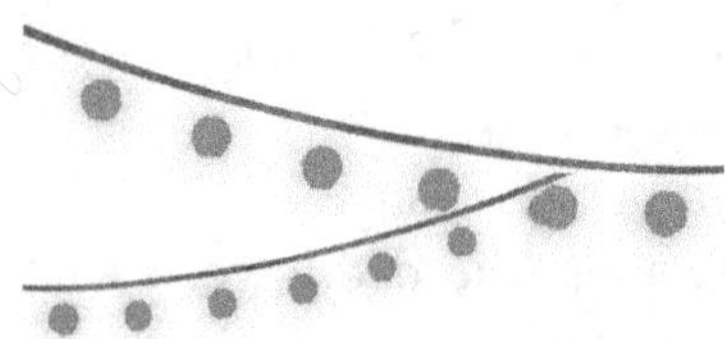

Boston: Answer your damn phone, Annabel.

Me: I'm no longer speaking to you which extends to text messaging.

> Boston: Don't be like that. I'm heading out today and it would be a good idea to talk before I go. We both re-upped for four more years, you know.

I rubbed my chest and tried not to let the hurt of that affect me. Linc had wanted to get away from me so badly he'd signed up for four more years in the Army. Hell, maybe the Army could use me as a recruiter. I'd have men flocking to join just to avoid me.

> Me: There's nothing to say. You don't trust my judgement even though I've practically raised myself. You've been gone, Boston. You don't get a say over what I do.

> Boston: You'll always be my little sister. I know what guys like Lincoln are thinking. You deserve better than that, so don't worry. He won't be bothering you again.

"Ugh!" I threw the phone down on the couch and paced my tiny apartment. Spunky pranced around my feet, snorting against my ankles as if she too was incensed by these pigheaded —no offense to Spunky—males trying to tell me what was best for me.

"How am I sad over a guy I barely knew?"

Spunky didn't answer me. I scooped her into my arms and stroked her short back. She head-butted me with her snout until we both got settled on the couch. I was no stranger to sadness and disappointment. You don't get through the death of your parents and then living with foster parents and an alcoholic distant relative who has zero ability to nurture without either sinking or swimming. And I was swimming, dammit. Like my life depended on it. Boston had escaped the grief that came after our parents died by going into the military, and while I may not have the medals or the scars to prove it, I'd become a badass in other ways.

I clicked on the television and let the mindless nature of it keep my thoughts from tripping over themselves. I could either let this latest experience set me back or I could put it behind me and learn from it.

Spunky let out the loudest snort I'd ever heard from her. I looked down at her cute little face and felt myself smile for the first time in a few days.

"I agree, Spunk. We're going to thrive. We're going to forget all about those men and live our best lives. Tonight, we wallow. Tomorrow, it's pedicures for both of us. How's that sound?"

She bleated over and over again while I giggled. I was still mad and sad and a host of other emotions I wasn't astute enough to identify, but I was going to put this all behind me and thrive. The next time I met a potential Mr. Perfect, I'd be ready for him and he'd be ready to man up and be with me no matter the adversities.

Quite frankly, maybe it was for the best. Linc clearly wasn't the man for me, and he'd done me a favor by leaving.

Yep.

Totally.

CHAPTER FOUR

$\mathcal{L}$incoln

THE POUNDING on the front door was nothing compared to the pounding between my skull. A black eye wasn't uncommon for me, but a black eye plus a hangover was. I didn't overindulge in alcohol much anymore. Figured I'd drunk my fair share my first couple leaves in the military and was making it up to my liver now. Well, before last night, that is.

Shit. I could barely remember last night. Pretty sure some grizzly guy named Nugget gave me a ride home and pushed me through my front door, where I'd fallen on the floor and spent the night.

"Open up, Linc!"

I squeezed my one good eye shut and even that movement hurt. "Go away." Shit. My voice came out softer than a girl's.

The door opened suddenly and it clipped my leg. Pain bloomed on my shin and made me forget about my headache for a second. "Oww..."

"Jesus Christ, you're a mess," Tank grumbled from somewhere up above me.

I wasn't planning on opening my eye anytime soon today. It had been approximately thirty-six hours since I'd last seen Keva, and if I couldn't gaze upon her full breasts, I wasn't inclined to gaze upon anything. Especially Tank's ugly mug.

Hands like vise grips grabbed me by the shirt and lifted me into the air. My one good eye shot open. Instinct took over and I made a wild kick in the general vicinity of Tank's crotch. It was a dick move—pun totally intended—but I'd already let him mess me up once. I wasn't in the mood to accept a second beatdown.

"Fuck!"

Tank let me go and I managed to stay on my own two feet. The room spun but I was made of tougher stuff. A little hangover couldn't keep me down, but the sudden nausea had other ideas.

"Oh shit." I ran from the room, pinging off the wall and then steadying myself as I reached the bathroom in time to puke. I flushed and then turned on the water in the sink. The reflection in the mirror was a shock. The beard that I'd shaved twice a day for years had started to grow out. My one eye was swollen shut and sporting some gnarly shades of blue. But it was my overall haggard appearance that had me straightening up and shoving down all the hangover symptoms. My head still throbbed but I'd suck it up and deal with it like a man.

I couldn't fail being a civilian already.

Needed to get my shit together. Quickly. Like, right fuckin' now.

I pushed away from the sink and headed back to where I'd left Tank doubled over and grabbing his junk. He tossed me a dirty look and stood up straight. We glared at each other for a while before Tank broke first. He patted me gruffly on the shoulder and shot me one of his lopsided grins.

"You look like shit, dude."

I slapped his hand away and returned the grin. "Fuck off. You're the one who gave me the black eye."

"Deserved it too."

I dipped my head, suddenly serious. "Yup."

"We gonna talk about it?"

I waved him toward my almost empty living room. "Sure. Have a seat on my new couch."

We sat on the floor with our backs against the wall. Tank was bigger than me by about twenty pounds but we were the same height. The guy was a beast, and there wasn't anyone else I trusted to watch my back. He'd been with me through some sticky situations, each of us counting on the other for our very lives.

Which made sleeping with his sister even worse.

"I'm sorry, you know. I had no idea or I never would have." Keva's name remained unspoken, but we both knew what I was apologizing for.

Tank stared at the opposite wall, his jaw flexing hard. "She's an adult and can make her own decisions." Then he swiveled his head and looked me dead in the eye. "I know you wouldn't have done that. Not on purpose. But I need you to leave her alone from here on out. Don't talk to her. Don't speak to her. Don't even look at her."

"We live in the same small town now, Tank." I hadn't thought this through—I was too busy acting out and moping about the whole thing—but I'd probably see Keva quite a bit in the coming days and months.

Tank pushed away from the wall and put his beefy fist in the center of my chest. "Promise me, Linc."

I was nodding before I'd come up with a plan. "Sure, man. I promise."

He pulled his fist from my chest and held out his hand. I shook it and it was as good as done. I wouldn't even acknowledge that Keva existed. She was just a girl. A hot, sweet, and funny one who'd turned my head for a day, but she didn't come before the guy who'd supported me in life-and-death situations over multiple years.

I said the first thing to pop into my head.

"I should probably move."

Tank frowned and dropped my hand. "Move? Where?"

I shrugged. "I don't know yet. Man, you should have told me your sister was here."

"I didn't know she was here. She was in San Jose last we chatted. I still can't believe she moved away from her best friend, Jenika."

I narrowed my eyes. He was always writing her letters when we were deployed. Seemed close. Shouldn't he have known she moved towns?

"Why didn't she tell you?"

Tank sighed and slumped back against the wall. "Annabel is a handful. You dodged a bullet, bro. She's stubborn and impulsive and not exactly happy I left for the military."

"I thought you said you needed out after your parents died? That you were acting out and going down a bad path?"

Tank nodded. "I was. Going into the Army saved me, but I left Annabel." His head dropped and I watched him struggle to take in a deep breath. "Never leave a man behind, right?" He lifted his head and looked at me. I nodded. "But I left my sister, and I'll have to live with that forever."

I could see from the slump of his shoulders and the lines between his eyes how much pain my friend was in. We all had baggage, some of us more than others. Tank's was heavy and nuanced and layered in repressed grief. You don't experience the death of your parents at age eighteen and not have scars from it.

As for me, my baggage was light and unimportant. I had a duty to help out my friend. With privilege comes responsibility, a phrase that had become the backbone of who I was as a sergeant in the Army.

I put my arm around his shoulders and squeezed tight. "What if we just go back in for another tour?"

Tank's head came up, hope shining in those eyes. "Really?"

I chuckled. He'd been begging me to stay in longer, but I'd wanted to try my hand at civilian life. Turns out I was shit at it. Day one and I'd already fucked up royally. Maybe another four years would make the difference.

"Sure, why not? Let me place some calls and see what I can do. I don't want to go overseas, but maybe some other part of the country would work."

Tank and I went out for food, settling my stomach and reinforcing my plan. By the time we came back to the house, I'd made the call, had a new assignment for us on the other side of the country, and found a little storage place to house my shit. It was only when I lay on my mattress that night, staring up at the ceiling and inhaling Keva's scent that was still clinging to the room that I began to doubt my plan.

I'd only had a taste of civilian life, and while I'd had the time of my life, I'd fucked it up. Keva was probably pissed at me. Understandably so. Probably thought I was using her, just like Tank had claimed.

She didn't know that I couldn't stop reliving those precious hours together. Couldn't stop thinking about the way her smile could calm my racing thoughts. Couldn't stop wondering what we could have become if she hadn't been Tank's sister.

I flipped onto my side and tried to find a comfortable spot. It was a good thing I was leaving Hell. There was no way I could live here and not search for her in a crowd. Seek her out. Try to talk to her. Get her to smile at me just one more time.

She was like a sunny day to a guy who hadn't come out of his dark cave in years. I craved her.

Only space and time would get her out of my system.

A lot of space and a lot of time.

eva

"KEVA, HONEY? YOU OKAY?" Lucy's voice came through the bathroom door, laced with motherly concern. I couldn't blame her. I'd been puking every morning for a week now. The stomach virus I thought I had should be gone by now, but it hung around like BO in a subway.

Which was why I had a pregnancy test in my hand, my whole arm shaking with nerves and nausea.

"I'm good. Be out in a second!" I called back, amazed I had a voice at all.

I couldn't catch my breath. I couldn't even blink. I just stared at that little stick and watched a second line slowly appear and get darker with each passing second.

If I thought I was done puking for the day, I was dead wrong. I buried my head in the toilet and offered up the contents of my stomach and possibly my spleen and kidneys too. When I had nothing else left to give, I sat my ass on the floor, swiping at the sweat on my forehead, and trying to corral my racing thoughts into something that made sense.

I was pregnant.

At twenty years old.

My head dropped to my arms and I held myself in a ball. Maybe if I held myself together physically, I could hold myself together emotionally too. I heard the door crack open, but couldn't find the energy to lift my head. Lucy's perfume hit me a second before her arms came around me.

"It's okay, Keva, honey. Don't cry." She rocked me like I wished my own mother would, offering me comfort that had nothing to do with her being my boss. I already loved working for her, but this moment would crystalize my love and respect for Lucy Sutter. "It's not the end of the world, I promise you that."

I wasn't sure how much time passed, but she eventually got me to my feet, helped me wash the mascara off my face, and cancelled all the appointments for the day. She gave me the crackers she had in her bag—probably for one of her kiddos—and stayed by my side in her office until I got a handful of them down.

"Alright. Would you like to talk about options or just take a few days to think about it all?" she asked kindly.

I put the bag of crackers aside and took a steadying breath. "Can a brain completely rewire in the span of a day?"

Lucy smiled softly. "I think so. People's lives can change on a dime. We adjust and find our happiness where we can."

I found myself nodding along. It certainly felt like my world had changed on a dime. My hand found my stomach before I realized what I was doing. It felt the same. Not quite flat, a little soft, and definitely warm.

"I'm keeping the baby," I whispered to the world at large.

Lucy reached forward and held my other hand. "Okay, then. I know you don't have a lot of family, so if it's okay with you, I'd like to be your family. Your support system."

Her soft smile went wavy and the tears were back, streaking down my cheeks and splashing against my blue blouse. I nodded and she carried on as if I wasn't losing my shit in her office and she had no obligation to help me like this.

"First things first. Let's get you set up with a great doctor. Mine is fabulous and I can call and get you an appointment. Then I'd like to see if we can trade in your car for a new one. That thing is a turd on wheels. Not dependable enough for a pregnant mama."

I swallowed hard. This was a lot and I knew I had so much to deal with to make sure I could provide a life for this little one of mine. Yet my brain kept going back to Linc's face when we were eating pizza together. The way we'd smiled at each other and I'd felt like I'd found my person. Perhaps I'd gotten that all wrong. Maybe he wasn't my person but he had to step into my life briefly to give me my person. My baby.

"My car is fine, I'm sure." I stood, letting go of Lucy's hand. I needed some time to think. Make a list. Plan out a budget. Tell my friends. Find a way to make some money so I could afford all the bazillion things a baby would need. Was there a market for pregnant strippers?

Lucy stood up too, putting her hands on my shoulders. Her face was stern. "Congratulations, Keva. You're going to make an amazing office manager."

"Huh?" It was official. I'd puked up my brains along with other essential organs. Her words didn't even make sense.

Lucy smiled. "You've been promoted to office manager, which comes with a really nice raise. Plus we have an extended maternity leave and the finest medical insurance. You go home and rest, and I'll get the paperwork together." She turned back to her desk. "Effective immediately, by the way."

My chest squeezed hard with emotion, and I didn't think I had words left to speak. "Lucy..."

She winked. "Go home and rest up. I'll call you later to check in."

I didn't even feel my feet as they walked down the hallway. I did, however, remember to dart back into the bathroom and snatch up the pregnancy test. I tucked it into my pocket and looked down at my flat stomach.

"It's you and me, baby," I whispered, nearly choking on the words.

I'd give myself today to cry and feel sorry for myself. I'd wallow hard. I'd eat all the ice cream and go through every box of tissues I had. I'd mourn the loss of Linc and the life I thought I'd have for myself.

And then tomorrow, I'd lift my head and carry on like I always did.

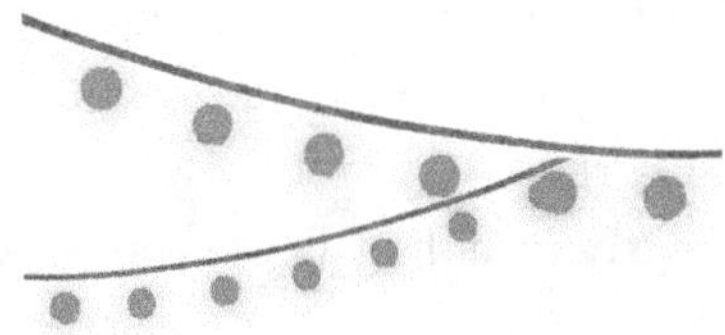

My feet were killing me. And my hips. And my back. Dear God, my back. I honestly thought the sleepless nights would come when Lucas was a newborn, but they were already hitting and I wasn't due for another two weeks.

"Take it easy on my bladder today, okay, kiddo?" I rubbed my belly as I searched for my flip-flops. I'd given up on regular shoes. My ankles had apparently decided that cankles were the wave of the future. My baby shower was today and I wanted to enjoy it. I'd spent most of this pregnancy battling tears at night, anxiety every single day, and feeling like I'd be a failure as a mother. I wanted little Lucas to have the best of everything and I wasn't sure I was it.

"We're here!" Audrey sang from my front door.

I rushed out of the bedroom. Well, rushed as fast as a nine-months-pregnant woman could. It was more waddle than run.

"I'm so excited!" I squealed, seeing my three friends crowded in my doorway with blue balloons, platters of food, and festively wrapped gifts. "Come in, come in!"

They put everything down on the table I'd pushed into the living room last night and then came to give me hugs. These three women had become my besties over the last nine months. We'd been heading toward a good friendship before I became pregnant, but once I announced it, they'd flooded into my life to lift me up and help me through. Lucy had become the mentor and bonus mom I never knew I needed, while these three bitches had become my support group. Sadly, Jenika had begun to call less and less. Funny how a life crisis could ruin some friendships and build others.

"Knock, knock." My neighbor, Janice, poked her head in the door.

I waved her in and waved away the waft of cigarette smoke. Janice lived in the other half of this duplex, a retired widow who spent her time smoking out on her patio because she had nothing else to do. Her words, not mine. She'd already offered to watch Lucas whenever I needed the help. I didn't think I'd need a babysitter for awhile—since Lucy had already given me three months off of work after he was here and offered a bring-your-baby-to-work office policy—but I appreciated the offer.

"I'm just going to say this now and will then forever hold my peace." Paisley settled her gaze on me and I prepared myself. She didn't mince words, a trait I usually appreciated. "Do you think you should tell Boston about the baby?"

I sighed and sank into the rocking chair I'd bought just last week, trying to get comfortable when there was eight pounds of baby stuck under my ribs. My brother was a touchy subject for me. I wasn't happy with him in general. Even before the Linc incident. He'd always been so much older than me. Six years was an eternity when you were kids. When Mom and Dad died, he'd left abruptly for the military, leaving me behind. I'd bounced from foster home to foster home, before being placed with a distant relative. An alcoholic relative. To say I had abandonment issues was an understatement.

"Last time I saw Boston, he was punching the father of my baby in the face. I think it's best we leave him out of the equation. When he finally gets discharged, maybe I can have a serious conversation with him then."

Marlo sat on the armrest of the chair, looking serious as always. "We just want you to have family around to help out so you don't have to do everything yourself."

I patted her leg. "Everyone in this room is my family. You're all Lucas and I need."

And that was the truth. They'd all helped me move to Blueball when staying in Hell became too painful. I saw reminders of Linc everywhere, which usually led to an emotional spiral that ended in tears. Plus, I was literally just down the street from Marlo, which could come in handy when the baby was here.

Thankfully Paisley did not bring up the one subject I had forbidden them from talking about. In a moment of weakness in my second trimester, I'd written a letter to Linc and told him about Lucas. I didn't expect him to drop everything and come racing back. That's not how the military worked.

But I had mailed that letter.

And he hadn't written me back.

In fact, the whole letter came back with a scribbled Return to Sender on it that broke my heart. The last vestige of hope I'd been clinging to, along with the memories of that one magical day together, officially shattered.

Janice and the girls swarmed around me for a group hug, pulling me from the memories I tried to bury under the responsibility of being a single mom. Lucy barged through the front door like the hurricane she always was.

"Sorry I'm late! Hey! You started the group hugs without me?" She nearly tackled our huddle, pushing and shoving until we were all laughing.

Bain, Lucy's husband and the only male in sight, was only allowed in because he was carrying a brand-new crib they'd gotten for me. We ate cake and opened presents. We opted not to play silly baby shower games and just talked. Lucy and Janice eventually left to go home and the girls stayed. They opened a bottle of champagne and served me sparkling cider. They put together all the baby items I'd been gifted—along with cursing when Paisley couldn't stand the way Marlo was using the screwdriver—while Audrey painted my toenails because she felt like having pretty toes was essential in case I went into labor anytime soon. They stayed the night and I went to sleep with a smile on my face for the first time in this pregnancy.

When I actually did go into labor eight days later, Audrey was right. My toes looked fantastic up in those stirrups. But I labored alone, minus the doctor and nurses. Everyone had offered to be in the room with me, but for some reason, I had to face this moment alone. I wanted it to just be me and Lucas. I needed to push him out into this world all on my own, as if beginning in the way I meant to go on was essential to keep my heart from fracturing in two.

When the doctor placed his warm, wet body on my chest and he began to blink his eyes up at me for the first time, my heart fractured anyway, falling completely in love with him in a way that changed my world yet again.

The old Keva officially died and the new Keva, the one that would be the best mother in the whole damn world because this precious little baby deserved it, was born.

Me and Lucas.

Always.

Forever.

CHAPTER SIX

resent Day

Lincoln

"I'VE ONLY GOT five minutes, so make it quick, huh?"

Tank still had a few months before he was discharged, and as much as he griped at me, I knew he was counting down the minutes until he could move to Blueball too. I had been too, but wouldn't you know it, the Army had pulled me in for longer than the four years I was expecting. But all that was behind me now.

I glanced around the parking lot of some roadside diner that had seen better days. The coffee had been strong though, and that was exactly what I needed. The sun was setting and turning the overflowing dumpster into something that was actually beautiful.

"I'm just giving you one last chance to say no."

Tank was silent. I held my breath.

"Nah. Go for it. You've been a sad sack for years. I'm tired of seeing your pretty blue eyes tear up every night."

I scoffed. "Fuck off, Tank."

He laughed, the sound still jovial when most guys I served with in the Army had laughs that had turned hard and brittle. "You know what I mean. Shit, I've never seen a guy so whipped from a single day with a girl. If my sister is what you want, you have my full permission to give it a go. But if you break her heart or do something stupid, that black eye I gave you will look like child's play."

The anxiety that had been eating away at me as I drove up the coastline melted away. We'd had this conversation already, but I hadn't quite believed my ears. I'd found myself waiting for him to take back his stamp of approval.

"She still hasn't contacted you back?"

Tank lost the jovial tone real fuckin' fast. "Nah. Not a word."

I shook my head. "So you don't even know if she lives in Hell."

"Guess you'll have to let me know."

A sudden need to be on the move in the direction of Keva had me wrapping things up. "Alright, then. I should get to Blueball tonight. I'll let you know if I see her, but my job starts tomorrow, so I may not get out that way for a bit."

Tank was quiet again before speaking so low I had to strain to hear him. "Just take care of her if you find her."

"You know I will."

I hung up and shoved the phone back in the pocket of my leather jacket. Tank and Keva had some bad blood to work out, and as much as I wanted to help make that happen for my best friend, I had my own shit to work out with Keva. For all I knew, she was already married and moved on, that day with an Army guy a barely recognizable memory. Sadly, my heart hadn't moved on at all. I'd carried every single minute of our time together on replay in my head for the last five years.

And now it was time to see if there was anything left

between us. If there wasn't, I'd walk away and never look back. But I couldn't do that until I at least tried.

Two hours later, I'd driven right past Auburn Hill on my way to Blueball. Unlike last time I visited, I was on my Harley and not some pathetic banana-yellow scooter sputtering on its last few gallons of gas. Also unlike last time, I didn't have a light-heartedness that drew naïve young women to me like moths to a flame. The permanent scowl on my face these days usually kept those young, happy ones away. It had only been just shy of five years, but it felt like a lifetime.

Mama's ringtone filtered up through my pocket as I slowed for a stop sign. The woman was relentless. I'd literally just said goodbye to her a few hours ago. Then again, I'd been giving her heart attacks for years now being away in the Army where she couldn't boss me around like the mother hen she'd always been. I thought writing to her every single week I was gone would make her feel better but I'd been mistaken on the level of love that woman had to give. I let her roll to voicemail and zoomed down the road, eager to get to Glamper's Paradise before it got too dark. The sooner I acclimated to my new life in the next town over, the sooner I could seek out Keva.

Downtown Blueball looked like one of those towns you'd find in a Hallmark movie set: pretty, charming, and full of busybodies. Back when I'd tried civilian life for a day in Hell, I'd wanted to blend in. Become a local. Shoot the shit with the guys and swap fishing stories. Flirt with the old ladies as I bought my groceries.

Now I just wanted to hunker down in my trailer in Blueball and let the world carry on without me in the middle of it. If I could have lived in an isolated tent out in the forest without my mama worrying about me incessantly, I would have.

The directions my new boss, Gannon Hart, had given me over the phone a week ago were spot on. I turned onto the road that would take me to his property, but instead of a sleepy camp-ground, I saw a million cars ahead, parked haphazardly in the street. Safe to say Blueball didn't have parking enforcement.

Bright lights lit up the tall oak trees in the distance. Loud country music hit my ears as I came to a stop and pulled the helmet off my head.

Looked like Glamper's Paradise was having a party.

"Shit." My lip snarled up in dislike. The last thing I wanted was to be involved in a fuckin' party. I stored my helmet and grabbed my duffle bag, slinging it over my shoulder.

Maybe I could skirt around the party and find the trailer Gannon had promised me. He'd told me it was on the back half of the property, tucked away with only one other trailer in viewing distance. Sounded almost like heaven. The ground was uneven and there wasn't a pathway in the direction I was going but so far so good. No drunken partiers had crossed my path and the volume of the music was dimming. There was just enough moonlight to get around the party like a thief in the night and find my trailer, the one marked with a wooden sign painted with a set of drums. Funny thing was, I used to play drums as a kid. Hadn't picked up sticks in years though.

The trailer was painted baby blue on the bottom and white on top, looking more like an Easter egg than an RV. Couldn't possibly hold more than a twin bed and a sink and toilet. It was fuckin' perfect.

The door was unlocked and the hinges didn't squeak as I stepped inside. The place smelled clean and everything was tight but cozy. I threw my bag on the bed and flipped the one and only light switch I could find on the wall just inside the door. Nothing happened.

I stepped back outside with my cell phone flashlight and made a full circle around the trailer until I found the electrical box in the back and flipped the breaker on. The RV lit up with a warm yellow glow, along with string lights zigzagging across the outside of the trailer from the overhanging trees. A single Adirondack chair and a round table made up my porch, with a square of fake grass underfoot. This shit was amazing. Way better than most of the conditions I'd been living in since I left for the military at eighteen.

I felt a grin split my face. I lifted my hand and felt it, just to make sure it was actually there. Hadn't had much to smile about in a long time. I sank into the porch chair and tilted my head back to stare up at the string lights. A man could get used to this, that's for sure. Perhaps that had been my issue five years ago when I'd tried to become a civilian. I'd tried to fit in with society when that was an impossible endeavor. Hiding out here in the woods in this mini trailer was more my style.

I reached out and flipped the light switch back off, the stars above reappearing and winking as clouds rolled by. When that sight got to be so soothing I thought I might fall asleep in the chair, I took one last look over in the direction of the party before heading inside.

People milled about everywhere, some of them dancing below a particularly huge oak tree, while others sat at picnic tables and ate while they talked. My gaze snagged on two women in particular.

One was tall with honey-blonde hair and a girl-next-door kind of vibe with her sundress. But it was the shorter one with dark hair that caught my attention. She had her hand on the taller one's face, holding her still in what looked like a death grip of authority. The dark-haired woman sported curves that instantly had me staring and wondering.

The hair on my arms rose, and I calmed my heart rate on instinct. If anyone looked this way, they'd see nothing but shadows and darkness. I could blend in without even trying, a skill you have to learn to survive in the Army. But I was anything but calm.

Because that dark-haired beauty?

That was my Keva.

No doubt in my mind. I could probably pick her out of a lineup blindfolded. Not one woman had ever had this effect on me, except for her. And she was currently standing a hundred yards away with a frozen wide-eyed stare. Before I could come up with a plan, she was moving, grabbing her things and rushing off into the packed crowd. I took one silent step forward before halting.

"Not like this, asshole," I muttered into the darkness.

The worst thing I could do was rush into a situation without scoping it out first. It was enough to know that Keva was here in the general vicinity. Now I could ask some questions, see where she lived, maybe even bump into her "accidentally" and on my terms. When I had just the right thing to say. When odds were good she'd be receptive to my apology. No use rushing headlong into a situation when I had zero clue about her life or circumstances. I wasn't exactly going into war, but I was battling for the woman I never should have walked away from.

I repositioned the chair so I could see through the trees, straining my eyes to catch another glimpse of her, but even after an hour, she didn't reappear. My heart hammered away in my chest at the possibility, right back to where I was the day I met her. Instantly and positively in love with the damn woman.

By the time the party wound down and I collapsed into bed, if it wasn't for my heart still beating away unnaturally fast, I'd believe that I imagined her entirely.

CHAPTER SEVEN

eva

I NEEDED A CELEBRATORY DRINK. I'd helped Gannon put together his marriage proposal to my best friend and hadn't made one sarcastic comment about love or men the entire time. I mean, really. Maybe an award should come with that drink.

In all honesty, I was happy for Paisley and Gannon. I'd put all my baggage around love on hold and seen them for what they were. They were so adorable it made me a little sick to my stomach with jealousy. Janice, my next-door neighbor who'd become like a mother to me, handed me Lucas. She watched him so much I had to admit that she and I were both raising him.

"Hey, baby." I kissed his little head and breathed him in. "Did you get some cake?"

He shook his head and kicked his legs. He was doing that more and more these days, wanting to be running around instead of in my arms. It made my heart ache to give him space, but I knew I had to do it.

"No, Mama." He tugged on my hand, pulling me in the direction of the dessert table. He blinked those blue eyes up at me and I was toast. All the late nights and dirty-diaper blowouts and counting pennies to buy him clean clothes and crying myself to sleep right alongside a crying baby had been worth it to hear him call me mama.

"You want anything, Janice?" I asked over my shoulder.

Janice shook her bleached-blonde pixie cut and edged toward the quieter side of the glamp-ground. I knew where she was going. She needed to light up a cigarette and inhale that nicotine. She'd tried to quit a dozen times over the last few years, but always gave in. Thankfully, she never smoked around Lucas, which would have been a deal breaker for me. And I honestly didn't know what we'd do without her.

Lucas pointed at each of the desserts he wanted to try, but as the number increased past five, I made him narrow it down so he wouldn't be up all night on a sugar high. Marlo waved me over and we went to go sit with her at a picnic table. We ate our desserts and watched everyone dancing, Paisley and Gannon in the middle of it all, softly rocking back and forth to a fast-paced song.

"Those two." I shook my head and Marlo snorted.

"I know." Marlo put her head in her hand and stared at them. Almost wistfully.

"Marlo? You okay?" Marlo was never wistful. Stoic, deadpan, and realistic to a fault, but never wistful.

"Keva!" We both swiveled to see Audrey hit the table with her hip, unable to slow down her run. She didn't even wince. She'd been off flirting with any and all single men at this party. This was actually the first I'd seen her.

"What is the matter with—"

She cut me off. "He's here." Audrey was breathing so hard I started to get alarmed.

"Who's here?"

I could see the whites of Audrey's eyes all the way around her brown irises. She flicked a glance at my son and it was official. I was panicked. If something affected Lucas, I went into full mama-bear mode. It just happened. A program of nature for mamas to protect their young. I rose from my seat and grabbed her face, pulling her attention back to me.

"Who, Audrey?"

Her fish lips, squeezed between my fingers, opened and closed. Then her eyes turned sympathetic, and the blood froze in my veins.

"Linc."

My legs gave out and I sank to the picnic bench. Alarm bells were ringing out so fast and furious in my head I didn't even hear anything else Audrey had to say. The girls knew we didn't mess around with that name. I'd banned them from talking about him somewhere during my third trimester when my hips decided to ache as badly as my lower back. My breath started coming faster. There just wasn't enough oxygen out here in the woods. Stars that should have been up in the sky swam across my vision.

Movement registered and then pain bloomed across my cheek. Marlo had slapped me in the face. My eyes shot open and all the sounds around us came roaring back. Along with a healthy dose of anger.

"What the fudge, Marlo?" I was aware of Lucas still sitting just two feet away from me.

Marlo and Audrey loomed over me looking concerned. Marlo shrugged. "I've always wanted to do that."

In some ways, I was thankful she'd used such harsh measures. My brain was suddenly laser focused. I pushed them away and stood, mama on a mission. "Tell me everything and then I need to get out of here."

"Daire Beneventi heard a motorcycle pull up and went to check it out. You know how he is with motorcycles." We all nodded. Daire lived in Hell but everyone heard his Harley gunning up and down Coast Highway on the regular. "Anyway, he told Izzy that Linc was back, who told Lucy, who told me."

"I need to get out of here," I said quietly, brain spinning. "I need to get Lucas out of here."

Marlo put her hand on my arm, and I appreciated the gentler touch. "He looks nothing like him, Keva."

All three of us looked down at Lucas who had a ring of blue frosting around his little mouth, along with a couple pieces of sprinkles clinging to his cheeks. He lifted his head, as if he felt our stares. His denim-blue eyes were a dead giveaway, in my opinion. Everything else was me, right down to the dimple on one side, dark hair, and the round face.

"Maybe you should go," Audrey hedged. "Just to be on the safe side. Get some time to think."

I nodded, already collecting our things. Janice came back toward the table smelling like an entire ashtray.

"We leaving already?"

There were exactly five people in the world who knew my secret: Audrey, Marlo, Paisley, Lucy, and Janice. I trusted them with my very life, so I knew Janice would understand once I told her the problem.

"Yeah. Change of plans. You can stay, though. I'm sure one of the girls can drive you home."

"No, no. That's fine." Janice was wringing her hands.

More alarm bells went off in my head. I had a bad feeling about things. Then again, I always had a bad feeling about things. Janice was not a hand wringer. She was stoic and direct, taking everything in stride as long as she had a cigarette nearby.

"What is it?" My heart couldn't really take much more excitement, but maybe hearing it all at once would be better than stringing out the bad news.

Janice glanced at the girls behind me and then down at Lucas before coming back to me. "My son called me yesterday. They're pregnant."

"Oh, congratulations!" I knew how much Janice wanted to be a grandma. She'd been playing the role with Lucas since before he was born, but nothing was as precious as your own blood.

Her hands did not stop their wringing.

"I, uh, need to sell the duplex."

And there it was. The bomb I'd always been waiting for.

Janice rushed to explain. "They're in Des Moines, as you know. I just can't see myself living so far away from my first grandbaby. I know I'm putting you in a rough spot and I hate that, but I don't know what else to do. I don't know how I'm going to leave you two."

I didn't give her a chance to say anything further. As the tears gathered in her eyes, I pulled her into a firm hug. This woman had been everything to me the last few years, stepping in every single time I needed help. Without hesitation, without a thought to her own health and happiness. I didn't know how any single mama was able to make it without their own Janice.

Now it was my turn to return the favor.

"I'm so happy for you, Janice." I pulled back, holding her hands in mine. "You have to go. Your first grandbaby? You won't ever get this time back. Just tell me when we need to be out, okay? Don't you worry about us. You got us through the sticky part. Lucas sleeps through the night and is potty-trained. He's practically ready to head off to college."

I tried for a laugh, even though my heart was breaking. Even though panic was beginning to make breathing difficult. Lucas got up from the table and ran over to wrap his arms around my leg, probably guessing his mama could use a hug. The boy was intuitive, so in sync with me that we seemed to know when the other needed comforting or a laugh. Janice hugged me again and then picked up Lucas, spinning him around and making him giggle.

"Come on. Let's get you home." Audrey grabbed my huge bag that held every toy and snack known to comfort three-year-old boys and slung it over her shoulder. "We can meet at your place tomorrow and discuss everything."

The sounds of the party faded away the further we walked.

My gaze darted left and right, already on edge. I wasn't ready to see Linc again. Might never be ready.

We were almost to my car when Paisley and Gannon came rushing up. "Hey! You guys leaving already?"

Marlo pulled them aside, whispering furiously while I threw my bag in the trunk and Janice got Lucas into his booster seat. I heard Paisley gasp. Then she was hugging me from behind.

"Where will you go?" she whispered, echoing the same question that was running through my brain on repeat.

"Not sure, but I'll figure it out. I always do."

I felt her stiffen and release me. I slammed the trunk shut and spun, slapping a big-ass smile on my face. "Congrats, you two. Sorry to leave early."

Gannon stared at me like I'd grown a second head. Then he pulled the hat off his head and slapped it against his thigh. "Oh fuck. You're about to cry, aren't you?"

I scowled at him. I'd made an effort to smile and he wanted to accuse me of crying? "No, I'm not!"

Paisley stepped between us. "You can stay in one of our trailers. Gannon, didn't you say you had one on the back of the property that's not ready for renting yet? Could we give it to Keva and Lucas?"

Gannon was already nodding. "Sure do. It only has one direct neighbor, so it should be safe for you two."

Paisley frowned while I ran that idea through my head. The trailer would be smaller than what we were used to, but beggars can't be choosers. Besides, Lucas would think it was an extended camping trip. What little boy wouldn't want to camp out under the stars every night with a full forest and glamp-ground for him to play in?

"What neighbor? You didn't tell me about a neighbor." Paisley was focused on her fiancé.

"Yes, I did. It's the guy I told you about. The one Bain recommended. He agreed to start this week, which is just in time. I can't keep up, and I don't like you having to help out when you get home from work."

Just like always, the rest of us faded into the background when those two were sparring. They were crazy for each other. If I wasn't facing a shit show of epic proportions right now, I'd be happy for them. As it was, I needed to get out of here before we ran into Linc. And before I burst into tears over losing Janice and our housing in one fell swoop.

"I don't mind helping, but I'm glad you pulled the trigger. Do we know if he's a decent guy? I don't want him near my best friend if he's not trustworthy." Paisley put her hand on Gannon's chest.

He grabbed her hand and kissed the back of it. "Bain wouldn't recommend him if he wasn't. If anything, it'll be good to have him nearby for protection. He's ex-military."

Time stood still. The noise of the party faded entirely. Everyone around me moved in slow motion. Even the warning bells went silent. There was just one thing I heard and it was the final bomb to be dropped this evening.

"His name's Lincoln Angelo."

Next thing I knew I was sitting in the front seat of the car, staring dully out the windshield with Marlo fussing around me. Thankfully she didn't slap me again. Paisley and Audrey were shouting. Gannon was trying to get a word in edgewise, but those two weren't having it. Janice was playing with Lucas in the back seat, trying to distract him from the crazed adults around him.

"What the fuck, Gannon?"

"Have you lost your damn mind, cowboy?"

"I don't—"

"No, you don't get to speak right now. You've stepped in so much shit."

"Someone explain to me what's going on!" Gannon finally bellowed, shutting everyone up. Even Lucas craned his head to see the giant of a man out the back window.

I patted Marlo's hands, but pushed her out of the way. I slid out of the seat and somehow stood on my two shaky legs. Everyone looked over at me, shock, concern, and confusion written on everyone's faces. I shut the door, making sure Lucas didn't hear what needed to be said. While I was proud of Paisley for not sharing my secret with her fiancé, this cluster illustrated that I should have let him in on my secret sooner.

"Linc is Lucas's daddy, but he has no idea."

Gannon's mouth flopped open and then he snapped it shut. "Lucas has no idea? Or Lincoln?"

I shook my head, feeling tired down to my bones. "Neither of them has any idea."

Gannon looked ready to punch a wall. Or maybe me.

I didn't blame him. He'd been deprived of his own child for the first five years of her life. He had some firm opinions on keeping that sort of thing a secret from the father.

"This isn't right," he growled.

I nodded, finally agreeing on something with the man. "Nothing about any of this is right."

CHAPTER EIGHT

incoln

THE METAL CEILING WAS UNFAMILIAR. The smell of pine trees registered as abnormal. I blinked a few more times and my brain caught up with my body. I remembered where I was. Blueball. In a trailer. At my new job.

The knock that had woken me up came again. I threw off the covers and sat up, instantly awake.

"Coming," I croaked, sliding into my jeans and buttoning them up as I made my way over to the door that was made for smaller humans than me. I had to duck down to see who was outside. For a quick second I thought it was Tank based off the shoulder width that blocked out the early morning sun. But this guy had tattoos up and down his arms and a pair of blue eyes my best friend didn't have.

"Morning," the guy rumbled. "Sorry for the early wake-up call. I heard you got in late last night."

I leaned against the trailer doorway, looking relaxed. I was anything but. "I did."

The guy put his hand out. "Gannon Hart."

I straightened, now at ease knowing who he was and why he was at my doorstep. "Hey, Gannon. Nice to meet you. Lincoln Angelo. Thanks for the trailer."

Gannon's mouth quirked up in what might be described as a grin. "Sorry it's so small. Once I get a few more units we can trade yours out so you can at least stand up straight in it."

"Nah, I wouldn't worry about it. I don't plan to be inside much." I hooked my thumb over my shoulder. "I just need to grab some shoes and I can help you with whatever you need."

Gannon took the hat off his head and messed with the bill. "Actually, I was hoping you'd help me out on a personal level. My fiancée's best friend is moving into that trailer." He pointed to the pink-and-white trailer right across from mine. "I was hoping you could go to her place and help her move her things here. I realize this is an odd job to give you on your first day, but I could use the help."

"That's what I'm here for." I reached down for the boots I'd pulled off last night. I didn't care what tasks I did. For now I just needed a place to live and a paycheck.

"Yeah, well, here's the thing." Gannon sounded so nervous I looked up while I jammed my feet into the boots. "It's come to my attention that you already know my fiancée's best friend."

I frowned. He must be mistaken. I didn't know anyone here.

"Keva Mooney."

Her name stopped me cold. All kinds of emotions danced through my veins hearing the name that had kept me going the last five years, but the only one to settle in was caution.

"You sure me helping is what Keva wants?"

Gannon jammed his hat back on his head, looking like my command sergeant when shit was hitting the fan. "Keva already knows the plan and she's expecting you."

I guessed that would have to be good enough for me. He handed me a piece of paper from his back pocket. I could barely read it. Thankfully, my command sergeant also had terrible handwriting and I could decipher it. It was an address. Keva's, I presumed.

"Yes, sir. On my way." I reached back into the trailer and grabbed my keys.

Gannon clapped me on the shoulder. "Thanks, Lincoln. But drop the sir bit. You're not in the military any longer."

I gave him a head nod and walked through the glamp-ground, breathing in the smell of the forest. It would take me some time to get used to being discharged. Over twelve years of my life wouldn't go away in a day or two. My Harley was exactly where I'd left it last night, but I had to brush off a layer of pine needles before I climbed on.

I used the maps on my phone to plug in her address and get on the road. She wasn't far away, still in the town limits of Blue-ball. I wondered when she'd left Hell. I wondered a lot of things about Keva. By the time I pulled up to her duplex and put down the kickstand, my heart was hammering inside my chest. I'd been in a lot of stressful situations in my life, but none of them prepared me for this. Women were as unknown to me as my enemy in combat. Probably more so. No telling how they'd react.

Swinging my leg over, I straightened my T-shirt and wished I'd stopped to brush my teeth. Not that I thought I'd be kissing Keva today or anytime soon, but it seemed like brushing my teeth was just one small thing I could have done to make sure this first interaction went well. Rushing in like a bull in a china shop and thinking later just seemed to be how I did things when it came to Keva.

I stepped up onto the stoop and tried to see through the curtains that were pulled tight across the front window. Sucking in one last deep breath, I put my knuckles to the plain door and gave it a good knock. And then I waited. And waited. When no one answered, I knocked again.

This time I heard a clunk from somewhere inside the house

and then a cry that was half wail. Alarm flooded out the nerves and suddenly I was back on the job, racing into a situation to save lives no matter the cost. I tried the doorknob and found it locked. The cries got louder and I calculated the merits of blowing this damn door down. If Keva was expecting me, she would have answered the door, right? So if she didn't answer and there was now crying, I had to assume she was injured. My shoulder was plowing into the door before that thought had fully formed in my head. The cheap door gave way with a splinter of wood.

"Keva!" I shouted, running through the tiny walkway between the kitchen and a little dinette set.

My gaze darted left and right, assessing the situation as I ran. I found the source of the crying when I saw a little boy in the middle of the living room with a cardboard box on its side, tangled around his legs. Teddy bears and knickknacks were scattered on the floor around him.

But what really caught my attention was the wet and naked woman who ran into the room the same time I did, only from the opposite direction. Her dark hair dripped into her eyes and slid down her body. And holy shit. What a body. Curves everywhere and in all the right proportions that made a man want to drop to his knees and beg her to let him touch her. Her breasts swayed tantalizingly as she came to an abrupt stop just a few feet from the boy. Her eyes went wide and everything just kind of froze. Even the little boy stopped crying.

"Keva?" I managed to ask around a strangled throat. Every bit of saliva in my mouth had dried the second I saw Keva naked.

She didn't answer me. One blink of those huge blue eyes and she let out a scream that told me where the little boy got his vocal power. She leaped faster than Tank that one time he pissed off a local in a high-stakes card game and the guy had shot at his feet like we were in some old-time western movie. I got a delicious flash of her ass before she had two throw pillows pressed to the front of her body, blocking out all the glorious bits I'd had carnal knowledge of years ago.

Fuck me. She'd gotten even prettier these last five years.

"Oh my God! Get out!"

My brain was a bit slow—considering all my blood had pooled far south—but I finally put a hand over my eyes and dropped my head. I had a partial view of the little boy, who looked back and forth between us while he extricated himself from the cardboard box that had fallen over. All I could think about was that apparently Keva still didn't like wearing underwear.

I put my other hand up in a sign of surrender. "Gannon said you were expecting me."

There was a beat of silence.

"I'm going to kill him."

I had a pretty good read on people after living all over the world and there was no doubt in my mind that Keva was going to make Gannon pay in ways he would not enjoy.

"Soo...you *weren't* expecting me?" I hedged. Her being naked was my first indicator that she hadn't been, but sometimes I was a dumbass and needed to verify before my rock-hard head could believe it.

"No, I always greet strangers in my birthday suit," Keva snapped sarcastically.

I took a second to rearrange every memory I had of her in my head. She hadn't been mean or sarcastic five years ago, but I knew people changed over time. Even goddesses like Keva Mooney.

"Well, we're not exactly strangers," I drawled. Which, given more time and thought, I would have realized was not the right thing to say.

She inhaled sharply. "Go stand outside my broken front door. I'll be back once I'm dressed."

I hooked my thumb over my shoulder. She was kicking me out already? This was not going well. "Outside?"

"I'm not letting a *stranger* hang out with my son while I'm getting dressed. So yes, out!"

I peeked a glance over my hand, and while I should have heeded her angry tone and the way she still declared us strangers, I couldn't help but focus on the pink cheeks and how lovely she looked, even soaking wet.

"Out!"

"Okay." I backed up, still covering my eyes, but making eye contact with the little boy. "Bye, buddy."

The back of my legs hit a chair and I grunted, barely managing to stay on my feet. I spun around and walked out without the self-blindfold so I didn't kill myself on furniture before I made it to her stoop. While she got dressed—and probably came up with a thousand reasons for why she hated me—I took a look at her door. I'd have to borrow some tools from Gannon and come back later to fix it.

"Strangers," I grumbled to myself. Fuckin' hated that word.

The door swung open and Keva was back, dressed in a pair of jeans and a fitted sweater that made her eyes sparkle. She put her hands on her lovely hips and I realized that sparkle was simply anger directed at me.

Shit. I was fucking this up. Badly.

"I'm sorry. I didn't mean to barge in unannounced. I thought you were expecting me and then I heard crying and thought you were hurt." I held out the splinter of wood that had been her doorjamb up until a few minutes ago.

She rolled her eyes and took the piece of wood, her pinkie ever so slightly brushing against my hand. I was so far gone for this woman, I considered this whole interaction a win just for getting her to touch me.

"I really don't need help moving."

I shrugged, regrouping. Keva didn't seem like she'd be receptive to me coming on strong. Or even coming on weak. "You're going to be living right next to me, so I might as well help."

Keva sighed and I tried not to let the disappointment on her face hurt my feelings. "Listen, if you can borrow Gannon's truck, that would be the most help. I'll have boxes ready to go by this afternoon."

I nodded, intensely relieved that she was going to let me help her, even in this small way. "I'll call him and ask right now, but I'm sure he'd be fine with it." I paused. "Is that your son in there?"

Keva's spine straightened and her eyes were sparkling again when she met my gaze. "Yes, he's mine."

I nodded. "Thought so. He's got your coloring. Traded the piglet for a baby?"

For a quick second, by referencing the girl I knew five years ago, all the coldness in her gaze left, leaving her with a look so warm I felt like I'd stepped back in time. Then it was gone again so fast I thought I might have imagined it.

"Baby pigs are a lot of work. Figured taking care of my son was more important."

I was beginning to feel like a bobblehead. "For sure. What's his name?"

Keva folded her arms across her chest and I couldn't stop my gaze from dipping down for a split second to see the effect it had on her cleavage. Damn, the woman was built like a walking, talking advertisement of everything a man loved about a woman's body.

"His name is Lucas. See you later, Linc."

She stepped back abruptly and swung the door shut. It bounced right off the ruined doorjamb. "You're going to fix that too," she snapped from behind the door.

"Yes, ma'am," I replied. I'd fix every little thing wrong with this place if she just kept saying my name. I'd waited years to hear her say it again.

I walked to my Harley in a daze, the image of her wet, naked body imprinted on the back of my eyelids. I might just see that moment for the rest of my life and die a happy man. As I zoomed back to Glamper's Paradise, I had time to put together a plan. A plan to get on Keva's good side.

Because that hadn't gone well. At all. But I was still in the game, baby.

Because Keva had come to the door, fully dressed—with no fuckin' ring on her finger—and wearing perfume.

No woman puts perfume on for a man she despises.

CHAPTER NINE

Keva

Me: Your husband is on my shitlist.

Paisley: So what's new?

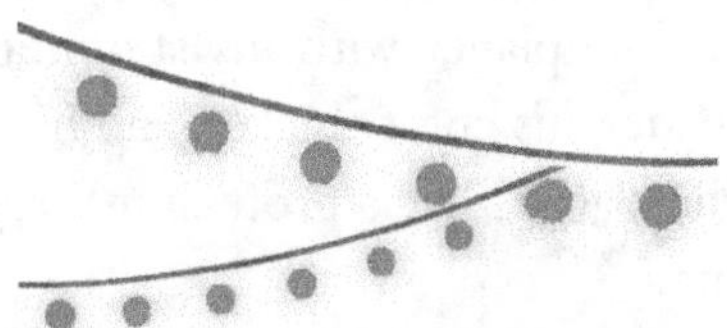

LUCAS WAS WHOLLY unaffected by a strange man barging into our home. He went back to playing like he had been when I hopped in the shower with the bathroom door open so I could hear him.

But me? Holy shit, I was dying inside. The man who'd haunted my dreams and waking thoughts for several years before I gave up on him entirely had finally come back. And his first view of me? Fucking naked.

I shook my head and grabbed my brush to get these snarls out of my wet hair. Of course I'd been naked. It was like all my high school nightmares coming true. My body wasn't what it had been back when Linc had seen me naked the first time. I had stretch marks and saggy skin where I'd stretched to accommodate a growing baby. Boobs that had breastfed and never quite shrunk back to their original shape. Never mind the lost sleep and hectic schedule that meant I hadn't darkened the door of a gym since high school physical education class. I was still young but my body had seen a few things.

No wonder Linc had looked like he got hit upside the head with a two-by-four. The second I heard Lucas scream, I'd come skidding around the corner, breasts a-swinging.

I moaned and dropped my head into my hands. He'd looked shocked all right. But he'd looked damn good too.

"Fucker," I mumbled under my breath.

While I'd been making another human being, he'd been lifting weights and packing on muscle to taunt every warm-blooded woman on the planet with his stunning physique. His shoulders were broader, his chest thicker, and his lower body had grown to fill out those jeans like a professional rugby player. Life was exceedingly unfair.

"Nothing you can do about it, Keevs. Just suck it up and get on with it," I told my reflection as I swept my hair up into a messy bun on top of my head.

"Mama?"

I looked down to see Lucas in the doorway, staring up at me. I'd gotten used to never having privacy. I'd woken up too many times to see Lucas standing right next to my bed staring at me in the dark because he couldn't sleep. Little kids did some creepy shit.

"You ready to pack up our boxes and check out our new house?" I injected as much enthusiasm as I could into my voice. I wasn't looking forward to living in a small trailer, but knowing we'd be living right next to Linc was the terrifying part. My secret would eventually come out. I was sure of it.

"Janny come too?" he asked, eyes wide with excitement.

My heart sank. I wanted to give my little boy everything, but no matter how hard I tried to protect him, he was going to be faced with disappointment at times in life. Like right now. I crouched down and tried to be honest but compassionate.

"No, baby. Janice is moving to a place called Des Moines, Iowa, to be with her son and his family."

Lucas's bottom lip trembled. "We famiwy too."

I nodded, heart breaking for him. "Yes, we're family too, but her grandbaby is about to be born and babies need a lot of help. Janice helped you when you were a baby, but now you're a big boy. She needs to go help this other baby, you see?"

Lucas frowned, but the lip trembling stopped. He nodded. "Otay." He ran to the living room singing at the top of his lungs a song from a terrible old movie I never should have allowed him to watch. It was about a unicorn being the last of her kind and her search for more just like her. It was oddly addicting and truly terrible voice acting, but Lucas had loved it.

I'd barely gotten two boxes packed when there was a honk out front. Lucas went running for the door with me running after him. No matter how many times I told him not to answer the door, his curiosity got the better of him.

"Lucas, wait!" I shouted as I ran after him out the door.

We both came to a halt in the front yard when we saw Linc climbing out of Gannon's big truck. He had a grin on his face that made my internal organs tumble about.

"Hey, you two. Got the truck."

He tilted his head to the obvious truck and then tucked his

hands in the front pockets of his jeans. His T-shirt had to stretch quite a bit as his muscles flexed. I blinked and cleared my head. I had zero time to be thinking those kinds of thoughts.

"Great. I, uh, still have some boxes to pack though." I put my hand on Lucas's shoulder to steer him back in the house.

"I got extra boxes too. And tape, and packing wrap for any breakable things."

My gaze swung back to Linc. That was thoughtful. And way overboard for a stranger. I also knew I was almost out of boxes and hadn't even gotten to my kitchen yet. I couldn't exactly refuse his boxes.

I rolled my shoulders back. "Thank you." With that curt acknowledgement, I went back in the house and had Lucas help me throw his clothes into a box in his room. I could hear Linc in the living room, taping up the bottom of the new boxes.

"You able to fit all this in the trailer?" Linc asked, leaning against the doorframe of Lucas's bedroom. It was so strange to see him here, just inches from the walls I'd painted a light blue when I was pregnant. I refused to acknowledge how close the blue of the walls was to the blue of Linc's eyes. Purely coincidence.

"Whatever won't fit I'll put in storage for the time being."

"You're welcome to store some in my trailer. I don't have much, so there's a few empty cupboards."

I closed the box and Lucas ran to fling open his closet. Linc was suddenly there in my space, taping the top of the box with a tape gun, overwhelming me with his heat and the scent of his skin. I straightened and moved away, promising myself to keep my distance. I appreciated the help moving, but that was all this was. A helping hand from a stranger.

"Hey, Lucas." Linc's smooth deep voice, saying my son's name, flowed over me. I was glad my back was to him and he didn't see the way my eyes slid shut. I just needed a second to gather myself. "You ever play with an engine?"

I spun around, opening my mouth to speak for Lucas, but my son beat me to it.

"Whas a gin?"

Linc smiled down at Lucas and all those internal organs that had melted officially ignited into a lake of fire that they'd never come back from. "Come on out here and I'll show you." He lifted his head. "Do you mind?"

I shook my head no even though I wanted to scream yes. Yes, I minded. Yes, I was nervous about Linc spending time with my son. No, I didn't trust Lucas with anyone but a very small group of people I'd personally vetted. No, nothing about Linc being back in town was sitting well with me.

The two walked out of the room and my mouth fell open. I spun around and sank down on Lucas's mattress. My hand came up to rub my chest. My heart was pounding. Is this what a heart attack felt like? Surely I was too young for this, right?

The two of them walked exactly the same.

I squeezed my eyes shut and tried to slow my heart rate. Emotions I'd kept stuffed down for years were starting to bubble back up. I'd left behind my emotional self when Lucas was born so I could handle raising a little baby on my own. I didn't have time for pesky emotions or to question if what I was doing was the right thing for all parties involved. But apparently I had time now because I was feeling all kinds of emotions.

I got to my feet and went out into the living room to see Linc helping Lucas lift a bright red plastic thing out of a box.

"This is a toy car engine. We can get it set up and I'll show you all the stuff you can do with it."

"Oh, Linc. We don't have room for that." Yes, practicality was always top of mind with me.

He lifted his gaze and looked so sure of himself I found my head nodding in agreement. "He can leave it at my place, then."

Lucas squealed and immediately began to play with all the parts under the hood, squeaking, honking, and making it light up when he used his play tools correctly. When he was fully engaged in self-play, Linc got up and helped me pack up the kitchen, the two of us moving around each other in mostly silence.

When his back was turned getting the glasses out of the top cabinet, I fanned my face with the packing material. I was aware of Linc's every move, every breath, every time his gaze swung my way. It was hyper-stimulating and ultimately frustrating. What was he doing back here? Why was he helping me? Why was he being so kind to my son? Shit, *our* son.

"Hungwy, Mama." Lucas slipped into the kitchen and hugged my legs. I rubbed his back and checked out the time on the stove. It was well past noon.

I felt Linc's gaze on us before I even lifted my head. "How about we try that place called Grass? I saw it on my way over here. Looked pretty good."

"Oh, I'm sure I have something here we could eat."

Linc smiled and my heart fluttered. "I need to meet people, being the new guy in town. And you and Lucas need to eat. Kind of makes sense to take a little break."

"I like Dago," Lucas said excitedly.

I interpreted. "The owners are Diego and Mandy. Diego always gives Lucas a lollypop after we eat."

Linc clapped his hands together. "Then it's decided."

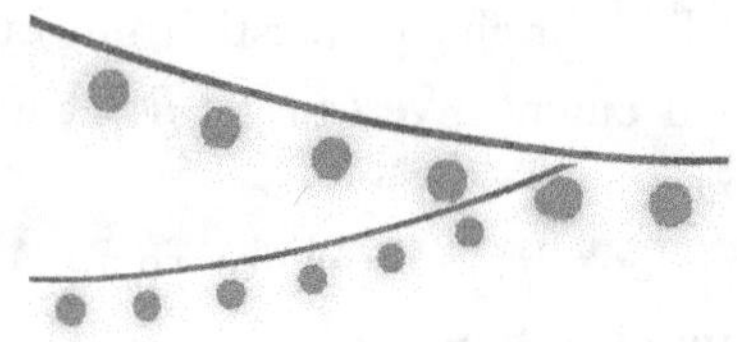

"Hey, you must be Keva, right?" the pretty redhead said from behind the register. "I'm Mandy. We haven't met yet, but Paisley says such great things about you."

Grass was a sit-down place, but you ordered at the register first before taking one of the many tables set up in between walls that had bright green fake grass encased by wood borders. Seemed weird at first to have grass on the wall, but it was actually like sitting in a garden once you got used to it.

I shook her hand. "Nice to meet you. Diego spoils my boy rotten and he's been so great with Paisley and Gannon."

Mandy smiled like only a woman can when she knows she's married to one of the good ones. "He's a keeper, for sure. I made him go to a doctor's appointment today so he left me in charge. Lord help us all." Her laugh was booming as she shifted her gaze to the man next to me. The one I couldn't get out of my head. "And who's this handsome fellow?"

"Hi, I'm Lincoln Angelo." Linc shook Mandy's hand, giving her a charming smile. The man couldn't seem to help himself. He was just a beautiful specimen and the ladies seemed to notice. Between his looks and that voice, a woman didn't stand a chance.

"Well, hello, Lincoln." Mandy turned to me and waggled her eyebrows. "Nice work, Keva."

I startled, catching her meaning. "Oh! No. We're not—"

"Well, hello there. What's your name?"

I spun around, finding a woman crouched down talking to my son, who'd obviously gotten bored with our conversation and was making eyes at the woman behind us in line. Linc edged closer to me, his hand landing on my low back. It was his touch that had words dying on my tongue. My brain seemed to short-circuit when he was touching me.

The woman looked up and I remembered who she was. Rosemary, the principal at Blueball Elementary School. "Hey, Keva. Is this your son? I've never met him."

"Y-yes." I stepped away from Linc, his hand falling away from my back. "Rosemary, this is Lucas. Lucas, this is Ms. Roberts, the principal at the school."

Rosemary gently showed Lucas how to shake her hand. "Will you be joining me for kindergarten soon, Lucas?"

"Oh no, he's only three," I interjected. "Well, four next week. Not quite ready for kindergarten."

The words were out before I could snatch them back. I hadn't meant to lay out the timeline of Lucas's life like that. Not in front of Linc. If he did the math, he'd certainly have a lot of questions for me.

Suddenly, Linc's arm was around my shoulders, steering me back to the register. "We'd better order, sweetheart."

I looked up at him and the look he gave me had me biting my tongue. There was no easy grin in sight. Just denim-blue eyes that held questions. Lots and lots of questions.

Shit.

CHAPTER TEN

inc

Have I mentioned how slow my brain works sometimes?

I sat across from Keva the whole time during lunch being pissed off that she'd met some other guy so soon after being with me. I'd built up our connection into something huge and significant in my head over the last five years, and now I'd found out that she'd slept with someone else right after. I'd also felt a connection all day today packing boxes next to her, but she'd been quick to move away from me in public. Was I simply delusional? Did I see something in her that she absolutely did not see in me?

By the time we got back to her house to keep packing, I was in a mood.

"I'll pack up the truck," I muttered, moving off down the hallway to get away from her. I just needed a few minutes to breathe. To wrap my head around being insignificant to the woman I'd fantasized about for five straight years. Perhaps that was the problem. I'd built her up so much in my head there was no way reality could measure up.

I grabbed the top box in a stack of boxes in her bedroom, completely ignoring the way the room smelled like her—sweet baked goods in a field of wildflowers—in case anyone wondered. I walked out to the truck holding my breath and loading it up without looking over at her at all. I continued in this manner until there was only one box left. I stooped to pick it up, and even before I'd exited her bedroom, I felt the flimsy bottom give way. Heavy objects shifted and hit my boots in a messy pile. I growled and tossed aside the ruined box.

I grabbed a T-shirt first, surprised to find it wrapped around a manilla file folder. I untangled the mess only to realize the T-shirt had the word Army written on the front. Holy shit. It was my shirt. Had to be. And then my brain was taking me back to that day five years ago when we'd answered the door and she'd been wearing nothing but this shirt of mine. I'd gotten my bell rung by her brother, so I'd forgotten that tiny detail.

She'd kept my shirt. For five years.

I stooped over to grab the manilla folder while I tried to process if that really meant what I thought it meant. My heart was already dancing a jig even though my head tried to project caution. I jammed a few pieces of paper in the folder and then paused on an official-looking document. Lucas's birth certificate.

Fuck. I knew I shouldn't look, but curiosity got the better of me. My gaze scanned until I reached the section for the father's information. Blank. What the hell? Who would get a girl pregnant and then bail from the entire situation? Clearly, whoever he was, he was an asshole. My gaze took in Lucas's date of birth. I knew his birthday was next week, but for some reason, seeing the exact date in black and white hit me different. I sank down to the floor and tried to count backward in my head. My limbs went numb and that sixth sense that told me there was danger ahead was clanging out a loud warning.

"Fuck," I whispered, brain stunned and scrambling. Were

women pregnant nine months or ten? I dropped the birth certificate and used my fingers to count again. Same result.

Then I got smart and pulled out my cell phone. My older sister had used an app when she got pregnant a few years ago to determine when she was due. I plugged in the date I'd been with Keva and hit submit. The date it spit out was two days off from Lucas's birthday. The phone slipped from my hand.

"I'm going to take Lucas over to Janice's! Be right back!" Keva hollered from the living room where she had been packing up all his toys.

Anger, the kind that's laced with so much hurt you're not sure where one ends and the other begins, filled every square inch of my body. I stood, breathing like I'd humped through the desert with a sixty-pound pack on. I stalked into the living room and grabbed an empty box. Back in the bedroom, I threw everything into the new box and taped it shut in a daze. Keva met me outside as I threw it into the back of my truck.

"All set to head over? Janice will watch Lucas overnight so I can get things settled over there first."

I jerked my head down and pulled keys out of my pocket. I couldn't speak. I feared I'd open my mouth and yell and never stop. Climbing into the truck, I tried to wrap my head around Lucas being my son and Keva never telling me.

As a leader in the military, I asked for one thing from the soldiers in my care. Tell the truth. Always. We were on the same team and nothing was too embarrassing or too small to share with the group. Sometimes it mattered on the level of life and death. This little detail though? It wasn't small. It was fucking huge.

"You okay?" Keva asked, darting looks in my direction as I took the first turn a little faster than I should have with the bed of the truck jammed with boxes.

I nodded again, feeling like my jaw might crack if I ground my teeth any harder. She snorted but let it drop, looking out the window as the scenery passed. I glanced over at her, my hands tightening on the wheel as my body reacted to seeing her curves in those tight pants and sweater. My body hadn't gotten the message that we were pissed off at her.

The truck bumped and rolled as we went over the uneven ground to the new glampsite Gannon had given us. I could see why he couldn't rent these two yet. The hardscape wasn't in yet, nor was Keva's trailer decked out with lawn chairs and string lights like mine was. I'd give her mine so Lucas had a nice place to come home to.

Lucas.

Holy shit. I had a son.

Keva slammed her door shut, having slipped out of the truck while I was lost in my head. I scrambled out after her, catching her around the back as she pulled down the tailgate. Wind whistled through the pine trees that surrounded the site, cocooning us in our own private bubble. It was now or never. And I was done with being in the dark.

"Were you ever going to tell me?"

Keva froze, hands reaching for the very box that had spilled her secrets. She turned, face locked in a neutral expression. "I'm sorry?"

"You should be," I snapped, feeling out of control in a way I hadn't felt in a very long time. "If I hadn't come back, would you have told me about Lucas?"

She put her hands on her hips, pretty little nose in the air. "What about Lucas?"

My arms exploded out from my sides. "That he's my son, Keva!"

Her face went white and she sagged against the tailgate of the truck. Her gaze faltered, dropping down to my boots. I wanted to both comfort her and rail at her for being so goddamn manipulative. I took a step closer, not sure if I could keep my hands from wrapping around her neck, but needing her to look me in the eye when she told me the truth.

"Well?"

She looked at me again, but all the fight had left her body. "I tried to tell you."

That was as good an admission as I'd get. I took a step back, shaking my head. I needed to stay away from her or I'd do something I'd regret later. I dropped my head back and stared up at the sky, hands behind my head. When I was able to look at her again without wanting to shake her senseless, she had tears in her eyes. Oh no, she didn't. She didn't get to cry when I was the one in the dark, losing out on four fucking years with my own son.

"Didn't try very hard. Could have told your brother at any time. Could have called me up. Sent a letter. Come and visited. Paid a guy to fly a plane and write it up in the sky where I'd see. Lots of fuckin' options, sweetheart."

"How'd you find out?" she asked weakly, staring at my boots again.

I felt like I was going to jump right out of my skin. I crossed my arms over my chest and tucked my hands in my armpits. If I could have sat on my hands to ensure I didn't do anything stupid, I would have.

"Does it matter?" When she shook her head, I pointed to the box. "Probably shouldn't have kept my shirt wrapped around the birth certificate. I've got a thick skull, but even I was able to figure that one out."

Keva sighed like she'd been holding her breath for years.

"I can't believe you kept my son from me. I hate liars." I also hated that I still found her attractive despite those lies.

Her gaze snapped up, a flare of attitude propping her up again. Then she attacked the box, ripping off the tape like a crazed woman and flipping through all the crap that was in there. She held up a tattered letter like it was some kind of triumphant cure-all for this situation. She slapped it against my chest and looked up at me with equal amounts of tears and fire in her deep blue eyes.

"And I hate deadbeats." She snapped her finger against the letter. "Maybe you shouldn't have sent my letter back unopened."

And then she marched off into the woods to places unknown.

And fuck if I didn't watch her go, admiring the way she held her head high while her hips moved in a mesmerizing rhythm.

CHAPTER ELEVEN

*K*eva

Me: Lucas is with Janice tonight. Need a wine and bitch session. ASAP. I don't have a place, so someone needs to host.

Audrey: Tonight? Um, my roommate is having some people over tonight. Marlo?

Marlo: No one ever comes to my place for girls' night.

Paisley: An apartment with a view of the cemetery? No, thanks. Come to my place. Gannon was going to take Elise to a birthday party anyway.

Me: Done. Bring lots of sugar and alcohol.

Marlo: Oh boy.

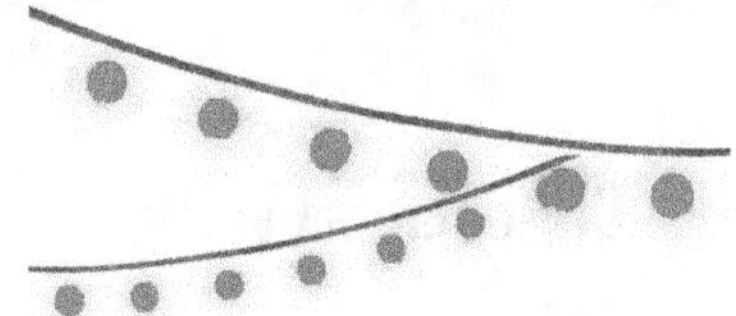

"OH, SHIITT." Audrey held out the word for dramatic effect.

I didn't need more drama. I had enough going on in my life as it was.

"Was he mad?" Marlo asked, moving the plate of brownies closer to me on the coffee table.

I took a swig of wine, feeling like I had enough energy to stay up for days on end. "No, he was perfectly fine knowing I'd kept him in the dark for years about his own son," I deadpanned.

"Okay, no need to get snarky." Marlo pouted. "I meant was he mad that he had a son or mad that you kept him from him?"

I sighed and put down my glass to scrub my hand across my aching forehead. "Sorry, Marlo. I'm just mad and scared and anxious and worried. I'm feeling all kinds of things, and I didn't mean to take it out on you."

Marlo reached over and grabbed my hand, giving it a squeeze.

"Let's talk about all that. What has you mad?" Paisley had on her psychologist hat. I could just tell from her no-nonsense tone of voice. Which normally would bother me, but I was at the point where I'd take any help I could get.

I snagged another brownie off the plate. My constant quest to drop the baby weight would just have to wait a little longer. "I'm mad because he called me a liar and then said he hates liars. I tried to tell him but he refused to listen! How is that my fault?"

Marlo let go of my hand so I could eat my brownie in peace. "You did. You sent a letter."

Audrey made a noise with her nose. My head snapped in her direction.

"What?"

She held her hands out in a gesture of peace. "Nothing, babe." But she and Paisley shared a look.

"What? Spit it out," I snapped.

"Well, it's just that one letter is, like, the bare-minimum attempt. You know what I'm saying?"

"For a matter as big as a surprise baby, I would think maybe a bit more effort would be expected," Paisley hedged.

I knew that. Deep down in my heart I knew I should have done more to contact Linc. But when that letter had come back Return to Sender, he'd hurt me. Crushed me. And I was about to be a single mom. I didn't have time to be hurt and mope about. I had a son to raise. So I got mad and that anger helped me put one foot in front of the other.

"That's the worried part of things. I'm worried I didn't do enough to notify Linc and he'll take that out on us. What if he's mean to my son?"

Marlo sat forward with a look so fierce I almost lurched back. "I've got a backhoe and land to dig a big hole."

Paisley put her hand on Marlo. "Whoa, there, vigilante princess. Lincoln doesn't strike me as the kind of guy to be an asshole to a little boy. What if he's just angry because he wanted to be there with his son and didn't get that chance?"

I threw my hands in the air. "Then he should have opened my letter!"

"Be that as it may, he's here now. He knows Lucas is his. And he might want to be involved." Audrey sat forward. "This could be a really good thing, Keva."

I thought about having to see Linc every day for the rest of my life, looking all handsome and not mine. No fucking thank you.

"Yeah, I mean, you could finally have that co-parent to help you out. You can share the responsibility and finally have some time to yourself." Paisley looked genuinely excited, like everything was already settled.

"I don't want time to myself!" It was a weak argument because I'd spent almost four years lamenting never having time to myself to these very same women.

"Why are you resisting having Lincoln in your lives?" Paisley asked, back to squinting at me over her wineglass.

All the fight seemed to leave me all at once. The adrenaline of the situation had finally burned away and I was left exhausted. I grabbed a pillow off the couch cushion next to me and hugged it to my chest. Maybe that would hold me together.

"I pinned all my hope on that letter. I had visions of him swooping back into my life and marrying me and we'd be this happy little family." I snorted. What an idiot I'd been. The Keva of five years ago seemed like a lifetime ago. "When he sent it back unopened, it broke my heart. He not only rejected me, he rejected Lucas." I could feel tears burning my eyes. Linc was just one in a long line of people who I'd given my heart to and they'd walked away.

My best friends, knowing my history, knew what it had taken for me to reach out to him for help. Marlo topped off my wineglass and Paisley came over to sit at my feet, her head on my knees.

Audrey was the first to speak. "Well, he knows now and he doesn't seem to be walking away this time. I think you might need to find a way to let him back in."

I opened my mouth to protest, but she cut me off.

"At least into your lives. Not your heart. Lucas deserves to have a father figure, babe."

And there went all the strength that was keeping my spine straight. I slouched back into the couch and let the tears fall. I would do absolutely anything for my son. Including letting the blue-eyed devil who'd rejected me waltz right back into our lives and stir shit up. If it would benefit my son, I'd set my skin on fire. And I had a feeling letting Linc back into my life would feel just as torturous.

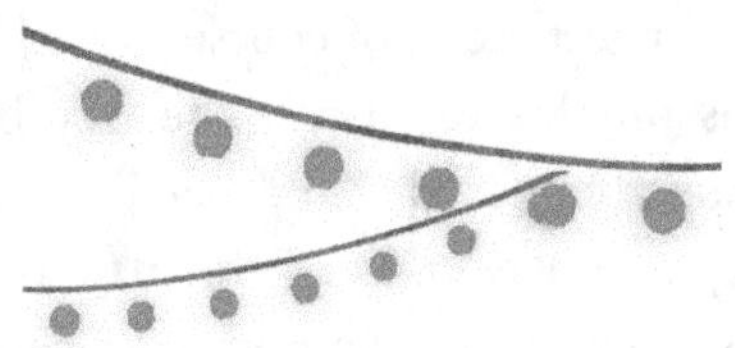

"Mama?"

I folded myself over his little bed, stroking my fingers through his wet hair. I was exhausted from putting away all our things in the new trailer, feeding Lucas a dinner that was marginally nutritious, and getting him bathed for the night. He'd be going to Janice's tomorrow before I went to work, but I'd have to find him a new daycare. Janice was set to leave at the end of the week.

"Yeah, baby?"

"Can I pway with Ellie?"

Lucas and Elise played together a lot when us girls met up, but now living this close, they'd be playing a lot more. "Sure. As soon as I get done with work tomorrow."

"Can I pway with the gin?"

I smiled at his little voice. I'd probably cry when he started saying all his words correctly. "The what?"

"The gin, Mama. It's wed."

Then it dawned on me. "Oh, the red engine that Linc gave you?"

"Yeah!" He threw his little arms in the air. His pajamas with the green dinosaurs were getting too small for him. Mentally, I added pajamas to my never-ending list of things to pick up this week.

"I'll check with Linc and see. Now how about we read a story? You get to pick tonight." Parenting tip number one: always redirect.

He picked the longest story, of course. I held back the groan and tried to focus on this moment. The way he snuggled his little body up against mine. How he liked to point at certain words with his finger as I read. Even the little-boy smell of him was precious. I'd simply sleep in another fourteen years when he moved away from home.

When his eyes finally slipped shut and his breathing evened out, I crept from the bed and put the book down. His door clicked shut with barely a noise. I had to turn slideways to slide down the hallway and out the main door. I'd planned to go outside and stare at the stars behind our trailer for a few minutes like I used to do at our old place, but stumbled to a halt on the stairs.

Our front yard was suddenly illuminated by a strand of string lights overhead. And there was fake grass and two white chairs just outside my door. Those hadn't been there earlier when we were moving in.

"Figured you two would use them more than I would."

Linc's smooth voice had me spinning around to see him sitting on the ground, his back against the tall oak tree that shaded both his trailer and mine. I blinked, wondering how long he'd been sitting there and why my heart was suddenly speeding up. I'd come outside to wind down for the night, not feel like I was in the middle of running a marathon. Not that I had any idea what that felt like or any inclination to want to know.

"Thank you," I managed.

I'd successfully avoided him all day. Probably because he'd been building a pergola with Gannon on the far side of Glamper's Paradise. Not that I'd been watching him hard enough to notice the sweat pattern on the back of his shirt or how his muscles flexed while holding up planks of wood. Nope. I was too busy moving in for that.

"I want in, Keva."

Damn him and that smooth-as-whiskey deep voice. It gave me shivers and made me think of hot, dirty sex out in the woods.

"What?"

"I read the letter you sent me, and I swear to God, I never saw it." Linc stood and walked toward me, looking older, but also just as handsome as I'd remembered him all those years ago. "If I'd seen the letter, I would have opened it. I can promise you that. I would never have left you and Lucas on your own. I can't roll back the clock, but I can be here now. Let me in. Please."

I had to squeeze my eyes shut to keep him out. I'd wanted to hear those words so badly when I was pregnant with Lucas. It was years too late, but the girls were right. I needed to let him back into our lives. For Lucas's sake. To be a father for Lucas, not a partner for me. With my walls firmly in place, I opened my eyes again.

"I think Lucas would like that."

Linc crowded closer. I could see the scruff on his chin that hadn't been there before. "And what about his mama?"

I swallowed hard. He did not mean what my stupid heart wanted him to mean. I knew this and yet my heart kept pounding out a rhythm of hope.

"I want what's best for Lucas."

Linc nodded. "You're a good mom, Keva. Lucas is lucky to have you."

And fuck if that didn't soothe some emotional wounds I didn't know I had. I didn't want his praise to mean anything, but it did. "Thank you."

Linc reached up, his big hand tucking a lock of my hair behind my ear. His barely there touch sent my limbs trembling. "I'm asking you to give me a chance to be a good dad. It's only fair."

I had to lock my knees and clench my hands into fists to keep from leaning into that hand of his. "I'm used to doing things alone, so it might take me some time to share."

Linc let go of my hair and put his hand on my shoulder. "I can understand that."

A flare of anger had me stepping back and pushing away the fog of desire that clearly still had ahold of me with this man.

"Can you though? Can you imagine being a pregnant twenty-year-old with no family? No home? No support system? You think you can handle a baby until you haven't slept in days and you don't have enough money to buy another pack of diapers and your car dies yet again." Just talking about it made my stress levels kick up. Lucas and I had gotten into a good rhythm, and with the help of my boss, my friends, and Janice, we'd somehow pulled through.

"Regardless of whether I should have done more to tell you, you don't get to waltz in here after the fact and be the good-time dad. If you want in on Lucas's life, you have to go all in. The good and the bad. The inconvenient and the hard. If you can do all that, then you'll deserve him."

Linc followed me, his eyes burning in the soft yellow overhead lights. "If you'd given me a chance to be there, you'd know I'm all in. I'm sorry for what you went through, Keva, I really am. But I'm here now and I'll prove I'm here to stay. All I need from you is to trust me."

He was even hotter when pissed, but I couldn't let him off the hook that easy. "Trust is earned."

"Same goes, Keva. Hard to trust a woman who kept my son from me."

I reached up and pressed my hands to his chest, shoving with all my might. He was a rock-hard slab of muscle, but I was a pissed-off woman. He didn't lurch back enough to satisfy me.

"I already explained that!"

Linc grabbed my hands off his chest and held my wrists

between us with just one hand. He was breathing as hard as I was. "Explain again how your phone didn't work?"

"Explain again why you just walked away without a word!"

My back hit his trailer. Shit. I didn't even know we'd been moving. Linc lifted my hands and pressed them over my head, pinning me against the trailer. He stepped in so close I felt his hard body at the top of each inhale. My heart was hammering so loud he had to hear it.

He dipped his head and sniffed my neck, a delicious slide of beard that burned my skin. I shivered, which he obviously felt because when he lifted his head, he sported a cocky grin.

"I've thought about you every day for five years, woman."

And then his lips were on mine, stealing my breath and making the world spin out of control.

CHAPTER TWELVE

inc

"So that's where I want to build a beach volleyball court. And across from it I want to take the existing fire pit and expand it." Gannon pointed out the locations on his property, walking me through his vision.

"Maybe some river rock for a seat wall around the pit. Outdoor furniture for socializing. Some tropical plants around the perimeter for screening," I added, seeing his vision come to life inside my head. This place could be the intersection of a high-end resort and communing with nature, glamping style.

Gannon clapped me on the shoulder. "I knew hiring you was the right decision, no matter what those harpies say."

I winced. "Sounds like Paisley's not too happy with me." Pretty sure Keva wasn't happy with me either. After I kissed her two nights ago, she'd been avoiding me. Which was hard, considering our living arrangements, but she'd managed it.

"Nah, Paisley'll get over it once she sees Keva's happy." Gannon shot me a look that had me wondering if he was about to punch me in the face. Been there, done that, knew the look. "You intend to make Keva happy, right?"

"Fuck yeah," I responded without hesitation. "But cut me some slack. I'm trying to figure out how to be a dad within a matter of days. I had no idea he existed until last week."

Gannon lost the papa-bear look and chuckled. "Yeah, I know a thing or two about that. Didn't know Elise was mine until her mother showed up on my doorstep and dropped her off at five years old."

I'd figured there was a story there, but knowing the details gave me hope. That little girl adored her dad.

"So, what do I do? How do I enter his life now?" I shifted to stand in front of Gannon. "Give me some tips. Please."

Gannon tilted his head to the right. "Let's go sit on the stage."

We walked over to the wooden stage he'd built under the biggest oak tree, having a seat on the edge and staring out at the pine trees that dotted his property line. The air smelled different here, cleaner, somehow more peaceful.

"You have a different situation. The mom is still involved. You have to be there for Lucas while also not pissing off the mom." Gannon chuckled. "And the mom's a pistol."

I ran a hand through my hair. "Yeah, I know. It's one of the things I like about her most. She's always been like that. It's just more intense now." I stood and paced the dance floor. I had too much pent-up energy to sit. "Lucas turns four in a few days. Keva says she usually just does a cake and dinner with friends and family. I was thinking of putting together a little outing for his birthday."

Gannon nodded. "Sounds like a good idea. Just make sure you get Keva's buy-off on the idea. You don't want to look like you're upstaging what she normally does for him."

"I won't. I just want to try to start a new tradition. One that involves me too."

Gannon wiped his hands on his jeans and stood. "You play any instruments?"

I blinked, trying to keep up with his erratic train of thought. "Yeah, the drums when I was a teen."

He seemed to like that answer. "Good, good. I'll get a set so you can practice."

"What for?"

He spread his hands wide, encompassing the stage. "If we're going to start a band, you'll need some drums."

My boss was officially insane. I'd met crazy good guys like him in the service. Made one of them my best friend. "Are you a closet good-time guy, Gannon Hart?"

He glowered. "What the hell's that supposed to mean?"

I twirled my finger in the air. "You give off this asshole I-don't-smile-even-when-I'm-happy air, but you're secretly a guy who likes to have a lot of fun."

Gannon just glared at me for a beat or two before a grin broke out on his face. He ducked his head. "Don't tell anyone."

I burst out laughing, and he joined me. I'd been nervous about trying civilian life again, but my new boss was making it a welcome change. I could see myself being friends with this guy.

"You ever thought about buying into this place with me?"

My gaze snapped to his. "Excuse me?"

He gestured to the glamp-ground around us. "It's a lot for one guy to manage. We can see how things go, but it kind of makes sense to expand with the success we've been having, and I can't do that without you. Maybe you should be a part owner."

"I, uh, well..."

Gannon tugged on his baseball cap. "Take some time. Give it some thought. If you're interested, we can work out the particulars." He turned to walk away. A lot had happened this last week and my brain was having a hard time keeping up.

"Gannon?"

"Yeah?" He paused and looked over his shoulder.

"Thank you."

He dipped his head and walked to the golf cart. He was planning to check out the far side of the property today to see if there was room for a public restroom and showers for those who snuck over to the lake on the property next to us. As he zoomed off, I grabbed my phone out of my pocket and shot off a text to Keva before I could overthink it.

Me: I heard about an indoor play place about half an hour from here. Any chance we could take Lucas there for his birthday?

Baby Mama: How'd you get my number?

I sighed. Dammit, the woman was difficult with a capital D.

Me: Don't you think I should have the phone number for my son's mother?

Baby Mama: I think Gannon needs to quit sticking his ugly nose in things that are none of his business.

Me: So…about that play place…

Baby Mama: Fine.

Me: You get the cake for after and I'll get us matching hats.

Baby Mama: I'm not wearing a hat.

Me: Come on, Keevs. It's a pretty birthday crown. I promise you'll love it.

Baby Mama: My name is Keva.

Me: That's not how I have you inputted on my phone…

She didn't answer me, and I figured she wouldn't. The second our lips touched, she'd been all over me, her body pressed against mine, her tongue just as eager to taste. But the second it ended, she'd pushed me away and walked back inside her trailer without a backward glance. The woman wanted me. That much I knew. But she didn't want me just as much.

I walked over to her trailer and began to plant the flowers I'd picked up this morning from the local nursery with Gannon's truck. The trailer didn't offer a lot of room, but I'd make this living space a thing of beauty for my son.

And for his mama.

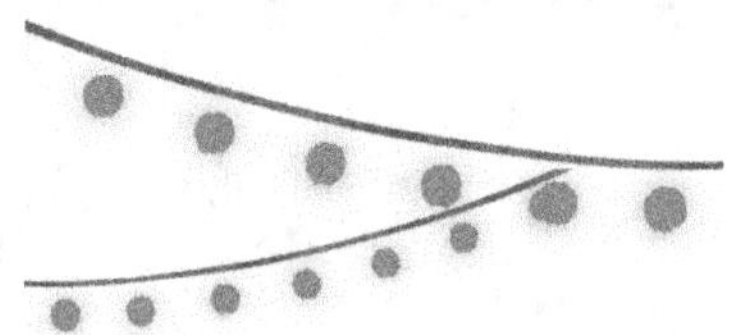

I hit the horn twice just to piss her off.

We both had the day off work and Gannon had lent me his truck again. I was starting to think I needed to sell my Harley and get a vehicle that would fit my growing family. Keva stuck her head out of her trailer and glared at me. Fuck, she was pretty when she was mad.

Lucas pushed past her in a full run and I hopped out of the truck to swing him up into my arms. He had on a shirt with two

T. rexes trying to fight and jean shorts that ate up his short legs. In other words: adorable.

"Happy birthday, Lucas!" I swung him around and then got a good look at him. I found myself doing that often. Just staring at him and cataloguing all his features. "Holy moly, you look so ooooold."

He giggled, his baby teeth showing. "I four!" He held up his fingers and I was insanely proud my son could count that high.

"Darn right you are. Let's get you in this car seat and we'll head to your surprise." I lowered him to the cab of the truck and he scrambled into the car seat I'd bought just yesterday.

"Does it have the right harness?" Keva was trying to push me out of the way to see the car seat. Her perfume hit me and I almost let her get away with pushing me out. At the last second I stood my ground and earned myself a growl from the little lady.

"Lincoln."

"Keva," I drawled back, pointing at our son. "Part of you trusting me. I researched car seats before I bought it."

She put her hands on her hips. "They're tricky to install just right—"

"Which is why I had Gannon and Paisley double-check it for me." I put my hands on her shoulders and dipped my head to get in her space. She'd put on makeup today, accentuating those deep blue eyes and long lashes. If she'd quit frowning, she'd have the perfect dramatic eyebrow shape all the women were trying for these days. "Just relax, and let me take you and Lucas for some fun."

She rolled her eyes. "I don't do fun."

"No shit," I deadpanned.

She drilled both index fingers into my abs and I let her go. She wasn't exactly smiling, but she wasn't frowning any longer.

"Hurt your fingers?" I asked her back as she walked to the passenger side of the truck.

She snorted and hopped in.

The ride to the play place was filled with chatter from the

back seat. All the talking Keva used to do was now coming from Lucas, and I was soaking it up like a sponge. Keva had to interpret a few times, but I was already starting to understand some of the words he mispronounced. When we entered, Keva tried to pay but I batted away her wallet.

"My treat, remember?"

She shrugged, but put her wallet back in the tiny purse she had strapped across her chest. The strap accentuated her boobs, a fact I'd noticed straight away and now couldn't stop noticing. They were bigger than I remembered, but that made sense given she'd birthed a baby. In my opinion, there was just that much more to love on. If she finally let me, that is.

We rode a few rides and then took a break to get cotton candy. Keva tried to protest, but I argued it was his birthday. We both turned pleading eyes on her and she relented.

"Fine, but if he pukes, it's on you. Probably literally."

I'd had all kinds of bodily fluids spilled on me in the military. "I'll take that chance."

I handed Lucas a huge cloud of blue cotton candy and he didn't waste any time pulling off a fistful and shoving it in his mouth. We walked in between the various rides and attractions, the sounds enough to make me rethink this as our destination today. I didn't do well with loud noises. My heart rate was up, and I was having a hard time convincing myself that everything was okay. This right here was the part of civilian life that I'd been dreading. The not fitting in in normal situations.

"Linc? You okay?"

Keva's question pulled me out of the breathing exercise I'd been doing any time anxiety threatened to get the best of me. I wiped my forehead, surprised to see that I'd started sweating. "Yeah, I'm good."

Keva tossed the rest of Lucas's cotton candy in a nearby trash can. Lucas's little hand slipped into mine and he held it tight. Keva took his other hand. As a family unit, we walked over to the area that had ropes and tunnels and slides. It was quieter over here and I focused on the feel of my son's sticky hand in mine. It calmed me more than the controlled breathing.

"I pway!" Lucas suddenly let go of us both and turned to shove our hands together. Then he bolted into the play area and climbed up a rope ladder.

Keva and I looked down at our hands. We were both sticky and hadn't planned on holding hands, but I suddenly needed that more than I needed air. I slid my fingers between hers and held on tight. She let me, her gaze lifting and focusing on Lucas as he climbed through the first tunnel. We just stood there, frozen, watching our son together while ignoring the fact that we were holding hands. It took a few minutes but my breathing finally normalized.

"Thanks for bringing him here."

I looked at Keva, who was still steadfastly not looking at me. "No way in hell I'd miss another birthday."

She inhaled sharply, lifting her nose in the air. I braced for something scathing to leave her mouth. "You're good with him."

My mouth opened but no sound came out. I tugged on our conjoined hands and managed to pull her gaze from Lucas for a moment. "Did it hurt?"

"Did what hurt?" She turned to look back at Lucas, and I appreciated how well she looked after our son.

"Saying something nice about me."

She scoffed and tried to pull her hand away. I held it even tighter.

"I'm kidding. Thank you. I'm not nearly as good with him as you are. He's a lucky boy to have you as his mother."

Keva swallowed thickly. "Thank you," she whispered.

"I'd like to tell Lucas I'm his dad."

Keva pulled her hand away then, keeping one eye on Lucas as she glared at me and crossed her arms over her chest. "He's not ready for that yet. It'll be confusing."

I pushed down the anger that flared, knowing it was just

masking the hurt her statement caused. She didn't trust me enough yet to tell Lucas the truth.

"I think you're stalling."

She made that scoffing noise again that I was coming to hate. "No, I'm not. I think I know my son better than you. You've known him, what? A week?"

"Only because you failed to tell me about him," I snapped back.

"Should have opened the letter, Angelo." Her voice was rising, causing a few heads to turn.

"Should have tried harder, Mooney."

We both glared at each other, chests heaving in anger.

"Excuse me. Is that your son?" A voice came from behind me.

We both spun around to see Lucas puking on a girl's shoes at the bottom of the slide. She screamed, and Lucas burst into tears.

CHAPTER THIRTEEN

Keva

WELL...THAT could have gone better.

"Happy birthday, baby," I whispered in the dark, knowing Lucas was already asleep.

The kiddo had been exhausted by the time we got to dinner and cake with my friends and Janice. Nothing like vomiting and crying on your birthday. To be fair, Linc had been great. I'd had more than a flash of annoyance with him for buying Lucas cotton candy, but then Linc had jumped right in to clean it up. He'd even exchanged emails with the little girl's parents, promising to send them money so they could buy her a new pair of shoes. Then he got Lucas laughing telling him stories about throwing up on a hike and not being able to stop because he was being chased by a wild animal. I wasn't sure if the story was real or not, but it made my boy smile, so I didn't question it.

Now he was waiting for me outside my trailer, his handsome self sitting in one of the Adirondack chairs he'd set up for me.

Despite all the fighting we seemed to do, I couldn't deny that my body was attracted to him still. He had this solemn look about him that made me think he was the bad-boy type. And then he'd swing our son up on his hip and run through the parking lot, both of them laughing their heads off, and he became so much more than a pretty face. And a hot body. And a fond memory.

The girls had given great advice about letting him back into our lives for Lucas's sake. Just one look at his toothy smiles today with a birthday crown on his head was enough to make that an obvious good decision. But I was finding it harder than I thought to make sure Linc didn't creep back into my heart too.

Probably because underneath all my stiff-upper-lip bullshit the last five years, if I really dug deep, I was certain my heart had never gotten over Lincoln Angelo.

I stepped outside and closed the door softly, pulling my sweater around me tighter. The nights were getting cooler these days, which reminded me I needed to start thinking about Halloween costumes for Lucas.

"What's the frown for? I haven't even opened my mouth yet."

I hazarded a glance at Linc. I could barely see him in the dark, sprawled in the chair, his legs out in front of him and his hands folded on his flat belly. His head rested against the back of the chair, looking entirely at ease out in front of my trailer. He hadn't turned on the string lights which made everything seem more intimate.

"I was adding Halloween costume to my mental checklist of things to do." I stepped over his legs and had a seat in the other chair, realizing that it put my leg entirely too close to his. I tried to fold my legs under me, but that made the armrests dig into my knees painfully. I finally gave up and let my legs rest right next to his. He shouldn't be the only one who could manspread.

Linc rocked his leg into mine, nudging me. "You always have a mental checklist running?"

I smirked. "Always. I used to leave myself sticky notes but Lucas went through a phase of trying to eat them when he was teething, so I switched to a mental list."

"Have you had boyfriends?"

My head whipped in his direction. He was looking at me intently, but he still hadn't lifted his head from the chair. "None of your business, Angelo."

He held his hands up with a smirk. "Whoa, don't start with the last names. I just meant, is this unusual for Lucas to be around a guy or is he used to having your boyfriends around?"

My skin felt like it was on fire. This was not a conversation I wished to have. "You're not my boyfriend."

Linc sat forward so suddenly I almost jumped. "Not yet anyway. Answer the damn question, Keva." His elbows rested on his knees, putting his hands brushing up against my leg.

"No, no boyfriends." I was flustered, which is the only reason the truth came out.

Linc's gaze didn't waver. "That Lucas has met? Or no boyfriends period?"

I huffed. "Period."

A grin grew on his face. A smug grin that made me angry. "I've been a little busy working full-time and raising a baby on my own. There hasn't really been time for dating."

"That's too bad." Linc stood up, towering over me, his eyelids drooping into a look that set the blood in my veins on fire. He'd looked the same way at me five years ago when I was wearing nothing but his T-shirt. "How about orgasms?"

My jaw dropped. His hand came up and pushed a lock of hair behind my ear. Why did that simple gesture make my limbs feel tingly? The side of his thumb traced a line across my cheek, stealing the breath from my lungs.

"No," I mumbled, not quite sure what his question had been. The truth of the matter was that I hadn't been with anyone since him. A fact that irritated me to no end, yet there was nothing I could do about it. I'd been telling the truth: there was absolutely no time for dating in my life.

Linc folded in half, his hands reaching out to grab mine. Then he was pulling me out of the chair.

"What—"

"Shh." He turned me around so that my back was to his front and then he sat back down, pulling on my hips so I ended up sitting in his lap. His arms banded around my waist, his nose nuzzling into my hair. "I wasn't here to give you a lot of the things you needed, but I'm here now and I can give you this."

My heart pounded against my ribs. His scent, the one that I'd started to forget over the years, hit me full force. He felt different below me, bigger, harder, simply more man than he'd been five years ago. One of his hands left my waist and ducked under my sweater. I held my breath. He moved ever so slightly, his fingertips dipping below the waistband of the leggings I'd worn knowing I'd be eating cake today and didn't want tight jeans digging into my skin.

"Say yes, Keva," Linc whispered in my ear.

I shivered, suddenly hot out here instead of cold. I'd said no a lot the last five years, denying what I wanted in order to give Lucas what he needed. What would be the harm in saying yes right now? Surely it wouldn't mean anything beyond tonight. Weren't the girls just saying I deserved just a little bit of time for myself? I felt like I was teetering on the edge of a cliff, ready to toss myself into the abyss for just a moment of pleasure. I'd purposely avoided cliffs like this for five straight years. I'd learned my lesson when the pregnancy test came back positive. Hadn't I?

"Yes," I said on an exhale, not at all sure if I was being an idiot or the smartest woman who'd ever lived.

"Good girl," Linc purred, fingers pushing down into my leggings. He paused for only a moment when he realized there was no barrier in the form of panties.

"Keva," he groaned, his forehead dropping to my shoulders like he was tortured by my undergarment decision. His fingers seemed delighted, spreading me open and finding my aching clit with a precision that made me gasp.

Linc's arm held me tight, not letting me squirm away from his touch. He flicked that bud and then abandoned it to find me soaking wet for him. With another deep groan I felt through my back pressed to his chest, he slid a finger inside of me. God, that felt so good. My eyelids drooped shut.

His thumb came back to my clit, somehow strumming while his finger pumped. Sensation I hadn't allowed myself, except for the odd night here and there where I used some of the toys I'd collected, came roaring back. I tried to squeeze my thighs together, but Linc kicked my feet wide with his boots and held me open for him. The man was everywhere, behind me, under me, surrounding my legs, and most importantly, inside my body.

It took an embarrassingly short amount of time before the feverish buildup had me arching away from him. My legs began to quake and everything below clenched around his fingers. My head fell back to his shoulder while he whispered dirty things in my ear. I let out the tiniest of gasps that sounded to my ears like a shotgun in the middle of the dark forest. And then I was trembling all over, riding out the best orgasm I'd had since we made Lucas.

Linc stayed still, his fingers still inside me as I blinked my eyes open to see the pine trees and stars overhead. He turned his head to kiss my cheek.

"I haven't been with anyone either," he said on a voice that had lost its smooth quality.

I lurched up and he reluctantly pulled his hand out of my leggings. He didn't let go around my waist though. I twisted to see him. He couldn't possibly be telling the truth. "You haven't been with anyone since me?"

He looked me right in the eye and said it again. I shook my

head, realizing he spoke the truth and finding that somehow incredibly hard to believe.

"Why? Did you get hurt? Never took leave? Somehow the women didn't like tall gorgeous men with muscles and tattoos where you were stationed?"

His cocky grin had me realizing what I'd said. "You think I'm gorgeous?"

I swatted at his chest. "Focus, Angelo."

He grabbed my hand and held it to his mouth where he kissed the back of it and then inhaled nice and long through his nose. I realized he was smelling his hand—the one that had just been inside me—and nearly died of embarrassment right there on his lap. I snatched my hand back while he chuckled.

"Oh, I'm focused, sweetheart."

I rolled my eyes and tried to get back up. He held me tight and shook his head at me.

"Does this mean I owe you an orgasm too?" I snapped, not at all relaxed and sleepy any longer.

Linc shrugged, looking like he was holding back a grin. "I wouldn't say no..."

"Gah!" I pushed his hands off me and stood, wrapping my sweater around me as if that would ward off the charm and irritation of Lincoln Angelo.

"This didn't happen," I stated clearly, while also keeping my voice down because Lucas was asleep just feet away from where his mama had let a man take advantage of her. Okay, I was lying about the "taking advantage" thing. I'd said yes and enjoyed the hell out of it while it lasted. It was only now, when I had to deal with his cocky grin, that I was regretting it.

Linc stood slowly, studying me seriously in the shadows cast by the moon overhead. He lifted his hand to touch me, but I shifted backward. His hand fell to his side.

"Where's the girl who was wild and crazy and rode on the back of a stranger's moped all the way into the city? The girl who swore she could read minds?"

I thought back to myself back in those days and tried not to be embarrassed. I'd been young. Carefree. And also careless. Those days were long gone.

"I've changed, Linc. I had to grow up in an instant so I could help a little boy grow up."

He dipped his head and shuffled his feet. When he lifted his head again, his eyes were soft. There was absolutely no fight left in him right now.

"And you did a great job. Better than I ever could. Thank you for taking such good care of our son. I know I asked you to let me into Lucas's life, and you have. But I have to warn you. I want into your life too. It's not enough to just take care of Lucas. I want to take care of you. When was the last time someone took care of you, Keva?"

His words were too much. Too close to the wound I hid deep in my heart. My eyes burned with tears and I turned to go inside. With my hand on the doorknob, Linc made his position clear.

"I'm going to take care of you, Keva, whether you want me to or not. I know you don't trust anything I say, so I'll just leave you with this. Actions speak louder than words and I plan on shouting."

I yanked the door open and went inside before the tears spilled down my cheeks. Linc was right about one thing: I didn't believe him one bit. Life had shown me over and over again that there was only one person I could count on: myself. I didn't plan on relying on yet another person who would let me down.

I'd take the orgasms and leave the man out of my heart.

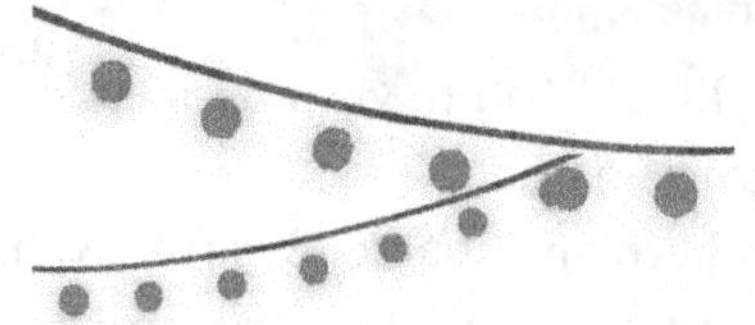

Baby Daddy: That totally happened, by
the way.

CHAPTER FOURTEEN

inc

"We're saying goodbye to Janice this morning and then it's take-your-kid-to-work day for me apparently." Keva wouldn't even look at me as she was stuffing her overfilled bag in the back seat of her car.

I had to jump out of her way as she spun on her heel and stomped toward the trailer, kicking up dust and pine cones in her wake. Her hair was up in a severe bun. Her spine was stiffer than my dick last night when she fell apart in my lap. Gone was the soft moans and the eyes as wide and soft as a deer. This morning's Keva screamed stress.

"Let me help you," I said calmly, following behind her as she stepped up into the trailer.

"No time, Angelo."

I shook my head and continued on my course anyway. Lucas was reaching up high to put his cereal bowl in the tiny kitchen sink. I grabbed it from him and got it in there before the left-over milk spilled down the front of the new shirt he'd gotten from Lucy for his birthday.

"Good morning, Lucas."

"Hi!" He shot me a cheesy grin of all teeth before turning around and running back to get a tiny backpack that had cartoon sharks all over it. He slung it over his shoulder and looked so adorable I forgot all about his mama's bad mood.

"Excuse me," Keva trilled behind me. I shifted to the side and she grabbed yet another bag off the counter, her blouse brushing against my arm. The flowery perfume she seemed to always wear hit my nose and I was right back to that chair in the dark, with her in my lap.

"Let's go, Lucas!" she barked in my ear. The daydream vanished.

"How about I go with you?"

That got her attention. With one hand on the doorknob she finally met my gaze. "Why?"

I frowned. "Why? Because you seem stressed and maybe I can help."

She shook her head and went out the door, Lucas hot on her heels. "You can't help."

This fucking woman. I pushed off the counter and followed her out, careful to lock the door behind me. While she got Lucas in his car seat, I climbed into the passenger seat and buckled my seat belt. For every reason I had for being obsessed with this woman, I had another reason for disliking her. It was like she had no concept of sharing. I was here now. Lucas was my son too, and I wanted to be there for him in every capacity.

Keva slid behind the wheel and sighed, giving me side-eye but keeping her mouth blessedly closed. She drove all the way to Janice's house in silence, Lucas babbling in the back with his dinosaur toys. When we got there, Keva sighed again.

"You miss your old house?" I asked quietly.

She stared out the window at the duplex, shoulders slumped. "No. I already miss Janice."

"Janny leave, Mama?"

Keva instantly straightened up, plastering a smile to her face before turning around to answer Lucas. "Yeah, baby. She's got the baby to go take care of."

Lucas frowned, thinking this over. "I not a baby."

"Nope. You're a big boy now," Keva answered and I could see her eye twitch as she said it. She hid it well, but she was having a hard time with this transition. She hid it for Lucas, but she couldn't hide it from me.

"You no call me baby, Mama."

Keva inhaled sharply. "I've always called you baby. I might call you baby when you're older than Linc."

Lucas cracked up. Apparently I was as old as those dinosaurs in his hands. "Otay, Mama."

We climbed out and said goodbye to Janice right there in the front yard. Lucas cried for a minute but then got busy playing with the new toy Janice had bought him. Keva held the woman tightly, and when she finally stepped back, I could see how hard she was fighting to keep her emotions under control. I took the keys from her and got both of them back in the car. With me behind the wheel, we pulled away from the curb and Keva and Lucas waved until we disappeared around the corner.

Lucas crashed his dinosaurs together, babbling in different voices as he let his imagination run wild in the back seat. I looked over at Keva to see her blinking rapidly and staring out the side window. I didn't give a shit if she'd be mad at me for it, I had to hold her hand. Reaching over quickly, I grabbed her hand and squeezed her fingers. She squeezed me back, actually letting me comfort her in the smallest of ways. When she wasn't sniffling any longer and we were almost to Glamper's Paradise, I tried talking to her.

"I asked to be part of Lucas's life, and that means letting me in on the stressful parts too. Not just the cotton-candy-and-buying-toys part."

Keva gave me that side-eye again, but she didn't let go of my hand. "I know."

"Do you though? You bottle it all up quietly and only let it out when you're exploding. I'd like to step in before you get to the exploding part."

She opened her mouth to argue with me but I cut her off.

"For example, why are you taking Lucas to work today?"

She shut her mouth and tapped her thumb against my hand. "Ugh, fine. I'm having a hard time finding a daycare that will take him mid-year."

I frowned. I hadn't thought about that because she'd never told me about it, and quite frankly, I was still fucking new at this parenting thing. But I did know one thing.

"I'll take him today. And every day this week. Would that help out?"

"You can't—"

"Says who? Gannon has days when he has Elise with him."

Keva let go of my hand as I turned into the glamp-ground. I parked back in front of our trailers, turning to look at her.

Keva huffed, but she quit arguing. "Fine. But he needs to lie down for a nap around two or he'll be a beast by dinnertime. And he needs lunch, but you have to cut it up really well and stay on him about eating it. Otherwise, he'll play the whole time and forget to eat and then he'll crash. And don't forget to put sunscreen on him if you're going to be outside. He's pale like me."

"Keva," I interrupted, putting my hand on her arm. "I got this. You'll see."

She searched my face and then looked back at Lucas. "Okay, but I'm just a phone call away if you have questions."

"We got it. Don't worry." Feeling all kinds of happy to have my son with me all day, and to perhaps lower Keva's stress levels, I climbed out of the car and opened up the back. "Lucas, my man. You're with me today."

Lucas looked up from his dinosaurs and let out a cheer that

warmed my heart. I helped him out of the car seat, grabbed Keva's ridiculously stuffed bag plus his backpack, slung both over my shoulder, and held Lucas's hand as we walked away.

"Have a good day, Mama!" I called over my shoulder.

Keva was standing by the open driver's side, looking all kinds of worried with this decision. I had a feeling that was her normal state of being. And quite frankly, I couldn't blame her. She'd been solely responsible for this kiddo for years now. I'd be a ball of anxiety too.

Turned out, it really was take-your-kid-to-work day at Glamper's Paradise. Gannon had Elise due to a lice outbreak at the kindergarten, which made it even easier to get work done. The two kids played while we took turns working and watching over them. When we finally took a break for lunch, neither kid was sunburned or injured, so I deemed that a success.

We did a picnic with peanut butter and jelly sandwiches, grapes, cheese sticks, and juice boxes under the tall oak by the wood stage. When Elise had enough, she climbed into Gannon's lap and stole his hat off his head to plunk it down on hers.

"Paisey says I look better in hats than you, Daddy."

Gannon looked pissed. "No, she did not."

Elise just shrugged. "Face it, Daddy. She did."

I tried not to laugh, but damn. Gannon had his hands full with that one. Lucas threw one more grape in his mouth and then shuffled closer to me. He was watching his little friend while staying awfully quiet.

"How about you, buddy? You like hats?" I asked him as he got so close his arm was now plastered against mine.

Gannon and Elise began to argue before Elise tackled him and a tickle fight ensued. Lucas and I shook our heads and laughed at their antics.

"Linc?" Lucas was suddenly looking up at me, serious as can be with his wide blue eyes.

"Yeah, buddy?"

"I want a daddy too."

You could have shot an arrow right through my gut and I wouldn't have been in as much pain as seeing my son desperate for a father. I put my hand on his little shoulder and debated my words. I hadn't exactly gotten the green light from Keva, but fuck it.

"I'll be your daddy from now on, buddy. Would you like that?"

Lucas studied me very seriously, looking just like his mama. Then he smiled and stood up, throwing his arms around my neck. "Yes, Daddy!"

I held him close, blinking back tears. Fuck, this parenting thing was harder than anything I'd ever done. No one had prepared me for the emotional hit when you heard your child call you daddy for the first time. But all of it seemed worth it to feel my son's hug. To know that I'd be there to help him from now on.

"Come on, guys. I just had a great idea." Gannon's voice brought me back to the picnic. He and Elise were covered in leaves and dirt. "I think we should build a tree house for the kids."

I kept Lucas close while we helped clean up the picnic. Gannon explained his plan while we worked. Elise whooped and Lucas threw his arm in the air with a "Yeah!" that scared all the birds in the tree above us.

"Can it have a princess chair, Daddy?" Elise asked.

Lucas pressed in closer to Gannon. "A wookout too?"

Gannon shot my son a grin. "Can't have a tree house without a lookout and a princess chair. Damn right. This is going to be the best tree house you've ever seen."

The kids cheered while Gannon and I began to talk out the design. We got busy using the wood he already had from previous projects, finding the perfect tree within a few feet from the future volleyball court. We'd gotten the ladder complete and half of the first floor—because of course this thing was going to have multiple levels—when a delivery truck pulled up.

Gannon was practically giddy, swiping his face with the bottom of his T-shirt. "Guess what I bought?"

I shook my head. The guy was crazy. It could be anything. "An outdoor fan?" I wiped the sweat off my forehead. I could practically wring out my shirt. I wasn't looking forward to seeing how hot it got during the summer around here.

The delivery driver had to use a dolly to get the boxes off the truck. Gannon and the kids danced around him the whole time while I cleaned up our tree house project. I hadn't been checking the time, but it seemed like we were definitely past nap time based on the way the sun was already starting to dip in the sky toward the west. When the boxes were on the stage and the driver had gunned it back down the road, Gannon pulled me over.

"Open it!"

I frowned at the boxes while seeing three smiling faces staring at me. "What is it?"

"You gotta open it, dumbass," Gannon grouched before Elise pinched him and he yelped. "Sorry."

To keep him from being black and blue—the guy cursed as much as everyone I'd met in the military—I opened the first box as quickly as I could. When I got a good look at what was inside, I burst out laughing.

"What is it?" Elise squealed, coming over to look. Lucas followed but he was too short to see inside. I scooped him up on my hip so he could see.

"You bought a drum set?" I asked Gannon, dumbfounded. I thought he'd been joking when he brought it up before.

"Fu—freak yeah, I did." Gannon grabbed another box and opened that one, eager to get the whole thing set up. "We're starting a band, Lincoln!"

I scrubbed a hand over my face and looked at Lucas. He shrugged his little shoulders and then laid his head on my chest. Poor kid was beat. Should have gotten him that nap.

"What's going to be our band name?" I finally asked, giving in to the inevitable.

Gannon whooped. "That's right! Glampers R Us?"

I grimaced. "That's terrible."

"It's a brainstorming session, dummy. You try coming up with something better."

I smoothed a circle around and around on Lucas's back while he snuggled into me and blinked his heavy eyelids closed. Honestly, all I could think about was how my son was comfortable enough with me to fall asleep in my arms. Now if I could just get his mama to do the same.

"You look good as a dad," Gannon said softly, patting me on the back.

I couldn't have stopped the smile if my life depended on it. "Thanks, man."

The little guy was like a heat rock. While Gannon got the drums set up, Elise helped me lay out the picnic blanket on the ground under the tree, along with another blanket from the bag Keva had packed. I laid Lucas down and covered him up, letting him sleep. By the time the drum set was ready and Gannon had taken the golf cart to get his guitar from their house, Lucas was blinking his eyes open again. The nap hadn't been long, but hopefully it would keep him from crashing later and keep his mama from yelling at me.

We starting jamming out in a cacophony of noise while I tried to remember how to play drums. It was a messy start, but by the time Keva and Paisley walked over to the stage after work, we were rocking out an easy song that actually didn't sound too bad. The kiddos were dancing and giggling, not at all annoyed by our amateur sound. Several of the campers had come by to hang out and listen too.

Keva and Paisley clapped when we finally wound down. I put the sticks on the stage and stood up, stretching out my back. I hadn't played in years, but Gannon was right. It was fun as shit.

"Time for dinner and bed, my rocker family," Paisley called out, drawing the kids' attention to their presence.

Lucas went running for Keva, hugging her legs and shouting up at her, "Daddy's a wockstar!

Keva's head whipped up to lock eyes with me.

Shit.

That was not a look of love right there.

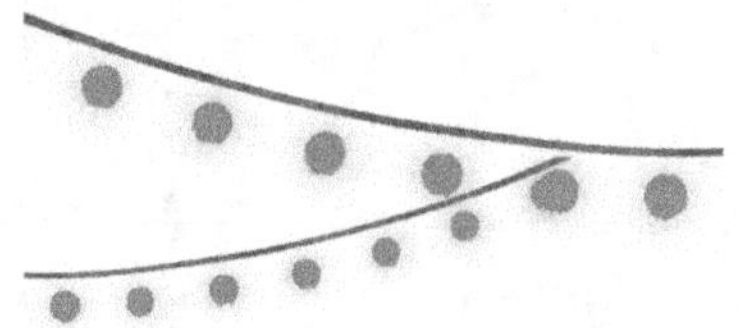

Gannon: How about Glamp-stars?

Me: ??

Gannon: Our band name, man!

Me: Dude. There's two of us. Hardly a whole band.

Gannon: You gotta think bigger, my friend.

Me: I'm thinking you might be delusional.

CHAPTER FIFTEEN

eva

ALL DAY long at work I'd been having some feelings that bordered on affection. Towards Linc. Which was straight-up crazy. The guy got on my last nerve...looking really fucking hot while doing so. He'd somehow gotten under my skin with his intense plea to be involved with Lucas and some of the small things he'd done around the trailer that showed he was thinking about us. Or was he simply thinking about Lucas?

Which would have been good, don't get me wrong. I really did want Lucas to have a father who was involved, but then Linc had pulled me onto his lap and given me the first non-self-induced orgasm in years and everything got murky. Was Lincoln really trying to get involved in *both* of our lives?

And why did that thought make me weak in the knees and giddy at the same time?

The knock on the window jolted me out of my deep thoughts. Paisley stood next to my car with a confused smile on her face. I opened the door and stepped out, gathering my things.

"I thought you might have fallen asleep in there," she drawled.

"Nah, just thinking."

"The boys are over there." Paisley pointed to the far end of Glamper's Paradise. We began to walk together in that direction, careful to stay on the brick pathway due to my heels. "Were any of those thoughts about your handsome baby daddy?"

I scoffed, elbowing her side. "He's not my baby daddy."

Paisley hooted. "Um, yeah. He's the father of your child, therefore he is by definition your baby daddy."

I could feel Paisley studying the side of my face. "Fine, but you don't have to say it that way."

"Why are you blushing?"

I stopped and spun, feeling all kinds of attacked. "You're like a dog with a bone."

Paisley smirked. "Guilty. Now spill the goods, woman."

I chewed on my bottom lip but knew there was no getting out of this. Paisley would harass me until she got the full story. It was just her bulldog way. "Fine. He may have given me an orgasm last night."

Paisley gasped, then danced around, looking ridiculous doing all that booty shaking in her clunky uniform. She finally stilled, grabbing my hands and leaning in close. "Tell. Me. Everything. Mouth, fingers, or cock?"

My face was on fire. "Fingers. I was sitting on his lap. Lucas was asleep inside the trailer." I rubbed my hand over my face, feeling all manner of mom-guilt. "I shouldn't have let him do it. I should have said no."

"No, no, no." Paisley pulled my hand away from my face. "You said yes, and rightly so. You still think Lincoln is hot, right?" I nodded. "And you like him?"

"Sort of, yeah," I admitted.

Okay, I more than kind of liked him, but I was having a hard time putting away all the hard feelings I'd clung to for almost five years when he was away. Warranted or not.

"Then enjoy the embrace of a hot man, Keevs." Paisley squeezed my hands. "Motherhood is not the sisterhood. It's okay to have orgasms."

A laugh escaped, and it felt really good to unload on one of my best friends. She was right. There was nothing wrong with enjoying a man. As long as I didn't let my feelings run amuck and start planning forever in my mind. It was just orgasms.

"Then let's go find him so I can get more of them."

Paisley threw her fist in the air. "That's what I like to hear!"

We found our crew on the stage, rocking out a country song that would have been better with a keyboard and a singer, but it wasn't half bad. And watching Linc's chest and arms flex against his tight T-shirt each time he hit the drums was all the foreplay I needed, apparently. A light sheen of sweat coated his tan skin, drawing my eye to his forearms and the way they flexed holding the drumsticks. The grin on his face when Gannon played the last note and fist-bumped him was enough to have me squeezing my legs together. A happy Linc took all his natural serious hotness and cranked it up to a level of scorch that had me sweating.

Paisley subtly elbowed me, a mischievous grin on her face. "You're drooling, bitch." Raising her voice, she called out, "Time for dinner and bed, my rocker family."

The kids came running and Linc focused his light blue eyes on me. Lucas nearly took out my knees in his excitement. "Daddy's a wockstar!"

I looked up sharply, all that desire crackling into anger. Daddy? Linc and I had already talked about this, and I specifically said not yet.

Linc winced, but helped stuff all of Lucas's things back in my bag before we walked back to our trailers in silence. I was fuming. I appreciated Linc's help today but that didn't give him the right to tell Lucas he was his father. That should have been a joint decision and done together. Linc placed Lucas's bag inside the doorway of my trailer after Lucas climbed inside to wash up. Linc didn't move out of the doorway, forcing me to look him in the eye.

"Look, I know you're mad, but I swear I didn't go out of my way to go against your wishes."

My hands were fisted on my hips. "Well, thank goodness. That makes it okay, then. As long as you didn't go out of your way."

Linc sighed at my obvious sarcasm. "Come on, Keva. Don't be that way. Let's talk this out."

I was too angry to talk it out. I knew I'd say something I'd regret later. "Listen. I need to make dinner first, okay? Let me get Lucas to bed and then we can talk. It's better that way."

Linc studied me for a long moment before stepping to the side and dipping his head. "Okay. I'll meet you out here."

I slipped past him and shut the door on his concerned face. I tried to stay present while I made a simple dinner for Lucas and me, but it was hard while I went over everything in my head about Linc overstepping boundaries.

After Lucas had eaten more food than had landed on the floor, I got the water started in the shower. He was way too big for the tiny bucket I kept in the shower for him to bathe in, but he didn't complain. He put so much shampoo on his head before I could stop him he was wearing a crown of bubbles almost taller than him. I couldn't help but smile. Somehow, just the sight of my son was enough to dampen the anger that had blanketed every other thought in my head.

"Let's rinse you off, your highness."

Lucas cracked up and did as he was told, letting me get all the soap suds off him before wrapping him in his favorite dinosaur towel. I dumped out the water and followed his wet footprints through the trailer.

"Did you have fun today?"

He let the towel drop and rummaged around for pajamas,

still completely unashamed of being naked. I used his towel to wipe up the wet trail he'd left. "Yep! Linc said he'd be my daddy from now on. Cool, wight?"

I swallowed hard and reminded myself to be happy for my son. "Yes, definitely cool. You like Linc, right?"

Lucas had his pajama bottoms on and then got his head stuck in the shirt. I rescued him, pulling his arm through so he could get his head through the neck hole. "Yep! He's building a twee-house! And he cut the cwust off my pb and j." His little face morphed into a puckered frown. "But he made me take a nap."

I swallowed a laugh. "You're supposed to take a nap, silly, but I'm glad you had a good day."

Lucas bounced on his little bed and then looked up at me. "Can I say goodnight to him?"

Oh, my heart. I brushed his dark hair away from his forehead. "Of course, baby."

He slipped out of bed and ran to the door of our trailer, pushing it open and leaning his head out to shout. "Daddy!"

I heard Linc's voice just a second later. "What's up, buddy?"

"Goodnight, Daddy!"

If I wasn't mistaken, Linc's voice sounded choked up when he finally answered. "'Night, son."

I squeezed my eyes shut and sucked in as much air as my lungs could take. I couldn't hold on to the mad. It was sucked out by the innocence of a little boy who simply wanted to love his father. I exhaled and turned around to scoop up Lucas.

"Time for bed, young man, or you'll have to walk the plank!"

Lucas squeezed his arms around my neck, smiling like the happy kid he was. He lowered his voice to a loud whisper. "We don't have a plank, Mama."

"Ahoy!" I tossed him lightly onto his bed. "I'll have to ask Daddy to make us one, huh?"

We read a pirate story that night, the joy on his face never leaving. Pretty sure the kid fell asleep with a grin still pulling on his cheeks. And as for me, I had some apologizing to do. I crept out of the trailer, taking time to twist the knob so it wouldn't make a clicking noise once it shut.

Splashing water had me turning around. Linc was on the side of his trailer, rinsing himself with a water hose. Water sluiced over his bare skin and traveled lower, getting caught in the swim trunks slung low on his hips. His head was tilted back, eyes shut as the water pelted his face and upper body. My mouth opened on a silent groan. It was like getting an unexpected front-row seat to a strip show. Not that I'd been to one. But I had a feeling it would be a lot like this. The man had added more tattoos to his body since I last saw it naked, each one ratcheting up his hot factor.

When his head came up and he blinked his eyes open, he smiled, leaning down to shut off the water. "Hey," he whispered, straightening and grabbing a towel slung over the awning of his trailer.

"Hey," I said back lamely.

He was rubbing that towel all over his body and I wanted to be the one to do it. I wanted to touch every hard bump of muscle and every dip in between. I wanted to trace every tattoo that dotted his tan skin and feel the tickle of his hair. I wanted to memorize every way in which he'd changed from five years ago. He'd been a young adult back then, but came back all man.

He finally tossed the towel near the door to his trailer and came over. "Sorry. My shower isn't working."

I blinked away my wayward thoughts. "It's okay. But you can always use mine if you need to." I sucked in a breath, wondering where the hell that invite had come from. I didn't want him in our private space.

Did I?

A drop of water fell from his hair and landed on his chest. Without even thinking, I reached out and caught it with my finger. And then my finger stayed, tracing down the contours of his torso. Linc inhaled sharply, his muscles flexing as I touched him.

"Keva?" he asked so low I barely heard him.

"Yeah?" I fluttered my eyelids up and locked eyes with him. His were hooded with the same desire I felt pooled in my gut.

"You still mad at me?" he asked. My finger came back up between his pec muscles, feeling the soft scratch of his light chest hair.

"I don't think so," I admitted. I didn't feel angry at all. I felt fucking horny.

He snatched my hand and held it firm in his grip, stopping my movement. "If you keep touching me, you're going to find yourself on your back."

My heart fluttered like a little slut at his threat. I wanted the press of a man against me, the heat of him between my legs, the fullness of his cock filling me. And not just any man. This one. Paisley was right. I was a mom, not a nun. I had a right just like anybody else to go after what I wanted.

With a defiant lift of my eyebrow, my other hand lifted to rip apart the Velcro that held his swim trunks together. Linc moved so fast I let out a little yelp. I was suddenly in his arms, my legs wrapped around his waist as he hustled us up and into his trailer. I didn't have a chance to check out his living space because my hands were too busy diving into his hair and kissing the ever-loving fuck out of him. My back slammed against something hard and I heard something clatter to the floor. His tongue was doing things to my mouth that had me dizzy. His hips thrust against me and my eyes rolled back in my head. Ribbons of pleasure furled out inside my body, heavy yet light at the same time. Even my toes went limp with hot, molten desire.

And then he stopped. My eyes fluttered open, my breath coming in embarrassing pants. His hair was a mess from my hands and it made me even more crazed. I tried to pull him back to me but he resisted.

"What do you want, Keva? Tell me, and I'll move heaven and earth to give it to you."

I swallowed hard around the emotion that was trying to push

through the fog of sexual desire. Dammit, I believed him. I knew this man wouldn't hurt me just like I knew my heart had always been his. Why else hadn't I been with anyone since him? At least now I could share my body too. He might destroy my heart, but at least my body would get what it wanted. I had the opportunity to take just a moment of pleasure for myself, the selfish kind of thing a single mom gives up forever.

"I want..." My words tapered off as he forced me to put words to what I was feeling. Back when we were together the first time, I didn't ask for what I wanted. I'd gone along with everything because it had been fun. I'd been too young, too inexperienced, too naive to comprehend the struggles of the real word. But not now. Now I was a grown-ass woman, fully capable of asking boldly for what I wanted.

I gripped his hair tight enough to make him wince. "I want your cock to ruin me, Linc."

$\mathcal{L}$inc

I BOWED MY HEAD, eyes squeezed tight while I tried to remain in control. This woman. Goddammit, this woman had ahold of me in ways I simply couldn't understand five years ago. Now I knew it plainly.

I was head over ass in love with her.

I also knew she'd junk punch me if I admitted that now. She didn't ask for me to make love to her. Didn't ask me to be part of her life. Hell, she didn't even say she wanted me. She just wanted my cock. If it wasn't so hot to hear her demand it, I would be insulted. As it was, I was too far gone for this woman to step back.

Lifting my head, I took in the sight of her physically and sexually on the edge for me, pressed between me and the kitchenette countertop, her cheeks pink, eyes heavy-lidded, and breasts heaving beneath the fucking blouse. Her prim-and-proper skirt was pushed up her thighs indecently to let me in.

I held her there with my hips, reaching back to the box

sitting on top of the kitchenette table, the one I hadn't taken the time to unpack yet. Right on top was a new box of condoms I'd bought before I came back to town with delusional hope of finding the same Keva. I'd found her all right, but she'd grown into a different woman. Understandably so.

But this? This Keva I knew. This hunger in her eyes, the way she gripped my hair, the eagerness in the way she clung to my body. This was familiar. I ripped open the box and took out the first condom my fingers found. Keva pushed down my swim trunks so they landed at my feet. She let out a whimper as she fisted my bare cock. My hands were shaking, but I managed to get the condom on while her hands stroked across my chest, exploring.

"I swear it's a new condom," I gritted out. "Not even my superhero swimmers will get past this one."

Keva smirked, then tugged the blouse over her head. "And I'm on birth control. Fool me once and all that."

Her wording bothered me, and I opened my mouth to explain that I'd never taken her for a fool, but she'd reached around and unfastened her bra. Her heavy breasts spilled out and I lost my train of thought. How could this woman be any hotter than what I'd built up in my mind the last five years? I cupped her flesh, watching in awe as she overflowed my palms. I dipped my head, finally getting my mouth on them. Flicking her nipple with my tongue, she whimpered again. When I sucked the tip into my mouth and continued to flick, she ground against me, holding my head to her breast in a death grip.

My Keva was a greedy girl.

And I fucking loved it.

I paid homage to her breasts, giving them equal time and attention. Fuck, I could play here for hours and not get tired. But Keva finally let go of my hair and gripped my cock, hand sliding up and down the slippery condom. When she cupped my balls, I'd had all I could take.

"Hold on to the cabinet above your head," I growled, batting her hands away before I embarrassed myself.

Keva instantly obeyed and even that turned me on. The movement thrust her breasts in my face, but I was on a mission to fulfil her request. I pushed up her skirt, noting a ripping sound but not having the restraint to go slower. Her sensible black panties were in the way, but I didn't want to take the time to remove them. Instead, I pulled them to the side and drifted my finger through the wetness.

"You want this cock, Keva?" I rubbed just the tip against her center, clenching my jaw against the tempting heat of her.

She whimpered again, but kept her hands above her head.

"You gotta say it."

I needed to hear her say it. I needed to know that she wanted something from me. That even though sharing our bodies wouldn't nearly be enough for me, I needed to know it was a start.

Keva opened her eyes wide and looked me dead in the eye. "I want your cock, Linc. I want it right now."

I shoved inside her heat in one long deep stroke, pausing as we both grunted from the shock of it. Keva felt like heaven, but not having her fully was hell. I knew this was only sex for her, but for me it was a physical commitment to how I wanted to move forward with my life. I wanted every moment to be with her and Lucas. She could ask for anything and I would find a way to give it to her.

Keva's legs squeezed my hips where they were wrapped around me. "I've missed this," she whispered into the dark trailer.

I knew she only meant sex, not me, which was just the reminder I needed. I'd give her what she asked for while working towards more. I pulled back until I almost fell out of her.

"Hold on tight, sweetheart."

And then I became a thrusting machine, giving her zero time to collect herself or to dictate exactly what she wanted from me, even while holding her heart back. Her ass had to be hurting where I was shoving her harder and harder into the edge of the counter, but she didn't complain. Her head was lolled against one of her arms as she held on to the cabinet above for dear life. The sounds of flesh slapping against flesh became the only discernable noise around us. It was obscene. It most definitely was not lovemaking, but it was still amazing fucking.

I captured a light pink nipple in my mouth and bit down. Keva keened above me. I let the nipple pop lewdly out of my mouth and continued to thrust hard and fast. Fuck, she felt good.

"Is this...what...you wanted?" I asked against her ear as I kept her hips in my tight grasp. Her whimpers began to string together into a continuous moan. I felt her tighten around me, and I knew she was close.

I let go with one hand and cupped her cheek, pulling her head away from her arm. Her eyes fluttered open and I held her there.

"Do not look away," I said through gritted teeth, continuing to pound into her until her breathing became choppy and her eyes went hazy. She pulsed around me with a breathy whimper, but never looked away, giving me the intimate contact I needed to spill right over the edge with her. Every wave of pleasure turned painful in its intensity, wringing me out until all I could do was cling to her and hope she felt it too.

This was not over between us.

It had never been over. Just on pause.

As I came back to my body, Keva's head rested on my shoulder, her breathing beginning to even out. I felt her warm hip under my hand, the tips of her breasts brushing against my torso with each breath. Her hands had left the cabinet at some point to lie around my shoulders. She was in my arms and in my heart. I turned my head and pressed a kiss to her temple. She stirred, lifting her head and staring at me in the dark.

"Did my cock ruin you?" I asked, unable to keep the grin out of my tone.

Keva let out a delicate snort. She pulled her arms away from me and sat upright. Well, as much as she could on the tiny kitchenette counter. Jesus. I could have found a better, more comfortable place to have sex with the woman I loved. Next time, for sure. And there sure as hell would be a next time.

"Yes. Gold star for you."

I was grinning. "Gold star? Damn, that's high praise. Do I get a homework pass too?"

Keva pushed against my chest and I reluctantly stepped back, pulling out of her. Though I kept my hand on her hip to keep her steady. She shuffled down her skirt and hopped off the counter before I could help her. She didn't waste any time distancing herself. I knew she'd do this and yet it still hurt. She was busy reconstructing walls to keep me out. Little did she know I'd just keep coming by and smashing them down until she gave up.

"I better get back to the trailer in case Lucas wakes up," Keva mumbled, pulling her blouse over her head. Her bra was crumpled up in her hand. I could see her nipples through the blouse, and even though I'd just had her, I wanted her all over again.

"I'll walk you over." I disposed of the condom and reached down to pull up my swim trunks.

"It's just right there, Linc."

I straightened, crowding into her space with an edge to my voice. "And I'll walk you over."

She sighed, but didn't argue further. Opening the door quietly, she walked across the open space between our two trailers. I kept pace with her, wishing I could pull her into my bed and not let her out of my sight. When she pulled open her trailer door, her intention of going in and closing it in my face without a polite goodbye was clear. I took matters into my own hands.

I pulled her back, spun her around, and slammed my mouth

to hers. She let out a gasp and my tongue dove in, tasting her one last time. I knew this kiss would have to last me until I could break down her walls again. She let me kiss her, but I could feel her holding herself away from me. I ended the kiss and stepped away from her.

"Goodnight, Keva."

She paused for a moment in the light of the moon and then scrambled to get inside like she'd forgotten for a second what she'd been trying to do. I waited outside until the light in her trailer went out some ten minutes later. Then I went back to my trailer and fixed the mess we'd made in the kitchenette, all the while reliving those moments inside of her.

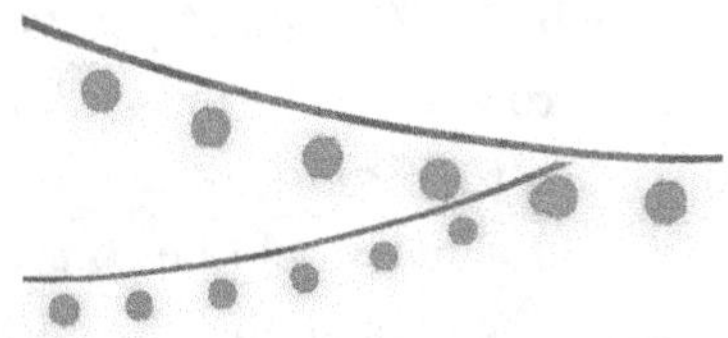

I had Lucas with me the next day too, a predicament I actually looked forward to. I wanted more time to get to know my son and for him to get to know me. To thank Gannon for his flexibility, I took Lucas to Crazy Beans, the local coffee shop, in Gannon's truck. We'd come to work with pastries and coffee treats, a surefire way to keep Gannon happy. Plus, I needed to thank him for loaning me his truck constantly. As much as it pained me to admit, I needed to get rid of the Harley. The time for riding motorcycles was over the second I found out I had a son.

As we waited in line and discussed which pastry was the

yummiest, I nodded hello to several people who looked familiar but I couldn't quite place their names. Then a tall woman came through the glass doors and I finally knew someone.

"Hey, Rosemary," I said as she got in line behind us.

The elementary school principal looked up from her phone and smiled when she saw us. "Lincoln, right? And this is Lucas."

My son smiled shyly up at her, moving closer to my leg just in case. I put my hand on his shoulder. "That's right. Hey, do you mind if I ask you a work question?"

Rosemary smiled. "Sure, go ahead."

"Well, we're trying to find a daycare for Lucas, but apparently it's tough since it's mid-year. Do you know of any places that have open spots?"

Rosemary tipped her head. "You know what? I think I might be able to help you out." She tapped around on her phone and then put it back in her bag. "Why don't you two swing by the elementary school tomorrow morning and we'll have Lucas take a trial run in the four's classroom? He just turned four, right?"

I nodded. "Yes, he did. That would be so great. I think he's ready to learn more than I can teach him when I have to work all day."

Rosemary crouched down. "What do you say, Lucas? Would you like to try out my school?"

After a second, he smiled at her and nodded. She grinned right back and I felt good about the whole thing. I just hoped Keva could come with me tomorrow morning and check out the school. I wanted her to feel comfortable wherever Lucas ended up.

I ended up buying Rosemary a pastry and coffee too, but I figured it was a small price to pay for her kindness. By the time I got back to Glamper's Paradise, Gannon was busy with helping campers. I took Lucas over to the tree house we started building and got him set up with toys in the shade. By the time the workday was over, I had the tree house completely built. We just needed to add fun decorations that would make the place come alive for little kids.

"Nice work, Lincoln." Gannon clapped me on the back and helped me put away the tools in the back of the golf cart. "The kids are going to love it."

"I've got some ideas for a telescope, a fireman's pole, and a fancy throne chair for the princesses."

Keva and Paisley walked over, both in their work clothes. It felt like life was falling into a warm and predictable rhythm. I could get used to coming home after a day of work to Keva and our son.

"Mama!" Lucas went running for her, wrapping his arms around her legs until she reached down and scooped him up. He let her hug him for a second and then was kicking to get down. "I go to school!"

Keva's head popped up to lock eyes with me, suspicion behind the curiosity. "Oh yeah?"

"We ran into Rosemary Roberts at the coffee shop, and when I explained our predicament, she said she'd get Lucas into the four's class. We can drop him off tomorrow and see how we all like it before we commit."

Keva's head tilted to the side and I sensed I'd misstepped somewhere, but for the life of me, I couldn't figure out where. She said she was stressed about getting him in somewhere. Well, problem solved.

"I already inquired about the four's class at the school and they told me it was full."

I shrugged. "Not sure what to tell you. Maybe someone dropped out the last day or two, but there's a spot now."

Keva's eyes narrowed and Paisley made a noise right by her side. Shit.

"What's wrong?"

"Oh, for fuck's sake," Gannon muttered under his breath. "Two unhappy women. Way to go, Angelo."

Keva turned to Paisley. "Does this sound like special treat-ment to you?"

Paisley nodded. "Almost like Rosemary wanted to do a special favor for Lincoln."

"No, that's not—"

"Almost like a flirting thing, am I right?" Keva asked Paisley, leaving me out of the conversation entirely, which I did not appreciate.

"It was not flirting!" I marched in between the two and gave Paisley my back. "I did not flirt and neither did she. I swear on my life."

Keva folded her arms across her chest. "You must have flashed those blue eyes. Suddenly you got my son a spot. Interesting."

Now I was mad and not just because she called Lucas her son instead of our son. "I didn't flash anything. I just wanted to help you out."

"Did you buy Rosemary breakfast? Did you have a cozy date?" Keva asked, tone almost mocking.

I was not answering that. "Are you mad because you just now figured out that flirting works or are you just jealous?"

Keva gasped and I heard Gannon chuckle. "I'm not jealous!"

I shrugged. "Sure seems like it."

"We're going to head on home, you two." Gannon patted me on the back and then he and Paisley left. Lucas was busy putting all his toys back in the giant bag Keva supplied each day.

Keva was staring at me, her eyes snapping with anger. And possibly jealousy if I was reading her right.

"Come on. I bought hot dogs to make for us tonight."

Keva lifted her nose in the air. "I don't want hot dogs."

I shook my head and walked over to collect the bag and steer Lucas toward our trailers. "Then make your own dinner, but Lucas and I are having hot dogs."

Lucas let out a cheer and eventually I heard Keva begin walking behind us.

This woman, man. She just might kill me.

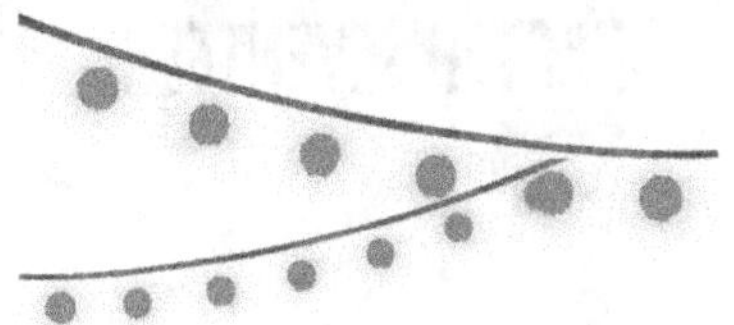

Baby Mama: Don't flirt with women when Lucas is with you, please.

Me: Well, shit. There went my plans for you.

Baby Mama: OTHER women.

Me: Oh gotcha. Well, that's no problem. I don't see other women but you anyway.

Baby Mama: That's quite the cheesy line.

Me: Not really. All I see is your red lips asking me to ruin your pussy. That memory pretty much blots out all other women for all time.

Me: What? No smart comeback?

Me: You were walking kind of funny today. Guess I did my job well.

Baby Mama: GOOD NIGHT, LINC.

CHAPTER SEVENTEEN

eva

"Come on, baby! The four's class waits for no one!" I pushed open the trailer door with my hip, calling over my shoulder to Lucas. I almost fell right out of the trailer as it opened too easily. My bags went sliding off my shoulders and I tipped. Strong hands caught me before my high heels got tangled in the metal steps.

"Good morning, sweetheart," Linc drawled in a morning voice that should have been illegal. He set me upright and pulled the straps of the bags off my arms entirely.

I blinked at the scruff on his face that had been trimmed up sometime between last night when he'd gone inside his trailer after dinner and this morning. His blue eyes were bright, matching his collared polo shirt. For a moment there I wondered what he'd actually done in the military. Linc's level of good looking was a deadly weapon that could have taken down entire nations.

"Morning." The greeting came out on a wobble, much like

my exit.

Linc threw the bags over his shoulder like they weighed nothing. His gaze drifted down my body, all the way to my toes before drifting back up. "You get prettier every day."

My cheeks went rogue and heated. I'd resigned myself years ago to the fact that I was now Lucas's mama and all flirting from the opposite sex was over for my lifetime. Then Linc swooped back in and suddenly I was blushing like a virgin schoolgirl.

"Wet's go!" Lucas charged out of the trailer, hopping down to the fake grass with a cheer as big as his backpack. I'd barely gotten him to go to sleep last night. The kid was so excited to be a "big boy" as he kept reminding me.

Linc put my bags in the back seat after Lucas climbed in. I watched them, still a bit dumbfounded that Linc was here and part of our lives. Linc straightened and shut the door after buckling Lucas in. He looked at me over the hood of my little sedan, eyes crackling with attraction.

"If you're not gonna get in, at least do a little spin and give me a show in that skirt."

I put my hands on my hips, irritated but also feeling highly complimented by his attention. "Lincoln Angelo."

He rapped his knuckles on the hood. "Keva Mooney. You wear heels like that, you better expect me to be lookin'."

"You're going to make us late," I groused, getting into the car as I heard him laugh. He climbed in next to me, and I booked it out of the glamp-ground.

Lucas babbled about all the things he wanted to do at "big boy school" while Linc kept darting glances at me. My face was burning and there was nothing I could do about it.

"Try not to flirt with Rosemary in front of Lucas, okay?" I snapped as we turned into the busy parking lot of the school.

Linc was quiet until I found a parking spot and put the car in park. "I know you're nervous about Lucas starting a new class, and I know my flirting makes you nervous too, but you don't have to keep pushing me away. You and I both know I never have and never will flirt with Rosemary."

Looked like I was the one getting schooled today. Sucking in a deep breath and hoping for some of the maturity that seemed to fly right out the window around this man, I managed to meet Linc's gaze. "I'm sorry."

Linc reached over and squeezed my hand. "He's going to do great and so are you."

I squeezed him back, immensely grateful to have someone here with me for a big day in my son's life. "Thanks, Linc."

My hands were shaking as I got Lucas out of his car seat. He almost ran into the crazed traffic of parent drop-off before I got his hand in mine. I somehow left his car door open and only remembered when I heard Linc close it for me and then run to catch up to us. My little boy was going to school and I was officially a mess.

We found the four's classroom right next to the outdoor playground area. The teacher came over to the open door to introduce herself. She was young and sweet, and I could tell Lucas instantly liked her. She held out her hand and he took it, walking away from me without even a backward glance. I gulped back tears and tried to focus on breathing.

I felt Linc's hand on my back making soft circles as we both watched Lucas join his new class. "Come on. Let's go get you some coffee before you head to work."

He steered me away from the doorway, which was for the best. Without him I might have stayed there for an embarrassingly long amount of time, watching Lucas and wondering where the time had gone. Linc took the keys from my hands and opened the passenger door for me. I climbed in and he even pulled the seat belt across for me. He had to adjust the seat way back to even get in behind the wheel, but he got us out of the parking lot without incident.

"He did great, thanks to you," Linc finally said.

I shook my head, blowing out a breath and trying to release

this emotion that had my throat clogged. "I don't know about that. If it was up to me, he'd stay a little boy forever and never leave my side."

Linc found a parking spot right in front of Crazy Beans. He held all the doors for me, which impressed me even when I didn't want to be impressed.

"What's your favorite coffee order?"

I scanned the menu, hyperaware of his warm hand on my back again. "Probably a mocha, but it's too sugary. I usually order a skinny latte."

Linc made a noise. When it was our turn, he stepped up and ordered two mochas. I tried to lean over to change my order, but he edged me out of the way and ran his credit card. When the barista turned to put two cups on the counter, Linc leaned in and whispered, "How about we just find a way to burn off those calories?"

There went my cheeks again. I had to bite my lip to keep the smile from blooming. I shifted down the line and studiously ignored Linc. He made it hard though, coming up right next to me and putting his hand on my back while he chuckled softly. He was a gentleman through and through—until he wasn't—and I was having a hard time not falling for the whole package.

"I figure you and I might need to get to know each other again."

That comment had me looking at him and ignoring everyone filtering in and out of the coffee shop around us. "What do you mean?"

He shrugged. "I only knew you for one day five years ago. Naturally, you've changed and so have I. I figure we need to get to know each other. I should know your favorite coffee. What you do when you want to relax. Your favorite color."

That sounded...nice. Too nice. "Get to know each other for Lucas's sake, you mean."

Linc pressed his lips together before answering. "Sure. For Lucas. But also for us."

The barista called his name before I could argue the point about there being no "us" and we stepped forward to grab our drinks. Linc surprised me by steering me out the door again and over to my car. "Do you mind showing me where you work?"

I guessed he was serious about this getting-to-know-me thing. "Sure, but then you won't have a car."

"Do you mind if I take yours? I'll come back early and we can go pick up Lucas together."

That sounded just about perfect. I nodded and we both climbed in. Linc was saying and doing all the right things. If I'd been looking for a boyfriend, he'd be just about perfect. But I wasn't. And certainly not a boyfriend who felt like he had to be with me because of our son. When we got to the fertility clinic where I worked with Lucy, he held the door again and followed me inside. I gave him the tour of the place and ended in the long hallway. No one else was here yet as we only had a few appointments early this afternoon.

Linc stopped me, his hand on my hip. "What I said earlier at the coffee shop," he began, stepping closer. His thumb began to sweep over my hip, turning me inside out even through a layer of clothing. "I want to get to know you, Keva. Not for our son's sake. And not just what makes you fall apart in my arms, but everything about you. Even the mundane things."

My hands landed on his biceps to push him back a step, but the second they touched him, they didn't do anything of the sort. In fact, I was pretty sure I pulled him further into me. Despite my better judgement, there was comfort to be found when Linc was near. The more I felt it, the more of it I wanted.

"I read books to relax and my favorite color is purple," I answered quietly.

Linc dipped his head and kissed my neck just below my ear. My eyes fluttered closed. "Where are you ticklish?"

My forehead found his shoulder, resting there as he kissed his way down my neck. "My belly." My voice was barely audible. Just a whisper of breath.

"Let me see." Linc pushed me backward, but he came with me. The door behind me flew open and we were suddenly in the bathroom. The motion-sensored lights flew on. There was no way in hell I was showing him my belly with these damn spotlights making the room seem like a dressing room nightmare.

When I just stood there like a deer in headlights, Linc pulled his head up to study me. His hard length was pressed between us, evidence that he wanted me and yet I couldn't quite believe it. "Keva."

I shook my head, feeling cornered and ready to attack. "You want to get to know me? I have stretch marks, Linc. Saggy skin. Wider hips than I had five years ago. I have the body of a mother, not a young girl anymore."

Linc gripped my hips. Hard. "Shut up. For fuck's sake. Quit talking about yourself like that. You're the most beautiful woman I've ever seen. More so than when I met you the first time. This body birthed a miracle. Our son." He dipped down to get in my face, looking angry. "Do you have any idea how hot that makes you?"

I blinked, still not quite sure if I was ready to believe him. He let go of my hips and stepped back. My heart took a nosedive. My insecurities had ruined the moment. Then he spoke.

"Lift your skirt and let me see you."

He was glaring at me, as if daring me to obey. I wanted to hide in these bright lights, but maybe showing him was better. Better that he know now before he got in too deep and broke my heart when he left. Because of course he would leave. People I cared about always left.

So I lifted my skirt, showing him my thick thighs, daring him right back.

He crossed his arms over his chest. "Higher. Around your waist."

My hands were shaking but I did it, shoving my skirt up around my waist and showing him the simple black thong that left everything out there. But once I quit worrying about myself,

I noticed that he had his fist pressed against his mouth. His jeans were tented, looking positively painful.

"Now turn around and grab the sink." His voice washed over me, that whiskey and smoke quality that had hooked me right from the beginning.

I turned, giving him a good look at my ass as I bent to grab the small sink. I didn't have time to worry about what I looked like because suddenly he was behind me, the sound of a zipper and the crinkle of a condom wrapper the only noise in the small room. I felt my underwear being pulled aside and then his hot length was pressed against me as he slid home.

My eyes rolled back in my head. My arms lost their strength and I went down to my elbows on the countertop. He filled me completely, edging on the side of pain. Linc grabbed my hips and began to move, every inch of him dragging against my walls with a precision that had me seeing stars behind my eyelids.

"This body," he said on a pant, thrusting inside me so hard I felt my whole body jiggle. "Is perfect." He pulled all the way out, his hands grabbing fistfuls of my ass, kneading the flesh before he plunged back into my body and set a brutal pace. "This body is *mine*," he growled.

And then he was reaching around and pinching my clit. I gasped his name and lost all control, spiraling into a different dimension with an orgasm that came on too fast. He grunted as he spilled into me, holding us tightly together until all the spasms stopped. Then he pulled out of me, grabbing my shoulders and spinning me around into his arms. He cupped my face and made me look him in the eye.

He looked pissed, wild, a bit out of control. I could barely breathe.

"We're gonna get to know all about each other."

It wasn't a question. It was a command. Normally I'd argue, but he held the upper hand. My skirt was bunched around my waist and I was still reeling from an intense orgasm in my place of work. So I nodded.

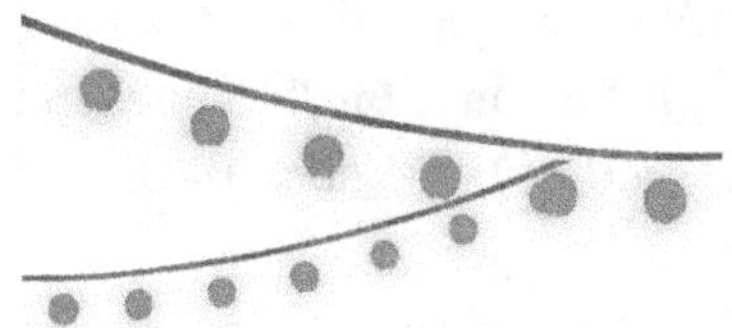

"Linc sure was all smiles when he walked out of here," Lucy drawled a few minutes later when I finally made it to my desk at the front of the clinic. My face burned. Oh no, what did she hear? "And your cheeks are a lovely shade of red. Did I interrupt something?"

With any other boss, I'd be mortified and wondering if I was fired, but this was Lucy. She'd been my friend and confidante for years now. She was the mother figure I always wished I had.

"We're getting along better," I hedged, pulling things out of my bag and avoiding her knowing gaze.

"You better date that boy before some of these single hussies get wind of him."

My mind instantly went to Rosemary. Apparently I'd turned into a person with a jealousy problem. "I, uh, I'm not looking to date anyone. You know that."

Lucy spun in my chair, looking like she wasn't going to get up and let me get to work anytime soon. "Well, sure. But that was before your baby daddy came back and put that blush on your face."

I rolled my eyes. "Why does everyone keep using that phrase?"

"Is the sex good?"

"Lucy!"

She grinned. "What? I've been married awhile. Give me the specifics."

I shook my head, but picked up a stack of file folders I needed to go through. "It's amazing," I mumbled.

Lucy stood up suddenly. "I knew it! Girl, you and Linc are fire together."

I put the stack down and took back my seat. "Oh, we're not together. Just scratching the itch as Paisley used to say."

Lucy giggled. "And look where that got her," she said, referring to them being married now. She grabbed my hands, looking down at me sternly. "Listen, Keva. Do not mess around here. That man is crazy about you and Lucas."

I squeezed her hands. "I know, but there's nothing there on a serious level. We're just...fucking. And co-parenting. Kind of."

"Mhm. I remember that first month after the birth of all three of my babies." Lucy shook her head, a soft smile on her pretty face. "It was that adjustment period, you know? Where you go from having that baby in your belly for ten straight months, just the two of you. It's so special. Suddenly you push that thing out of your body and everyone gets to hold the baby. You have to share and it sucks. You never had to share Lucas. Ever."

I opened my mouth but wasn't sure what to say. She was right. It had just been me and Lucas right from the start.

"Sharing is hard, Keevs. But you're one tough bitch. You can do it."

And then she walked away, leaving me with all kinds of things to think about.

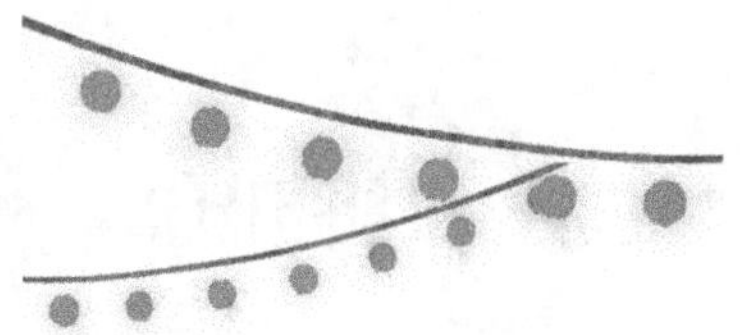

Baby Daddy: Pretty sure Lucy knew what we were doing in that bathroom.

Me: Pretty sure I've caught her and Bain in that same bathroom, so she has no room to talk.

Baby Daddy: Felt wrong to throw away my superhero swimmers in a place that likes to collect them.

Me: Maybe it's best you don't come to my place of work in the future.

Baby Daddy: That's not going to happen. Those pencil skirts and heels are like a siren call.

Me: Off to go buy mom jeans and flats.

Baby Daddy: Pretty sure even a muumuu wouldn't deter me...

CHAPTER EIGHTEEN

inc

A WHOLE WEEK WENT BY. Lucas was thriving in school, the weather was turning cooler, and Keva was still building that wall to keep me out. We'd manage to find some alone time here and there and she'd let me inside her body, but kept her heart under lock and key. Pretty sure there was even a dragon protecting that heart of hers.

After five years of celibacy, I never thought I'd be irritated about having frequent sex with a woman who made me out of my mind with a single glance but wanted no strings attached. But I was. Irritated, that is.

"What did that dirt do to you, bro?"

My lungs were heaving and I'd made quite the progress on clearing a path toward the northern end of Glamper's Paradise. Gannon and I wanted to make a safe path for glampers to hike and get to the lake on the property to the north of us. Technically that land wasn't ours, but no one lived there and glampers were sneaking over already. Might as well carve out a safe path for them so they didn't get lost.

I leaned on the shovel and wiped the sweat off my brow with my forearm. "Just working out some things."

Gannon set down the wheelbarrow of tree stumps we'd cleared earlier. "Yeah, I can see that. Anything I can help with?"

I was just angry enough to let words loose when I'd normally hold it all in. "Keva."

Gannon chuckled, taking off his hat before jamming it back on his head. "Yep. Women. I knew it."

"She's just...so guarded." I let the shovel fall to the ground and moved further into a shady spot. "I want to be an equal partner with her, but she doesn't trust me. She's slowly letting me help with Lucas, but anything beyond that, she shuts me out."

"I've gotten to know Keva since she and my wife are friends. She's a spitfire, just like Paisley. You're going to have to jump into the fire and probably get singed in the process. It's the only way to get through to women like that."

I wasn't sure if that was the best advice. Keva had been raising our son alone. She had a valid reason for being bitter and untrusting. Maybe what I needed was to come at things from Keva's angle. "I know you love Elise. Anybody with two eyes can see that, but what do you miss most about being kid-less?"

Gannon looked away, thinking about it. "That seems so long ago, it's hard to imagine. Uh, probably the loss of who I was before her. I was more carefree. I could go out whenever I wanted. I could go get drunk with my buddies and not have to be responsible twenty-four seven. It's the never getting a break that was hard when Elise arrived. If another parent is involved, there's two of you. You have backup. Single parents have no backup."

I nodded along, trying to envision how life had changed for Keva. While I'd been off making the life I wanted, she'd been shouldering one hundred percent of the responsibility. Then an idea hit me.

"Can I ask a favor?"

Gannon tipped his head. "Sure."

"Any chance you could babysit Lucas for me Saturday night?"

Gannon worked his jaw side to side. "I'll do you one better. We'll keep him for a sleepover too."

I started nodding, the idea bubbling up in my brain and taking hold. "I sincerely appreciate it."

Gannon clapped me on the back and then grabbed the handles on the wheelbarrow again. "I was in your shoes not too long ago. Just please go get your girl, huh? A pissed-off Keva isn't good for anyone."

His laughter echoed off the trees as he walked away. I spent the rest of the day making plans in my head. I wanted the night to be perfect. A way to show her that I not only was all in with raising Lucas, but all in with her too.

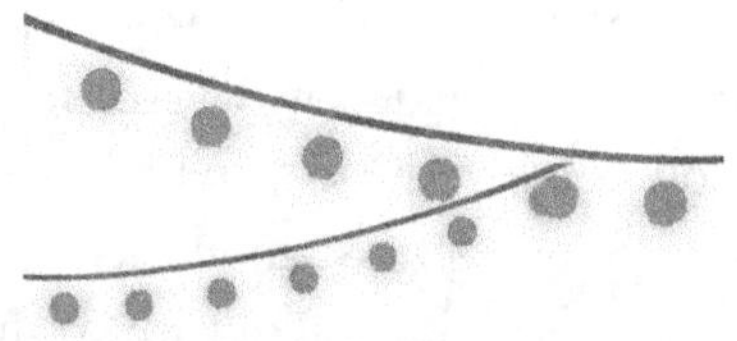

"What is going on?" Keva dug her heels in, bunching up the fake grass outside her trailer.

"We're going out tonight. Just go in and get dressed." I gave her lower back a push but she didn't budge.

"What about Lucas?"

She was cute when she was being responsible. I could barely

keep my hands off her in the pencil skirt and heels she wore to work every day. "I took care of it. He's at Paisley and Gannon's. All you need to worry about is getting dressed, okay?"

Her toe tapped against the ground as she studied me. I wasn't sure what she was looking for, but I must have passed inspection because she gave me a single nod and reached for the door. "Fine. I'll be out in a second."

"Take your time. We're in no rush." The woman was always rushing from one thing to the next. The last thing I wanted was for our date to stress her out. I settled into the chair outside her trailer and waved her in.

She was still giving me side-eye, but she finally disappeared inside the trailer. A minute or two later I heard her say something but couldn't make it out. She'd probably found the outfit I'd laid out on her bed. Paisley had helped me, so I hoped it would fit. Only a few minutes passed and Keva popped open the door in the navy-blue dress dotted with tiny white flowers. The bust was ruched—a word Paisley taught me—accentuating her gorgeous breasts, and the skirt was just short enough to show off her curvy legs but not make her feel uncomfortable. However, she was barefoot.

"What is going on?" she demanded, color dotting her cheeks and making her even prettier.

I gave her the once-over, insanely pleased I was taking her out on a date. Everyone would be staring at her, wondering how this stranger had gotten the prettiest woman in Blueball on his arm. I stood up and took her hand, kissing the back of it.

"I'm taking you out on the date I wished I would have the first time we met. The date you deserve."

Her eyes went wide and then she was glancing down at her pretty painted toes.

"Now where are your boots? I specifically asked for a pair of comfortable ones. Remember the day we met? Those boots were killing your feet."

"Linc," Keva whispered, head still bowed. With a deep inhale she looked up at me, her eyes filled with tears.

I squeezed her hand. "I told you I'm all in. With you and with Lucas. Let me give you a night of fun. You deserve it and so much more."

Keva tugged on my hand, pulling me in so we were eye level with each other. She kissed me quick, hovering there like even she was shocked that she'd initiated. I didn't let her get away with a tease. I cupped my hand on the back of her head and deepened the kiss. Her tongue dueled with mine, giving as good as she got. I was hard already, but I wasn't going to give in. I wanted more than the surface level she'd been giving me these last few weeks.

"Thank you," she whispered when we came up for air. "Be right back."

And then she was gone, probably getting those boots on. When she came back out, she'd slicked on that red lipstick that had caught my attention years ago. She was so stunning she took my breath away. I'd been obsessed with the girl I'd met five years ago, but I was in love with the woman she'd become.

She let me open her doors and even hold her hand in the truck I'd borrowed yet again from Gannon. I took her to the barbecue place Gannon had suggested when I asked. He said the dancing there was fun. He'd had a devilish grin on his face when he told me, so I wasn't sure if this was a good idea or not. Regardless, the food was amazing, the live music was great, and Keva was clearly making an effort to chat, letting me get to know her.

"Who's that over there? The one with the puffy hair?" I gestured with the longneck beer bottle in hand. The woman in question was thin as a rail but her dark brown hair was so puffed up on the top she looked like she might topple over.

Keva grinned. "That's Fifi Le Roux. She owns Chasing Tails, a dog grooming place in town."

Now it was my turn to laugh. "She looks like a poodle now that you bring it up."

"Linc!" Keva slapped my hand but dissolved in a fit of giggles. When Fifi ran to the dance floor to join in the line dance and immediately began to grind on some unsuspecting guy, we both laughed harder.

"Oh my God! She's humping his leg!" Keva gasped, laying her head on my shoulder while she laughed.

I leaned down and kissed the top of her head. This is what I'd wanted for tonight. A chance for Keva to have some fun. A woman shouldn't be stressed all the time.

"Looks like he likes it," I said back, eyeing the way the guy had turned and looped Fifi's long arms around his neck.

"That's Robbie Wells. He'll flirt with a fence post." Keva's hand rested on top of the wooden picnic bench. I put my hand on top of hers and laced our fingers together.

"Why does his shirt say 'Everyone talks shit to me'?" I didn't actually care, but giving Keva reasons to keep talking to me was my aim for the night.

"He's a mobile pooper scooper," Keva said dryly. Then she looked up at me and we both started laughing again.

"That's a fit made in dog heaven right there." I took one last swig of my beer and set it down. I stood up and tugged on her arm. "Come dance with me." I wanted to get my hands on her body. Show off to everyone that this gorgeous woman was mine.

Keva was already shaking her head before I got the question out. "Oh, I couldn't. I haven't danced in ages."

I pulled her up anyway, dipping down low to kiss her on the mouth. Yep. In public. I could feel her stiffen against me but I didn't care. "Just move side to side and I'll take care of the rest."

She followed me to the dance floor, but I could tell she was nervous. I pulled her in close and wrapped my arms around her waist, swaying side to side nice and gentle. Her flowery scent enveloped us as she lifted her arms and slid her hands around my neck.

"It's not a slow song, Linc," she whispered furiously.

"Don't care," I drawled right back. I shot her a wink and let my hand slide a little lower on her backside.

"Linc!"

"Shh, woman. Just dance, would you? No one is looking at you. No one is going to tell Lucas that his mom and dad were having some fun out on the dance floor tonight."

Keva snorted, but let her head drop to my chest. "You obviously don't know this small town quite yet."

I smiled above her head, moving us to the music, letting the songs switch, but never giving up my hold on her. She eventually relaxed in my arms, fused at the hips and swaying as one. I considered it a victory to finally get this woman to relax. My dick took notice of her soft curves but there was nothing I could do about that. I knew for sure she could feel me when she ground against my dick. I hissed and she laughed softly.

She pulled her head off my chest, eyes hazy, cheeks flamed. "You keep saying you want me."

I nodded, not sure where she was going with this. "I do."

She kept staring at me, those blue eyes refocusing the longer she looked. "I think I finally believe you."

I couldn't hold back the grin. "'Bout time, woman."

She rolled her eyes, but grinned back at me, finally letting me in just a tiny bit. "I'm not good at trusting."

"I know. That's why I'll just keep proving to you that I'm worthy of that trust you rarely give out."

Her thumb brushed against the back of my neck. "Thank you."

I squeezed her in tighter to my body. "No, thank you." I dipped my head and got right up close where only she could hear me. "Because in a couple minutes I'm going to take you home, peel that gorgeous dress off you, spread your legs, and take my time. No quick fucking tonight. I'm going to worship every inch of you. Wear out every muscle in your body. Make you shout my name."

Her eyes had gone wide, the color in her cheeks now spreading to her neck. "Oh."

I ground against her with the next drop in the beat, now harder than steel. "Yeah, *oh*. I've never gotten to take my time with you and I want to. Desperately."

Keva's breasts were crushed to my chest as her breathing quickened. "Then take me home, Linc."

I'd been waiting years for her to say those words.

I grabbed her hand and practically dragged her off the dance floor. Her laugh floating into the night sky as I marched us to the truck was the best sound in the world.

CHAPTER NINETEEN

 eva

"Open those legs, sweetheart."

Linc's work-roughened hand had slid high up my thigh and under the hem of my dress. I looked out at the darkened road as we bounced our way home in the truck. I felt feverish with desire for this man. It was even more than five years ago, a feat I didn't think possible.

"Probably not safe to divide your attention," I replied with a saucy smile. A little thrill ran through me. That was me, flirting. Apparently I did still know how to do that.

"You're lucky I'm talented with my hands." He didn't wait for me to comply, he just slid his hand up high enough to find the one and only pretty pair of panties I owned. He groaned at the feel of the lace, his fingers moving up and down. My thighs trembled but I didn't keep them closed. I gave in to what I wanted, opening my knees wide and letting Linc work me over without even touching my skin directly.

He made a left at the last stop sign and gunned it toward the end of the road where the glamp-ground beckoned us home. His finger slipped underneath the lace and I whimpered. The breath whooshed out of my lungs at the intense feelings that swept over me. It was like this one man held the key to revving my body. One look, one touch, and I was a heaving, sweating pile of needy nerve endings.

"Fuck, Keev. Already wet for me."

His jaw clenched tight and then he withdrew his hand completely to grip the steering wheel. I whimpered again for the opposite reason.

He wouldn't even look at me. "Not yet, sweetheart. I promised you more than a quick fuck in a borrowed truck."

"How about a quick fuck here and then a longer fuck in a bed?" Yes, I was desperate.

Linc's jaw unclenched and he actually smiled when he glanced over at me. The man was deadly with a grin. "I like you desperate for it, I won't lie."

The truck bounced over the uneven dirt road out by where our trailers were located. He put it in park and climbed out, pointing at me in warning when my hands went to the handle to let myself out. He came around and opened my door, holding out his hand to help me down. When my boots hit the dirt, he bent down and pulled me up into his arms in a princess carry. I yelped in protest, feeling the breeze on my bare ass as my dress pulled up.

"What the hell. Linc!"

He ignored me while he opened up the door to his trailer. Somehow he got us through the aisle and into his bedroom without knocking my new boots against the trailer. When he got to the bed, he dropped me, letting me bounce. The sparkle in his eyes kept me from complaining. Linc looked like he was having fun and it hit me that I wasn't the only one who could use a little fun in their life.

"I remember you giving me a piggyback ride that first day," I said lightly. I'd thought about that chivalrous move for months.

Linc shrugged and stood up to pull his shirt over his head and toss it to the floor. "I've always wanted to take care of you." He tilted his head with an evil grin. "But back then I mostly just wanted your tits pressed against me."

I laughed, propped on my elbows as I watched him leer at me. "Don't tell anyone, but I kind of liked the rough handling."

Linc's eyes lit up like I knew they would. He put a knee on the mattress and wrapped his hands around one of my boots. "Your secret is safe with me." Then he pulled the boot off and proceeded to get the other one off too. He moved fast, grabbing my dress and tugging it upward until he got it off my body. My bra was next, but he left me in the lacy panties. "Flip over."

"Say please," I teased.

Linc loomed over me, his fist digging into the bed right by my head. I was practically vibrating with needing him to touch me. "Let's get one thing straight. When we're in the bedroom, I won't be saying please. I'll make sure you're taken care of, believe me, but if you know what's good for you, you'll just do what I ask without the attitude. Can you do that for me, sweetheart?"

His hand dipped down, fingers dragging up my inner thigh. Goose bumps covered every inch of my skin. If he wanted me to comply, that was a good way to do it. "As long as I can give you attitude outside of the bedroom."

He winked. "Wouldn't have you any other way."

Holding his gaze, I lay back and lifted my arms above my head—delighting in the way his gaze latched on to my breasts— and then rolled, giving him my back. He hooked his hands at the sides of my panties and tugged downward. Even though the draft of cooler air on my ass made me squirm, I let him do what he wanted.

"Such a beautiful woman," he murmured, pushing off the bed and standing between my feet. And oddly enough, with Linc, I felt beautiful. I didn't feel like a single mom on the cusp of minivan life.

His fingers curled around my ankles and pulled my legs apart.

My breath came quicker. I wasn't the one in control here. I'd been the only one in control the last five years, so it felt odd to hand it over to someone else. Odd, but mixed with a relief so palpable I shuddered with it. His lips hit my ankles, kissing their way up one leg, then the other. The bed stifled my moan while I tried to keep still.

His hands kneaded my ass roughly. "Goddammit. So fuckin' beautiful." His praise made anything still stiff and unyielding in me melt. I had no defenses against his obvious adoration. "Your curves, Keva. They've always taken my breath away. I remember how you felt pressed up against my back on that damn scooter."

I lifted my head off the bed. "You remember that?"

His hands immediately left me. With a growl, he grabbed my shoulder and rolled me back over. He looked angry and I wondered what I said to change his mood so quickly.

"I remember everything about that day, Keva Mooney. I played it over and over in my head every single day I was gone." He shook his head. "Fuck, I fell in love with you and thought you'd long forgotten about me. I spent five years wanting you, missing you, wondering if you were happy." His gaze skittered away to the far wall.

Shock had me putting my hands on his cheeks and pulling his gaze back to me. "You fell in love with me?"

He nodded once, his five o'clock shadow scraping against my palms. "Yes. Fell that day and then stayed in love with you. It was only my friendship with your brother that made me stay away."

I blinked repeatedly, mind turning this news over and over in my brain. I'd spent five years assuming I was nothing but a quick fling. I honestly never thought I'd see Linc again let alone find out he was in love with me.

"You love me?" I asked on a whisper, too afraid to say it any louder.

His face softened as he continued to look down at me. "Yes. I love you, Keva. Been in love with you for five years and will love you for another fifty more."

My heart took off, racing as if I'd been handed the ATM card to an unlimited bank account. "Only fifty?"

His grin took my breath away. "You might be able to convince me to last a few more than that."

My fingers danced across his brow, then down his nose and across his lips. This man, this handsome, dedicated, sweet man loved me. I swallowed hard and took a step forward with a bravery I didn't know I had in me. Once burned badly enough, a heart stays closed. Or so I always thought.

"Make love to me, Linc."

He dipped his head and kissed me. "Gladly," he said against my lips.

He kicked out of his pants and I wrapped my legs around his hips. He reached between us and lined himself up with my body, sliding inside like he was made for me. He pressed his forehead against mine. We both groaned, our breath mingling along with our bodies. He began to move but I kept my arms around him, needing him closer. He was inside of me and yet still too far away. His chest slid across mine as my hands smoothed across his back.

"Linc," I murmured, feeling him hit deep inside over and over again, crumbling every single brick I'd put up to keep him out.

"I love you," he whispered above me.

I tilted my head back and kissed him as I shattered. He followed soon after, spilling into me with a burst of warmth, still telling me he loved me the entire time. I couldn't say the words yet but I hoped he knew. I fell asleep pressed to his chest, our legs intertwined and his arms holding me close. For the first time ever, I spent the night with a man, enjoying our bodies until the wee hours of the morning.

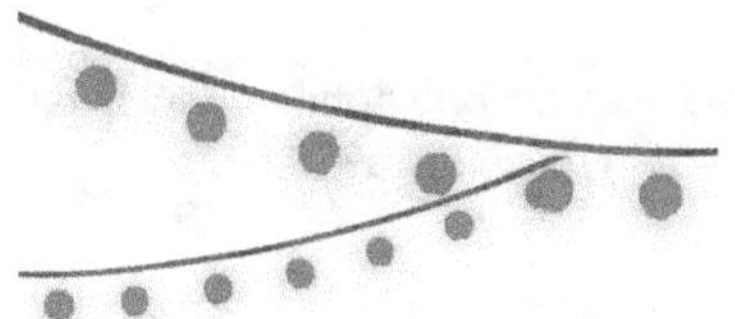

Paisley: The rumor mill says you and a certain newbie were getting quite frisky on the dance floor...

Me: The rumor mill can't be trusted.

Marlo: So you didn't take advantage of that gorgeous man last night? Disappointed in you, honestly...

Me: Ouch, Marlo! But if you must know, yes, we did enjoy ourselves.

Audrey: That's it? That's all the info we get?? We're besties, bitch! Spill the details.

Me: It was hot. Even hotter than the other times.

Paisley: WHAT OTHER TIMES???

Audrey: What she said.

Me: lol Let's focus on what's important here.

Marlo: We're trying to, but you're literally cockblocking us from those details.

Me: Has anyone noticed how thirsty Marlo's getting these days?

Audrey: Yes, but that'll be a discussion for a different day. Tell us what's important.

Me: I really like him.

Paisley: Of course you do. You did have a baby with him…

Me: No, I mean, I think I'm falling for him all over again.

Marlo: Would that be so bad?

Me: Well, I spent five long years convincing myself I was fine without him, so yeah, this feels a bit reckless.

Paisley: He and Lucas are adorable together.

Audrey: When I swung by the other day, I saw Linc working on your car.

Me: Wait, what?

Paisley: Didn't you notice that clunking sound was gone?

Me: I'm so screwed.

Audrey: Nah, you're fucked, which is where we all want to be, amiright?

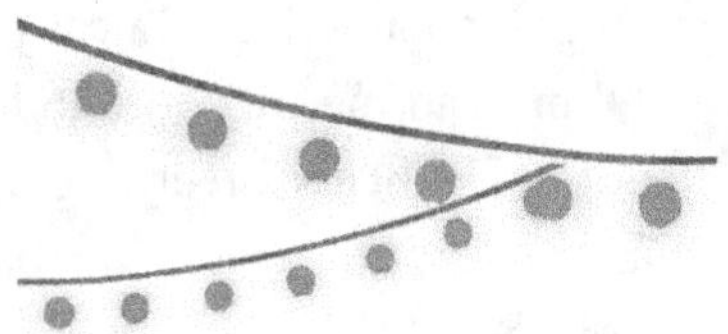

"Tell Daddy where we went today, Lucas." It still felt weird to call Linc daddy, but weird in a warm and fuzzy way. I stirred the ground beef sizzling in a pan on the little stove top in my trailer while Linc chopped the lettuce right next to me. We were making tacos for dinner. Like a real family.

"At the wibary, Miss Hattie said I could wead 'bout wombats!" Lucas wrinkled up his nose, stuck out his teeth, and sniffed around, acting like a wombat, when he really just looked like a cute little rat.

"That sounds amazing. Maybe I should go meet Miss Hattie too."

"She's weally pwetty." Lucas dropped the wombat act and had a seat at the dinette table.

"Not as pretty as your mama," Linc replied, elbowing me gently. I grinned at him, soaking up his compliment. Something had shifted between us last night. If I'd had any resistance left to keeping this man out, it was long gone now. I had to work on letting go of the past and think about what our future could look like.

"Lucas, can you get the ketchup?" I gave the meat one last stir.

"Ketchup on tacos?" Linc asked incredulously.

"He loves—"

A loud bang hit my ears and suddenly Linc's heavy body

pressed me against the cabinets, the pan of meat sliding across the cooktop in the chaos and spilling out the side. I froze, not sure what was happening. It sounded like Lucas had dropped the bottle of ketchup but Linc had me pinned like he was shielding me from an active shooter. His heavy breathing hit my ears while his heart hammered fast and frantic against my back.

"Daddy?" Lucas's voice wobbled.

"Linc? Babe, it's okay," I whispered, trying to move my head enough to see him behind me. His eyes were wide and glassy. "Hey, Lincoln? Look at me." It took him a second, but when he did lock eyes with me, my heart broke. The man was terrified.

Lucas began to cry, sensing the tension in the room, but my focus was on Linc. "Hey. We're okay. It was just the ketchup bottle. We're fine. Everything's okay."

He nodded once and then stepped back. A sheen of sweat covered his brow and his breaths were still unsteady. I put my hand on his chest and he flinched. Then he grabbed my hand and squeezed. I wasn't sure what just happened, but for the first time since he'd been back, Linc did not seem fine.

He let go of me and spun around, stooping down to pick up the ketchup bottle and Lucas. Linc tossed him up into his arms and cradled our little boy into his chest. When he spoke, his voice was jovial, but there was a tremor in it that had me nervous still.

"Did you see that? Daddy was so clumsy he made Mama spill the meat!" He twirled them in a circle and Lucas lifted his head from his chest. "Think we can eat a taco with a hot dog in the middle instead?"

"Ew, Daddy!" Lucas was laughing though and the tension drained from the trailer.

I got busy at the stove trying to salvage the meat. "I don't think we'll have to eat a yucky hot dog taco. Have a seat, you two, and I'll get the shells going."

They sat, bending their heads together and talking about something I couldn't make out. The whole while my brain was spinning. I'd been so caught up in my own head about raising Lucas by myself, I hadn't truly considered the hell Linc had been living in those same five years. I'd heard that it was rough to return to civilian life, and what did I do? Throw a surprise baby at Linc and a hell of a lot of attitude. He'd done nothing but try to take care of Lucas and me since he returned to town, but who was taking care of Lincoln?

Just before I turned to the table with the taco shells, I squeezed my eyes shut and vowed to do better.

CHAPTER TWENTY

$\mathcal{L}$inc

"You just going to stare at it all day long?"

I spun around in the dirt to find Gannon behind me. My heart was thundering, reminding me of what had happened in Keva's trailer the other night. The bastard had snuck up on me when I least expected it. Keva had left this morning with Lucas to drop him off at school. I should have been getting my workday started, but I had other ideas brewing.

"Gotta put a bell around your neck, bro," I grumbled.

Gannon guffawed and came up beside me to stare at my Harley. She was a thing of beauty. The one and only possession of mine that I'd had throughout my time in the military that I gave a damn about. The deep-purple-and-black paint job was pristine. Chrome flashed in the early morning sunlight like she was showing off for me. I spent a decent portion of my day wiping her down and keeping her clean.

And she had to go.

"What are we looking at here?" Gannon scratched the beard he'd been growing recently.

"Just saying my goodbyes."

His head whipped around so fast I thought he hurt himself. "You selling her?"

I shrugged, pretending that plan didn't hurt the bachelor I'd always been just a little bit. "I've got a son now, Gannon. I can't keep borrowing your truck to take my girl out either. I was thinking of heading out to the dealership and trading her in for an SUV of some sort. You mind if I take a couple hours?"

Gannon clapped me on the back. "I knew you were a good one." Then he tipped his baseball hat and moseyed off in the other direction.

I fired her up one last time, clicked my helmet in place, and roared down the road. I may have taken the long way that went out by the coast, but I eventually made it to the dealership in the city and found an SUV that would do. It had all the safety ratings I needed to cart around the two most precious people in the world, and it was black, a nod to my Harley. The paperwork took forever, but eventually I headed back home without a backward glance. The Harley had been perfect for my old life, but I wasn't that man anymore. I had responsibilities, and taking care of my family was more important than a well-oiled pile of expensive parts.

As I left the city and the pine trees began to thicken outside my windows, I started thinking about how much had changed in the last few months. Telling Keva I loved her after our date had made everything really fucking clear. In the military, I'd been a staff sergeant, leading my unit in various missions. Those soldiers had become my family, which meant I protected them at all costs. But I wasn't in the military anymore, and I felt like I'd lost that family. I'd been floundering and wondering where I fit in. Gannon had offered me a landing place in the form of a job and housing at Glamper's Paradise. But it was clear that Keva and

Lucas were my family now. I'd protect them at all costs. They were mine to support, mine to love, mine to lead.

I'd spent years hiding the fact that I'd fallen in love with Keva the first day I met her. A fist to the face by her brother, who was also my best friend, was enough to keep me silent on that issue. Boston had seen me suffering though, wondering why I never went out with him anymore when we were both on leave at the same time. When I finally told him how I felt about Keva, he'd taken it surprisingly well. He'd given me his blessing and that was all I needed. It felt really fucking good not to have to hide my feelings any longer.

When I finally pulled up to Glamper's Paradise, I veered left and headed for the group of people huddled around the outdoor fire pit. Normally I'd avoid people, but not when Keva and Lucas were part of the group. I put the SUV in park and climbed out. Keva lifted her head and there was a small smile on her pretty lips. Her eyes went wide when she saw my vehicle. Lucas saw me too and took off running. Man, I'd never get over the sight of my son's arms and legs pumping as he ran toward me with a smile on his little face. When he reached me and barreled into my legs, I swung him up in my arms and held him tight.

"Where's your Harley?" Keva said, still a few feet away. She wasn't quite running toward me like Lucas, but I did enjoy the fact that she'd come right over. She was a tough woman—and I fucking loved that about her—but I knew I'd wear her down eventually.

"Traded up for ol' Bessy here."

"Old Bessy?" Lucas squealed, giggling at the name and looking at the beast over my shoulder.

Keva, though, wasn't interested in the new vehicle. She was staring up at me, still in her work clothes and looking hotter than any woman in a fifty-mile radius. She wasn't frowning, but she wasn't smiling either.

"What?" I asked, bracing myself for something snarky. I've

learned that for each step forward with Keva, there's an inevitable step backward.

"You love that Harley," she said quietly.

"Loved," I corrected her.

Her eyes narrowed and the cool evening breeze made long strands of dark hair fly across her face. I reached up and pushed them behind her shoulder while she remained still. Lucas kicked his feet, obviously bored with ol' Bessy already, and I put him down so he could run back to Elise and the adults by the fire pit.

"Why did you sell it?" she finally asked.

I'd never had someone so averse to the idea of someone loving them before. So untrusting.

"You know why," I said quietly.

A long minute ticked by as she turned that over in her head. The crackle of the fire mixed with the sounds of the night descending all around us. The days were already short and the weather had turned cold seemingly overnight.

Then Keva launched herself at me and I caught her, wrapping my arms around her waist as her hands gripped the back of my neck. She pulled and I dipped my head down, certain she wanted to say something to me, but I was wrong. The woman kissed me, right on the mouth and in front of everyone, including our son. Her tongue slid along my lower lip, and before I knew what was happening, we were locked in the kind of kiss that had me indecently hard behind the fly of my jeans.

Someone by the fire let out a whoop and Keva pulled back, a sheepish smile on those lips. Her hands still held my neck though and I took it all as a good sign. I squeezed her waist and shot her a wink.

"Totally worth it."

We shared a knowing smile, and if it weren't for Lucas being a few feet from us, I would have carried her all the way to my trailer to strip that pencil skirt and blouse off of her.

"Do you mind if we chat real quick?"

My thumb brushed against her hip. "Of course."

While Gannon, Paisley, and the kids chatted with campers around the fire, Keva and I moved off to the side below a tall pine tree where we could still keep an eye on Lucas. The air was cooler over here away from the fire, but whatever was on Keva's mind was worrying me. She was the queen of mixed signals. Kissing me in front of everyone and then wanting to talk after. Letting me fuck her hard and fast behind closed doors but then acting aloof in public. I had a feeling her heart and her head were telling her completely opposite things. My job was to get her to listen to her heart again like she used to.

"What's going on?" I asked when she didn't start speaking.

She crossed her arms over her chest and then dropped them. Shuffled her feet and then looked away. I reached up and cupped her face, making her look at me.

"Whatever it is, just say it and we'll work through it together."

Her eyes looked big and vulnerable out here, but she finally nodded. "I was thinking about what happened in the trailer the other night."

My spine stiffened and my hand fell away from her cheek. I knew what she was referring to. Keva reached out and put her hands on my chest.

"I want to help, Linc. I can imagine being back to civilian life is tough after so many years in the military. I honestly am ashamed that I didn't ask earlier, but are you doing okay?"

Fucking great. One freak-out and Keva was looking at me like I was a head case. "I'm fine."

She nodded but stepped even closer, tilting her head back to maintain eye contact. "Okay, but I was thinking it might be a good idea for you to go talk to the therapist guy Gannon goes to just to make sure. I got his number for you."

"Gannon has a therapist?"

Keva nodded. "Yeah, he and Bain go to the same guy. I hope I didn't overstep but I just thought it might be good for you to talk to someone who might have some strategies to help you."

My brain was tossing that idea around. Before I left, a seasoned officer had advised me the same thing, but I'd brushed him off. I didn't like asking for help.

"Please don't be mad." Keva gripped my shirt. "I want to help but I don't know how to. I should have been trying to help earlier, but—"

"Keevs," I interrupted her, putting my hand over hers and trying to get her to release my shirt. "Thank you. Yes, I'll go see him. But under one condition."

Her shoulders dropped in relief. "What condition?"

"You go with me."

Her whole body jolted. "Go with you?"

I nodded, warming to the idea already. "Yeah. You've been through your own trauma, and I think if we're to move forward as a couple, we should hash out all the drama of the last five years."

"A couple?"

I grinned. "You're just echoing me now, sweetheart. Yes, as a couple. We're a fucking couple. The fact you can't get that through your head is reason enough to go, don't you think?"

Keva just stared at me and I stared right back, daring her to disagree. Then she shocked me again by lifting up on her toes and pressing a kiss to my mouth. Before I could deepen it, she stepped back.

"Okay. I'd like to try that if you will too."

I nodded, feeling elated and trying to hide it so I wouldn't spook her. We'd taken a few steps forward and I didn't need her stepping back. "Now how about we get the food out of ol' Bessy and have dinner together as a family before we put Lucas to bed?"

"You brought dinner?"

"I stopped to meet Diego at Grass. Got dinner for us and Gannon too since I ended up taking the whole damn day to buy the car."

Keva gave me a look that had me wishing we had a soundproofed bedroom in one of our trailers. She walked her fingers down my chest and I was done for. "You're pretty hot when you're acting all domesticated."

I reached around and smacked her ass, just to see her mouth drop open and her cheeks go red. "You can thank me later tonight after Lucas goes to bed."

She did thank me later as she chanted my name in barely a whisper. Her fists gripped the sheets in her trailer, and she didn't even flinch when I murmured I loved her before we both drifted off to sleep. No thanks were necessary when she let me sleep over with Lucas just a few feet away and her in my arms.

Like a real family.

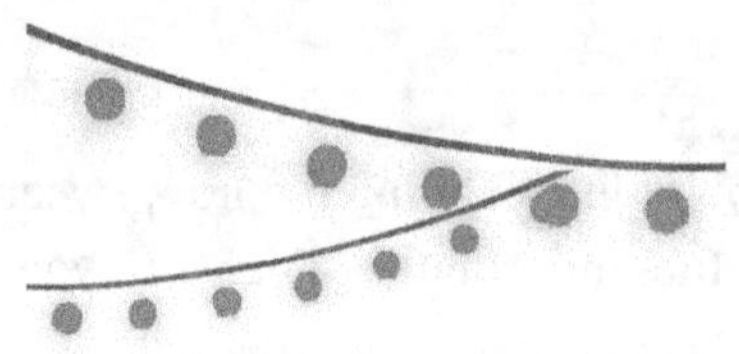

Me: Whatcha dressing up as for Halloween?

Baby Mama: Nothing.

Me: Damn. Going with the birthday suit, huh? Nothing is my favorite look on you.

Baby Mama: Linc

Me: Keva

Baby Mama: Is everything about sex to you?

Me: No, of course not. I'm a nuanced, deep person when you get to know me. You think maybe a French maid costume would be a good choice?

Baby Mama: For you, yes.

Me: Don't you mean oui?

CHAPTER TWENTY-ONE

eva

"OKAY, EVERYBODY CREEP INSIDE REAL QUIET," I whispered fiercely to the group of us assembled on Gannon and Paisley's porch. Marlo, Audrey, and I went in first, standing behind Paisley. My heart was about to beat out of my chest with happiness.

"Nice shirt," I snarked loudly at Gannon, playing my part perfectly. His new shirt said "I'm the dad."

Gannon and I still hadn't had it out yet about his part in bringing Linc home, although now I was happy about it. Not that I'd ever cut Gannon slack. The cocky guy deserved some ribbing for sticking his nose in my love life.

I heard the group behind us hush Elise when she began to giggle, hiding her and Paisley's mom in the middle of their huddle of people. As a group, they surged forward into the house, coming up behind us as planned.

"Dad?" Gannon sounded confused, which was perfect. His dad pushed through the throng of people and showed off his grandpa shirt. Then Paisley's mom pushed Elise to the front of the group for the final announcement about being a big sister written on Elise's shirt.

"I like Elise's shirt the best," Paisley's mom said on a grin.

Gannon sounded like he might need resuscitation, a job I wasn't volunteering for. Paisley put her arm around Elise and tugged her over to Gannon. There was a stinging happening behind my eyeballs, and if I wasn't mistaken, I'd need those tissues I'd shoved in my pocket just in case. I stepped back to Linc's side and put my arms around his waist. The room was hushed, expectant.

"I'm pregnant," Paisley announced.

I sniffled and even Linc squeezed me tighter as if he was having a hard time keeping his shit together too. Gannon let out a whoop that hurt everyone's ears and then he was spinning his girls around. The man was so happy I thought he might drop dead of a heart attack. When he got on his knees to kiss Paisley's flat stomach, the first tear rolled down my cheek. Linc murmured an excuse and slipped out the back of the crowd to disappear into the kitchen.

I cheered for my friends—and our perfectly executed baby reveal—and went in search of Linc. I found hm leaning against the countertop, head bent and focused on breathing by the sound of things. He'd been to the therapist I suggested three times already, and seemed to be heading in a good direction. I wasn't sure what set him off just now, but I wanted to help.

"Linc?"

He lifted his head, eyebrows pinched. The whites of his eyes were red.

"Hey," he answered, fingernails still digging into the granite countertop where he gripped it behind him. He tried out a smile, but I could tell it was forced.

I came over, putting my hand on his chest and peering up into his face. The steady heartbeat beneath all that muscle reassured me that he was okay.

"What's wrong?"

He opened his mouth and I knew I'd hear some bullshit he thought I wanted to hear. He was always trying to protect me and Lucas. I appreciated it, but when he was hurting, I wanted to know.

"The truth, Lincoln."

A single eyebrow climbed his forehead. "Oh, it's Lincoln now, huh?"

"It is when you're about to bullshit me."

His grin was real now. He let go of the countertop and put his hands on my hips. "I'm really happy for our friends."

"Me too." I stepped closer, leaning into his body. "And?"

Linc dropped his forehead to mine, staring deep into my eyes. "And I hate that I missed out on that moment with you."

My eyes fluttered shut as my heart began to ache. "Oh, Linc."

His hands left my hips to cup my face, making me look at him. "I would have given anything to be here when you found out. To assure you everything would be okay. To tell you I loved you. To tell you I looked forward to our son. I'm sorry I wasn't here. That'll be my biggest regret in life."

Another tear slipped down my cheek, this one for us. "I'm sorry I didn't try harder to tell you. I couldn't risk rejection. I'm sorry I let my hurt feelings keep our son from you. That'll be *my* biggest regret."

Linc moved just an inch, his lips fluttering over mine. There was apology in the kiss, the subtle brush of lips meant to soothe and heal the past. Then the inhale of longing led to a deeper kiss of promises and a future together. It was a perfect kiss for an imperfect couple.

"Oh Lordy, we got ourselves another set of lovebirds!" Audrey called out from behind me.

Linc and I broke apart, but he didn't drop my gaze. His eyes were burning, still connected and communicating even though our bodies shifted away. Marlo followed Audrey into the kitchen.

"I told her to wait, but you know Audrey," Marlo deadpanned, heading for the refrigerator.

"Hey! I said they were super cute, and if we waited for them to finish, we'd be waiting a long time. And that pregnant woman in there wants cake. You don't make pregnant women wait for sugar. It's like a pregnancy rule or something." Audrey grabbed the stack of baby-blue and light-pink paper plates and forks we'd hid in the vegetable drawer in the fridge. Paisley had assured us Gannon would never find them and she'd been right.

Marlo pulled the sheet cake out and rolled her eyes. "Remind me never to fall in love or have babies. I'll be walking around in public oblivious to the hickey on my neck like Keva."

I slapped my hand to my neck. "Shit! I thought I covered it enough."

Marlo and Audrey's laughter trickled back as they marched out of the kitchen. Linc's smirk was too cocky.

"Might want to wipe that grin and hide out until that erection dies down." I pointed to the obvious bulge in his pants and followed my friends back out to the party.

Linc followed my advice and found me a few minutes later, condition resolved. He leaned into my ear. "You're going to pay for that later. You think the hickey is bad. Wait 'til you can't sit down after a thorough spanking."

My cheeks heated and his smirk was back. I opened my mouth to dish out some snark but his cell phone rang. He pulled it out of his pocket, saw that it was his mother, and put it away again.

"You need to get that?" I'd seen her call him a few times in my presence, but he never answered it.

"Nah. I'll call her later."

I frowned at him while he snagged a plate with a thick slice of cake and dug in. I felt myself getting in deep with Linc and yet there was so much we still didn't know about each other. We did everything backwards in our relationship, skipping steps and tripping over ourselves. Maybe it was time to go back to the basics and date my baby daddy, the guy I was already in love with.

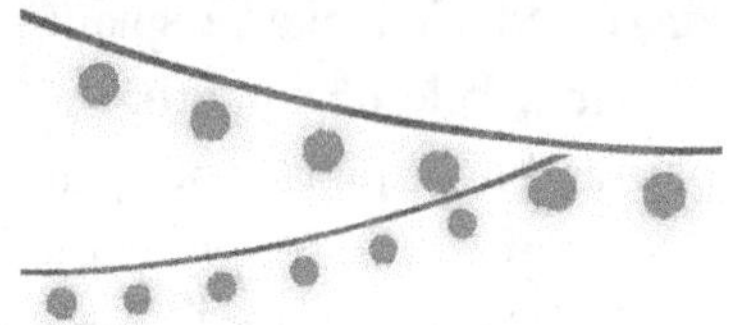

"Mama?" Lucas tugged on my sweater. He was adorable in a T. rex costume, holding the reins of the head, while the tail swished back and forth behind him.

"Yeah, baby?"

"Do I gotta do it by myself?" He stared at the next house like the doorbell might bite him.

"No way, buddy. I'll go with you." Linc stepped around me and gave our son a reassuring grin. Elise and Gannon had gone a couple houses ahead, Elise calmly telling Lucas that a princess couldn't trick-or-treat with a dinosaur. Paisley was back at their house, setting up for the after-party where the kids would collapse into a sugar-overdose heap of exhaustion.

"But..." Lucas wrinkled his little nose at Linc. "You not anything!"

Linc's gaze darted left and right before he leaned down and rescued an abandoned *Toy Story* hat that some Woody had left behind. It didn't fit his head and he looked so ridiculous my heart melted. Kids were trick-or-treating everywhere on this street. Blueball went all out on Halloween and this year was no different. We'd been offered hot dogs and kettle corn already and we'd barely made it down half a block.

Together, the two made their way up to each door, ringing the doorbell and shouting "Trick or Treat" at the top of their lungs. That had always been my job, and as much as I thought I might miss it, I was happy to stand on the curb and watch it happen.

We called it a night when Lucas tripped and lost his tail. He scraped up his knee, but bravely blinked back the tears as Linc distracted him with all the different candies in his bucket.

I pulled a Band-Aid out of my bag and smoothed it onto his knee. "All set, Mr. T. rex. You ready to head to Elise's house?"

Lucas nodded sleepily and didn't even protest when Linc scooped him up and carried him back to the car. He laid his head on Linc's shoulder and was out before we'd gotten him strapped into his car seat.

"What else do you have in that damn bag of yours?" Linc asked as we climbed into his new SUV. He tried to peer inside but I smacked his hand away.

"A woman never tells."

He shot me a look and started the car. "Okay, but seriously. What's in there?"

I moved my leg to cover up the bag. "I'm not telling my secrets, sir."

"Food? Weapons? First aid kit? Lipstick? Tampons?"

"All of the above and more."

Linc was looking at me like he wasn't sure if he was hurt that I wouldn't share, or if he just wanted to toss me over his knee and spank me for not sharing. I was just enjoying being playful with him. I hadn't been playful in a long time. Being able to trust him had awakened a part of me that had gone dormant under the stress of being a single mom.

"Are you ever going to tell me?"

I shrugged, watching the neighborhood go by as we slowly drove through the streets, watching out for kids still trick-or-treating. "Perhaps. Maybe one day when I owe you a big favor."

Linc's hand slid over to grip my thigh. He shot a glance into the back seat before turning to the front again. "I actually had a different favor in mind."

His hand started traveling higher on my thigh. "Oh yeah? What's that?"

"I was thinking." He paused to make a turn that would lead us out to Glamper's Paradise. "What if we had our own costume party tonight?"

He licked his lips and I could only imagine what images he had in his head. I opened my legs wider and his hand took advantage. "I mean, it would be a shame for the adults not to celebrate the holiday, right?"

Linc grinned and the sight of it made me happier than I'd been in a long time. "Exactly right. I'll put Lucas to bed, text Gannon our apologies for bailing on the after-party, and then meet you in my trailer. Bring the baby monitor."

I gasped softly as his fingers found where I needed him most. "Not my trailer, huh?"

His grin turned wicked. "Not for the things I have planned for you tonight. You need to be able to scream."

He stroked up my center and I leaned my head back, eyes sliding closed. "French maid? Nurse? How do you want me?"

His thumb found the bundle of nerves that had me panting. "I'll bring the costume. You don't worry about a thing."

Bliss.

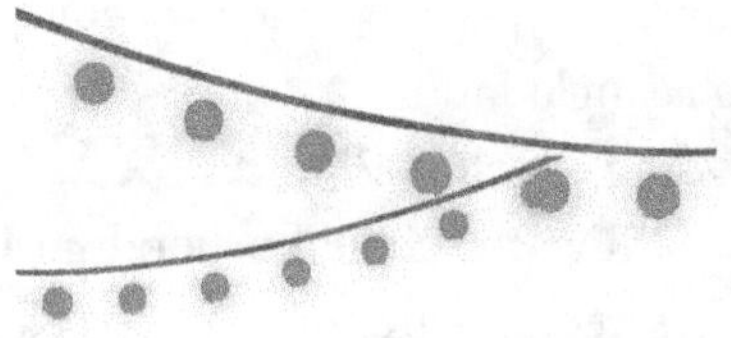

I was naked as the day I was born, lying on Linc's bed when he finally came in. He took one look at me and growled, stalking over and throwing something at me. I caught it mid-air, untangling the material to see a familiar T-shirt.

"Is this—?"

Linc pulled his shirt off and stepped out of his jeans. "Yes, ma'am. Now put it on so I can rip it off."

His beautiful erection bobbed as he pulled off his boxers. He gripped the base of himself and stood there watching me with hooded eyes. When I got the Army T-shirt on that I'd worn all those years ago, he rolled his lips in, looking like he was in pain.

"Just like that first day."

I nodded, too flooded with desire to put anything I felt into words.

"We're going to recreate that day, except this time, I ain't leaving. I'm going to wake up with you in my arms and your scent on my skin. You're going to whisper good morning and we're going to spend the next day together. And then the next. We clear?"

I nodded again, very much liking how he took control of things in the bedroom.

"Good. Now scoot to the edge of the bed."

I sat on the side of the bed, looking up at him, mouth watering.

"Now open those knees and slide one hand under the shirt. Tell me how wet you are."

I did as he ordered, my nipples rubbing almost painfully against the soft cotton. My eyes nearly rolled back in my head as I let my fingers slide through my folds. "Soaking."

Linc tugged on his cock once before gripping the base again. His chest began to heave, great gulps of air pistoning in and out. "Other hand under your shirt to grab your breast. Don't quit stroking yourself."

My fingers kept up a steady rhythm while my other hand

found my heavy breast. Linc stepped closer, fist still gripped tightly on his cock. I could see that bead of moisture seep out of the tip and I wanted to taste him.

"I wanted your pretty red lips on my cock that day, but we never got the chance."

"Let me." The words tumbled out of my mouth eagerly. Without missing a beat, I leaned forward and licked the tip of his cock. He hissed and I moaned. I could come just like this, touching myself and seeing him come undone from my tongue.

Linc ran his cock over my lips. When I opened my mouth, he shoved inside and cupped my face with his hands. "Fucking hell, Keevs. You're stunning with my cock in your mouth."

I bobbed down, letting him slide down my throat before pulling back. Lipstick stained his cock. Tears welled in my eyes and spit dribbled down my chin, but I'd never felt sexier. I kept my gaze on him the whole time, watching the way his muscles bunched as he held himself under a tight control. How his skin broke out into goose bumps. The granite-hard lock of his jaw. Then the complete adoration in his eyes when the first spurt of hot fluid hit the back of my throat. With a bark of release, he squeezed his eyes shut, fingers sliding into my hair in a tight grip. I swallowed hard and fast, welcoming him into my body any way I could have him.

Seeing Linc lose himself sent me over the cliff. My thighs trembled and my fingers faltered. My jaw ached and my lungs burned, but none of that mattered when the sudden orgasm crashing into me was blissful and unreal. I felt used and cared for, a complex mix that was hotter than the summer sun. Linc pulled out of my mouth and scooped me up, laying me down on the bed with him behind me. We lay like that for long minutes, both of us catching our breath.

The knock on the door had me sitting upright, pulling the sheet up and over me even though I still wore his T-shirt. Linc chuckled. "It's okay. Just pizza delivery."

I peeked over the edge of the sheet. "Pizza?"

Linc got off the bed and pulled on his jeans, barely able to tuck himself back inside. "Just like our first day together, remember? We'll eat and then we'll make love. Nice and slow. Won't quit 'til you're shoutin', sweetheart. I keep my promises."

I flopped back on the bed and let him take care of me.

CHAPTER TWENTY-TWO

$\mathcal{L}$inc

Me: Please step outside. I'm taking you to a
wine bar on a date.

IT DIDN'T TAKE LONG for the bubbles to appear. Standing
outside, I'd just seen the light turn off in Lucas's bedroom, so I
knew she was done for the night.

Baby Mama: Um...what about our son? Who's
sleeping.

I shook my head. The woman was always so practical and
always underestimating me.

Me: Just come outside.

A few seconds later, the trailer door cracked open and Keva
peered out. I stood there next to the self-contained fire pit I'd

bought after reading the safety ratings and knowing Lucas couldn't get into it by accident. The string lights were on and there was a fancy bottle of red wine breathing on the table set up in between the two deck chairs. Blankets were slung over the chair backs, ready for us to curl up in them.

I saw the moment Keva took it all in. Her shoulders peeled away from her ears and she lost the little line between her dark eyebrows. Guilt clawed its way into the good feeling I'd had about us all week. No matter how much I tried to let go of the guilt of leaving her to raise our son by herself, I couldn't seem to drop that weight. My therapist had suggested that it might just take time and repeated effort.

Stepping forward, I took her hand in mine and tugged her out the door and over to the chairs. I poured us both a glass of wine while the soft breeze made me glad I'd brought out several blankets. Gannon had promised this area got snow a couple times a year, and with how quickly the temperature was dipping, I believed him.

"This isn't the wild and crazy nights you probably envisioned when you got out of the Army."

I turned to her, wishing she understood how wrong she was. This was always exactly where I wanted to be. I'd had enough adrenaline to last me a lifetime. I had a seat, pulling her into my lap. She let out a soft laugh, feeling all warm and soft cuddling against me. I couldn't help myself and nuzzled into her neck, inhaling her familiar scent.

"The last time I was in your lap, these trees got a show."

I reached back to lay a blanket across us and simply enjoyed a snapping fire with my girl on my lap. "That night was like coming home for me."

Keva turned, holding her glass to her chest. Her eyes were darker out here, almost black. "I was so mad I let you touch me. Mad you could still get an orgasm out of me."

The cocky grin was inevitable, but she slapped my chest play-fully anyway. We sat in silence, just staring at the fire and sipping our wine, unwinding after a day of working and parenting. I wanted a thousand more days with Keva just like this one. I wanted to know everything there was to know about her. I wanted to anticipate her every need and care for her so completely she'd never doubt me again.

"Tell me about your parents," I said softly. I knew from my friendship with Boston that their parents had died when he was only eighteen. Keva had to have been much younger.

Keva sighed, taking another healthy sip of wine before answering. "I was twelve, Boston had just turned eighteen. It's all kind of a blur, to be honest. One day we were a happy family and the next my parents are gone, my brother is shipping off to the Army, and I'm moving in with a foster family."

My heart clenched, realizing how hard that must have been at twelve. She'd been all alone, facing a huge loss. "I remember Boston saying you were with an uncle?"

Keva nodded. "A few years—and a couple foster families—later, my father's stepbrother took me in, but he was a barely functioning alcoholic. I think he only took me in because he found out there'd be a check from the government every month that he could spend on alcohol. I mostly just lay low and counted down the days until I was eighteen."

I squeezed her tighter, wishing I could travel back in time and somehow rescue her. Wishing I could stop the tremble in her voice now when she recalled those years. "I'm sorry, sweetheart. No one should have to go through that."

She shrugged, but I could see the tears welled up in her eyes. "I lucked out finding that job with Lucy and meeting my friends. They rallied around me when I found out I was pregnant."

I dropped my forehead to her shoulder, angry at the situation and knowing there was no one to blame. No way to go back and change things for her. I could only move forward, taking exquisite care of her and Lucas and hope that that made up for being missing from their lives for five years.

"I think that's why I couldn't risk your rejection again," Keva said so quietly I barely heard her. "Everyone leaves me."

"Babe, no." I put down my wineglass and took hers from her hand so I could pull her in tight and look her in the eyes. A tear slipped down her cheek before she could swipe it away and it nearly ripped me in two. "That may have been the sequence of events in the past, but it will never be true now. I will never leave you. Lucas will never leave you. You're stuck with both of us forever."

She nodded, but continued to silently cry. "It's just my parents left. Boston left. You left. It's a pattern. And I'm terrified I'll fail Lucas in some way and he'll leave me too."

I pulled her into a hug, tucking her head against my chest and stroking her hair. "You're the best mother I've ever seen. Lucas would never leave you. I'm sorry for being one of the ones that left. I thought I was doing what was best for you, which was obviously horribly wrong. Now that I'm back, I promise you I'll never leave you. I love you, Keva, which means even if you don't love me back, I'll still be right here. I'll be your fucking shadow, taking care of you whether you let me in or not. Okay?"

Her hand, the one gripping my shirt in her fist, tugged on me. "But you'll die one day and leave me. Everyone will."

I shook my head, never feeling more certain of anything. "I don't believe that. Some people are made to be together through space and time. We had one day together and the universe tied us together forever with Lucas. I came back for a job and we stumbled into each other. We were meant to be, Keva Mooney."

She lifted her head and I kissed her wet cheeks. "Even when I die, I'll still be taking care of you until you join me in the afterlife. All my accounts list you and Lucas as my beneficiaries." I gave her a mock look of warning. "Now don't go and off me for my money. It's not a lot."

Keva's mouth dropped open. "When did you do that?"

She was cute when she was learning just how much I loved her. "The day after I found out about Lucas."

Her eyes welled up again, and admittedly, I didn't know much about women, but they seemed like happier tears. "You're a good man, Lincoln."

I shook my head. "Not sure about that, but I'll be a good man for you."

She cuddled into my chest, then lifted my shirt to wipe her face.

"Did you just use my shirt to wipe your snot?" I teased her.

She laughed softly. "You make a girl cry, you take the snot."

I kissed the top of her head.

"Now tell me about *your* family," she said quickly.

I grunted. "Not much to tell. My parents are still married and I have three older sisters. They're all a pain in the ass."

Keva looked up again. "Well, your mom reaches out a lot. That's not so terrible, is it?"

I tilted my head back and forth. "She's a bit smothering, to be honest. I think my going off into the military made it worse for her, but better for me. I couldn't take her constant mother-henning as a teen. She and my sisters would gang up on me and my dad was pretty gruff and standoffish, so I was on my own. I should call her more often now that I'm out, but I wanted to get my life together before she started in on all the ways in which I was failing."

"Well, I haven't witnessed what your mom is like, but if she's anything like me with Lucas, she probably just loves you so much she oversteps a bit without meaning to."

I grinned, recalling how great Keva was with our son. "Maybe you're right. Besides, I'm older and wiser now."

Keva smirked. "Wiser? You sure about that?"

I poked her in the belly and she squealed. "Got you, didn't I? I'm damn smart."

She grabbed my finger and pulled it away from her ticklish spot. "All I'm saying is that I don't have much in the way of extended family to offer Lucas. Maybe it wouldn't be so bad to involve your family. For Lucas's sake."

I groaned. "Dammit, woman. You know I can't say no if it has to do with him."

Keva smiled smugly. "I know." Then the smile dropped. "You actually have family, Linc. You should see them and let them love on you."

I pulled her hand up to my lips and kissed her soft skin. "Okay, I will. But only if you contact Boston."

In all the times Boston had complained about Keva ghosting him, her brother never mentioned that he had a nephew. I had a feeling he'd want to know. Whatever bad blood these siblings had between them, they deserved a chance to work through it, just like Keva and I had. There'd been a lot of misunderstandings, and if talking it out could provide Keva with more people in her life who loved her, then I was all for it.

Keva wrinkled her nose. "Ugh. Fine."

I pulled her into my chest and shifted her on my lap. We sat there together in the silence for a good ten minutes. I'd have stayed there all night, but I knew she needed her sleep.

"Should we give these pine trees another show, or would you like me to carry you to bed?" I whispered in her ear.

Keva lifted her head, eyes looking sleepy. "I think I'm turning into an exhibitionist."

I grinned like the wolf who found Little Red Riding Hood. "I'll keep the blanket around us if you take my cock out of my pants."

Her eyes lit up. "Think this chair can handle us both?"

"If it doesn't, I'll build you a new one tomorrow."

CHAPTER TWENTY-THREE

Keva

LINC and I fell into a domestic rhythm better than anything I had hoped to dream of when I found out I was pregnant. It was hard to let go of some of the responsibilities I'd been shouldering all by myself, but I was finding it rewarding when I did. Linc enjoyed taking Lucas to school, which gave me time to get ready and stop for a coffee before work, previously a luxury I never got to indulge in. We shared in the parenting and even the day-to-day things like keeping a stocked refrigerator or remembering to sign a form Lucas needed for a field trip. It was probably boring by most people's standards, but after all the stress in my life, I craved steady and easy.

There was nothing steady and easy about our nights though. The man drove me wild once Lucas went to bed, demanding and giving in equal measure until I wasn't sure if my legs would hold me. I might have been running on fumes with how late he kept me up, but I was smiling too hard to be bothered by a little thing like sleep deprivation. I was a mom. I was trained for sleep deprivation better than a Navy SEAL.

"Hello?"

The voice was cheerful but cautious through the phone. I had a split-second panic that maybe I shouldn't be doing this, but I pushed it down. We'd made a deal and I was just helping things along a bit. Linc deserved to have someone take care of him as perfectly as he took care of Lucas and me.

"Hi. Mrs. Angelo?"

"Yes, and who is this?"

I sat on the little couch in the trailer, hoping Linc wouldn't come home too quickly from his trip to the store for ice cream with Lucas. "This is Keva Mooney. You don't know me, but I'm close with your son. I've seen you call his phone a few times and I wanted to reach out."

"Oh, my. It's lovely to meet you, honey. Lincoln's told me about a special someone but he hasn't told me anything else. That boy is closed up tighter than a startled clam."

I chuckled at her description of Linc. "He is for sure. But here's the thing. We both want to be more involved with our families and I thought what better way than to get together for Thanksgiving. I know I'm a little late, but do you already have plans? Would you want to come up here?"

There was a brief pause in which I thought I heard a sniffle. "Oh, honey, just boring plans I'm cancelling right now. Give me twenty minutes and I'll have called all my daughters and told them we're headed up north. Blueball? Is that the town?"

"Yes, ma'am." I looked around the trailer, just now realizing that inviting a bunch of people to a tiny trailer was ambitious, if not stupid. "We live in a tight space, but I'm sure I can come up with something."

"Don't you worry about us. I'll sit in a tree if it means I get to see my boy. Nearly killed me when he went off in the Army."

"Being that I'm a boy mom too, I can understand that completely."

"Well, hug that son of yours tight, and I'll hug mine when I see you next week. How about you text me what you're planning to serve and I'll bring the rest?"

"Okay, sounds like a plan. Thanks, Mrs. Angelo."

"Oh, honey, if this is what I think it is, just call me Mama. I can't tell you what this means to me."

And just like that, plans were put into motion.

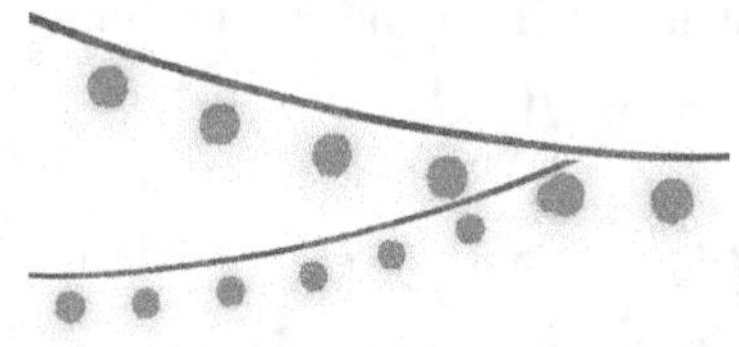

Linc stood in the doorway to my bedroom, a tiny space that barely held a bed and overhead drawers for my clothes. His hands were up on the doorframe, lifting up his T-shirt and showing off those abs I'd had my tongue on last night. His flannel matched his denim-blue eyes.

"What's your deal this morning, Keevs?"

I tucked the sheets under the mattress and smoothed out the comforter for the third time this morning. I'd been up since before the crack of dawn, alternating thoughts that I'd forgotten an important detail that would embarrass me in front of Lincoln's whole family or that Linc was going to kill me for keeping this a secret. I straightened up, thankful for my short stature when my head didn't hit the ceiling in this part of the trailer. I was already sweating in a sweater and jeans. I needed to calm down or I'd gross out his family with my sweaty hands.

"No deal. Just excited for Thanksgiving."

Linc frowned. "Still don't get why Gannon and Paisley aren't hosting inside their warm house."

My fingers started twisting together and I forced them to stop. I'd had to enlist the help of my friends in keeping this charade. Thankfully, even Gannon had kept his mouth shut, though I was sure the favor would cost me.

"Oh, come on. It's fun to be outside and I rented enough space heaters to feel like summer out there." I came closer, drawing my finger along the skin that was showing beneath his shirt.

Linc grunted and dropped his hands to let them rest on my waist. I knew that look on his face. "Think we have time? Lucas is with Elise."

I pushed him away. The man was too damn tempting for his own good. His family was due here any minute now. "No! Did you not get enough last night?"

He'd woken me in the middle of the night and taken me from behind, my face shoved into the mattress. Who would have guessed this single mom liked grunts in the dark and rough handling by her baby daddy to wake her up in the middle of the night? I wasn't sure when I'd adopted the hated "baby daddy" phrase in my own head but there it was.

His cocky grin turned playful. "I can never get enough of you. You know that."

I kept pushing him until he had to walk backward down the aisle of the trailer. "Stop batting your pretty eyes at me, Angelo."

"I don't have pretty anything, woman. Handsome, hell yes." He dug his feet in at the door and leaned down to steal a kiss. "I can't wait to show you how thankful I am for you tonight."

I pressed another kiss to his lips, nerves flaring. "I sure hope so..."

He frowned, but I reached around and opened the door, escaping into the cool air and coming face-to-face with three unfamiliar cars pulling into our glampsite. A gray-haired woman with very few lines on her pretty face stared out the windshield at us.

"What the hell is this?" Linc muttered.

I watched his face closely. Confusion turned to surprise and then finally to happiness. The breath whooshed out of my lungs when he hurried to open the car door for his mother. He helped her up and then she flung her arms around him, crying. My own eyes welled up as they stood there hugging while the rest of his family got out of their cars.

Linc's father approached me first, putting out his hand and shaking mine without a trace of a smile. He looked a lot like Linc, just without the stunning blue eyes and a few decades older. My nerves kicked in again when he didn't say anything. Then all the butterflies got pushed aside when three women pulled me into a group hug of laughter, perfume, and talking all at once. I gathered these were the sisters Linc had referred to.

Linc finally came over and pulled me from his sisters, putting his arm around my shoulders and formally introducing me to everyone. Each of the sisters was married and had kids, so the volume level was intense. Linc's mom interrupted his introductions like she just couldn't wait, pulling me into a bone-crushing hug.

"You're just as beautiful as my boy described. Thank you, honey." When she pulled back, she still had tears in her eyes and hell if my own didn't well up again. "You can call me Grace or Mama. Whatever you're comfortable with."

The long braid slung over the front of her shoulder wavered in my field of vision. I wondered what my life would look like if I still had my mother around. I blinked repeatedly, trying to pull myself together. This whole surprise was supposed to be for Linc's benefit, but it was soothing something in my soul too.

"If y'all want to come on back, we have a volleyball court, horseshoes, snacks, and a fire pit to keep warm."

The kids let out a shout and then the group was off, traipsing through the woods to the other side of the glamp-ground to find the festivities. Grace put one arm around my waist and one arm around her son's. Linc's dad was somewhere behind us, the shuffle of his feet through the fallen leaves letting us know he was there.

"Tell me everything about your life here."

"Well..." Linc hedged.

Just then we came around a thick line of trees to the clearing. Lucas and Elise caught sight of us over by the fire pit. Meatball jumped out of Elise's arms and snagged a marshmallow off the outer ring of the fire pit before anyone could yell at him. Lucas ran over to us with a toothy grin. "Mama! We got marmallows!" He already had marshmallow goo around the sides of his mouth.

"Mom. Dad. I'd like you to meet my son." Linc put his hand on Lucas's excited shoulder. "Lucas, these are your grandparents."

Grace let out a whimper and then she was swinging Lucas up into her arms to look at him. The woman was slight, but clearly strong from raising four kids and now a brood of grandkids. Thankfully Lucas let her look her fill, reaching up to play with her dangly turkey earrings.

"Lucas," she repeated quietly, like she was testing out the sound of his name. "Will you be Grandma Grace's favorite and sit by me today?"

"Can we eat marmallows?"

Grace grinned, walking away from us with her new grandson. "All the marmallows we can eat, my boy."

"That's it?" I asked Linc as we watched them walk away. "Doesn't she want to know how it all happened?"

Linc shrugged, putting his arm around me again. "Oh, she'll want to know everything, but she knows enough now to welcome our boy with open arms."

"And your dad?" I asked, watching the older man take a seat away from the group, like he was watching instead of being a part of the festivities.

"He's not a talker, but he'll come out of his shell eventually when it's just one on one. On the other hand, we won't be able to get my sisters to shut up."

My friends and his family blended perfectly, as if we'd all known each other forever. I leaned my head on his arm, feeling like all was right in my world for the first time in forever. I no longer felt like responsibility was crushing me. I had enough space to hope and dream again. "I think I love your family."

He kissed the top of my head. "They're your family now too."

I lifted my head, feeling like if I didn't finally say the words that were strangling my throat, I might die. "Hey, Linc?"

He just looked at me, his kind eyes so sure and steadfast. "Yeah, sweetheart?"

"I love you."

He didn't say a thing. I watched his Adam's apple bob as he swallowed hard. Then his arm tightened around my shoulders and he pulled me to his front, burying his face in my neck and inhaling. We stood just like that for long minutes, oblivious to the excited chatter all around us as Gannon and Paisley joined us and our new friend, Diego, from Grass, delivered the food I'd ordered.

Linc eventually pulled back to stare into my eyes. "Thank you," he finally whispered.

"For loving you? That was remarkably easy." Lord knew I'd tried to keep him out of my heart.

"No. For giving me everything I ever wanted in life and yet didn't dare to dream. You, our son, our families. For giving me a second chance. I'm the luckiest man alive."

He dipped his head and kissed me. We'd gone about this all backwards but we were finally where we were always meant to be.

Together.

"Thank God you're not mad," I said against his lips.

Linc lifted his head and raised an eyebrow. "Oh, you're in trouble for keeping this a secret, but I'm too happy right now to punish you. Besides, the punishment I have in mind is not suitable for an audience."

I shivered, already anticipating what kind of punishment he could provide me. "Tonight?"

He nodded, promising me all kinds of things with the way his fingers tightened on my skin. "Tonight."

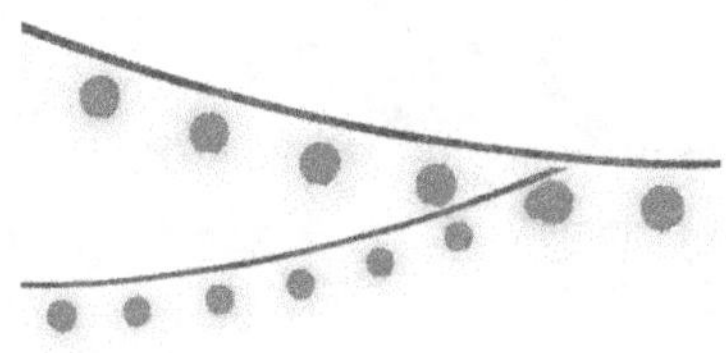

Me: Your dad whittled a pine cone out of a piece of wood at the party and gave it to me.

Baby Daddy: Wow, go Dad! He must like you.

Me: I'm confused.

Baby Daddy: Pine cones symbolize fertility.

Me: Umm…why's your dad giving a fertile pine cone to me?

Baby Daddy: Maybe my superhero sperm are hereditary and it's a warning?

Me: God help me…

CHAPTER TWENTY-FOUR

inc

I'D BEEN awake since three, staring at the woman next to me and wondering if I was about to fuck everything up. As the first stream of sunlight began to filter through the blinds of the little window by our bed in Keva's trailer, I held up the thin gold band that held a diamond I'd be paying off for several years, even after the hefty down payment. I could have sold my Harley and gotten a brand-new SUV, but I'd chosen one a few years older so I could use that money for the ring. Keva deserved a ten-karat diamond for raising Lucas on her own. Were mistakes made by both parties? Sure. But Keva had paid a heavier price than I had. And if she'd let me, I'd spend the rest of my life making her load a little easier.

Keva began to shift next to me. I closed my fist around the ring to hide it and kissed her cheek. She was so beautiful, far prettier than when I'd met her even. There was something about seeing her with our son, the way she cared for him with everything she had that made her far sexier than her younger, carefree self. She'd been so young before. Now she was all woman, and I was crazy in love with her.

"What are you grinning about?" Keva croaked, now fully awake and blinking up at me.

I used my thumb to push some hair off her cheek, careful to keep my fist closed. "Just recalling how you told me you loved me."

Keva's neck went pink and then it hit her cheeks. She rolled into me, burying her head in my neck and kicking me in the shins. "You say it like you're gloating." Her voice was mumbled but I caught the humor in it.

I skimmed my thumb over her shoulder and pushed the blanket down so I could get my hands on more of her. "Hell, yeah, I'm gloating. I got the prettiest woman in Blueball to admit she loved me back. I think that's the exact right time to gloat."

"Prettiest, huh?" Keva lifted her head, her hair all tangled around her face. She crossed her eyes and wrinkled her nose. "You can say that when I wake up like this?"

I leaned down and plucked a kiss from her lips, not at all bothered by the hair that tried to impede me. "Yep. Especially when I know the tangles in your hair are because I had it wrapped around my fist last night. And the pillow crease on your cheek is because I made you orgasm so hard you fell into a deep sleep to recover. Fuckin' beautiful."

She brushed the hair out of her face, biting her bottom lip as the blush took over her cheeks. "And the crossed eyes?" she teased, looking up at me through her lashes.

I used the pad of my thumb to gently close both eyes before kissing them. "Guess I better be more gentle with you. Must have fucked you cross-eyed."

Keva's eyes flew open and she cracked up, smacking my arm playfully.

"Got something I want to ask you," I said quickly before she went to crawl out of bed to get the day started and I had to share her with the tiny human we'd created.

She sat up, her back against the tiny headboard built into the wall of the trailer. "Let me stop you right there. I promise I don't have anymore secrets up my sleeve. No more surprise family visits."

I sat up too, facing her. "That's good, sweetheart, because I got a secret of my own."

Keva pulled her head back and frowned. "What?"

I opened my hand and held it out, palm up. The ring sparked there between us. Keva looked down at it and then sharply up at me before looking back down again.

"I'm not making the same mistake twice, Keva. I left you once but I'm never doing that again. You can put this ring on and marry me, or you can refuse it, but that doesn't change me being right next to you forever. Where your shadow goes, mine does too. I know you think people always leave you, but this is your chance to flip that script. Agree to marry me and let me show you what it looks like when someone stays. When someone loves you forever, no matter what happens. Say yes, sweetheart."

Keva's gaze finally popped up to mine, tears shining from her deep blue eyes. "When did you get this?"

God, she killed me. Little Miss Control Freak wanted to know the details of purchasing the damn ring before she'd give me an answer. "Sometimes you just need to know enough to welcome someone with open arms. To step off that cliff and trust they'll catch you. Do you trust me, Keva?"

She was breathing hard, like I'd asked her to run a mile and then give me an answer. I believed in her and I believed in us, but I needed to know that she was on board. That she was ready to take this next step in trusting one another.

Suddenly Keva was moving, scrambling up on her knees and putting her hands on my face. She got her nose up real close to mine, serious as could be. "You want to stay. With me and Lucas. Forever?"

I shook my head, quick to clarify when her eyes began to shutter. "I want to stay with *you*. Forever. I choose you for life. Lucas, and any other children we're blessed with, is an added bonus."

Keva sucked in a deep breath and then she tackled me, pushing me back on the bed and kissing my face. "Yes! Yes, yes, yes."

My heart started beating again, relief flooding every single cell in my body. But sadly, the ring was long gone. I grabbed Keva's shoulders and held her still enough to steal a kiss before twisting and pinning her beneath me. Tears leaked out the sides of her eyes and into her hairline, but she was smiling as wide as I'd ever seen her.

"Only one problem."

"What?"

"Pretty sure the ring went flying off the bed."

Her eyes went wide and then she was scrambling to get out from under me. "Oh crap. Where is it?"

We both scanned the floor but didn't see it. Expensive rings should come with built-in tracking devices. Keva dropped to her knees and began to look under the bed, her gorgeous ass in the air in those stupidly short pajama shorts she always wore and then complained she was cold. I was a half second away from grabbing that ass and telling her to forget about the ring when the door burst open and Lucas was standing there, rubbing his sleepy eyes.

"Whatcha doing, Mama?"

Keva nearly bashed the back of her head trying to come out from under the bed, but I got my hand between her skull and the bed frame in the nick of time. She sat upright on her heels and held up something green in her hand, smiling at our son.

"I found that Lego soldier we lost!"

Lucas cheered, took the soldier from her, and ran out the

door to play with his Legos. I spun in a circle, thinking of where the ring could have rolled. I wasn't panicked, but for the money I paid and for the seriousness of the moment, I really wanted to see that ring on Keva's finger. Keva cleared her throat and I turned back to her. She had a saucy grin on her face as she held her hand up, a shiny diamond winking back at me.

Fuck yeah. That was what I wanted to see. Keva with my ring on her finger. With a whoop, I grabbed her under the arms and pulled her up. She shrieked and wrapped her legs around my waist. I danced her around the room, which wasn't much of a dance considering two steps in one direction got you to the other wall, but I didn't care.

"Did you find annudder one?" Lucas asked from the doorway, watching us celebrate.

We both looked at him and then at each other.

"Something like that," I hedged. "How about we make some after-Thanksgiving pancakes?"

Lucas looked at me curiously. "What are those?"

I let Keva slide down my body. "Well, anything after Thanksgiving is either going to be pumpkin or turkey flavored. Which would you like for our pancakes."

Lucas's face spasmed into a look of horror. "Turkey pancakes?"

I nodded and moved toward the door. "Pumpkin it is!"

"And then we want to chat with you, okay?" Keva said behind me, kissing Lucas good morning. He ran off to play Legos again while Keva and I got breakfast on the table, easily moving around each other in the cramped kitchenette. I poured the first round of batter in the hot skillet.

"Got a question for you."

"Didn't you already ask me one?" Keva teased, twirling the ring around her finger.

"Well, that was the most important one, but this one is too." Keva put down the milk carton where she was pouring Lucas a glass and looked at me. "I was thinking that we should go house shopping. These trailers are great, but it would be even better to have more space."

A smile grew on Keva's face. "I'd love that."

I flipped the pancakes. "Alright. It's settled, then. You pick what you want and I'll make it happen."

Keva snatched the spatula from my hand. "Actually, I want to house hunt together. I want to do everything together from now on."

I twisted the knob and shut off the burner before turning to her and pulling her into my arms. "Everything, huh?"

I dipped my head and got my lips on hers, teasing her mouth open before diving in. She let me too, making me forget our son was only a few paces away. I wanted to tip her back on the table and spread her open. Seal the promise of forever with our bodies twisted together.

Then I heard a whistle of air and my ass was on fire. I jerked my mouth from hers and gaped. "Did you just swat me with the spatula?"

Her laughter was a tinkle of happiness. "I've always loved that ass. Feed me first though." She went up on tiptoes to get right by my ear. "Then you can fuck me, Sergeant."

I was already half hard just hearing those words from her lips. I smiled lazily, knowing I had my whole life with this woman. "Yes, ma'am."

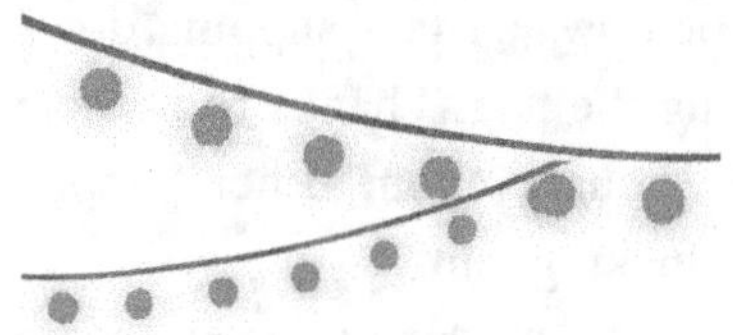

We were walking through the trees, on our way to the first annual After-Thanksgiving Corn Hole Challenge that Paisley had texted us about. Not going was apparently out of the question. Lucas had ahold of me with one hand and his other hand in Keva's. We counted to three multiple times, swinging him through the air to his squeals of delight.

"Hey, baby, what would you think about Daddy and Mama getting married?" Keva asked in a rush of breath.

Lucas looked up at us both. "Like Gannon and Paisey?"

"Exactly like them. We would move in together too."

Lucas shrugged. "Okay."

"Yeah? You sure, buddy?" I asked, wanting to make sure this was all okay with him before moving forward. If he needed more time to get used to me being around, I'd give it to him in a heartbeat.

"Sure." He looked up at me, eyes wide, looking so much like his mama it made me want to pick him up and squeeze him. "I'm otay sleeping on the floor. You're bigger. You need my big-boy bed."

My heart squeezed hard. I stopped walking, tugging on his arm and almost crying right there in the dirt. I crouched low and made sure we were eye to eye. "That's the kindest offer anyone has ever made to me, son, but your mama said I could sleep with her, so you can keep your bed when I move in."

His teeth were front and center as he grinned, throwing his arms around me. "Otay!"

I pulled him into a hug and stood, looking at Keva over his shoulder. She swiped away a tear slipping down her cheek and then she was joining the hug. Thanks to no help from me, she'd raised a son who thought about other people before himself. This woman was a fucking saint.

"Are we going to hug all day or throw some beanbags, huh?" Paisley's voice cut into our moment.

We broke apart and I put Lucas down so he could run over to Elise. Gannon pulled beers out of a huge ice chest and held them out to us. "First people to arrive get the first beer. It's a new rule."

I put my arm around Keva and steered us to the beer. "Dude, it's only eleven in the morning."

Gannon scoffed at my concerns. "It's a holiday. Rules about timing of alcohol don't count on holidays."

Keva accepted her beer and took a sip, grimacing. "Who else is coming?"

"Everybody," Paisley answered. "I texted everyone I had numbers for, so we'll see who shows up."

Paisley gasped and somehow knocked the bottle of beer out of Keva's hand when she grabbed it. "What is this?" she shouted.

Keva's diamond sparkled in the morning sunlight, but nothing rivaled the happiness on her face. "I said yes."

Paisley squealed, hugging the crap out of my fiancée. Gannon clapped me on the back with a congratulations, and the party began. More people came and everyone got to see the ring and offer their congratulations. I met half the town in between corn hole games and couldn't have told you their names, but they were all very welcoming. More importantly, Keva had a permanent smile on her face.

Gannon handed me another beer an hour later, seeing that I was carrying around an empty. "Never seen Keva so happy."

I took a sip of the cold beer, watching her show another woman her ring and the way they all squealed each and every time. "I'm going to keep her that way."

"The best men do," Gannon drawled, watching his own wife and the slight swell of her belly as she walked around the glampground.

I didn't know how I'd managed it, but with Keva by my side, I'd found a whole new life I actually looked forward to.

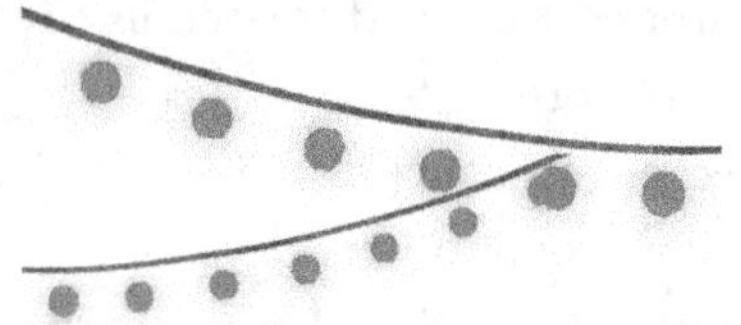

Me: You look hot showing off my ring on your finger.

Baby Mama: You look hot standing over there watching me when you should be playing corn hole.

Me: There's only one hole I want to be playing with.

Baby Mama: Wow, that was a bad line.

Me: Let's hope our son didn't inherit my inability to flirt. Although your flirting skills aren't much better....

Baby Mama: Hey! I can flirt! I'm just rusty...

Me: You can practice on me all you want, sweetheart.

Baby Mama: Is there a mirror in your pants? Because I can see myself in them.

Me: I take back my offer.

CHAPTER TWENTY-FIVE

eva

MY PHONE RANG three times in a row, the buzzing in my pocket
finally pulling me from the group of friends I was with and over
to the space heater closest to the beer coolers. I pulled out my
phone and saw that it was my brother calling. My finger hovered
over the ignore button, but at the last second, spurred by happy-
just-engaged hormones and the promise I'd made to Lincoln, I
hit the accept video call button. The screen flashed and then
there was my brother. Or an older, longer-haired version of the
brother I'd once known.

"Annabel?"

His voice had deepened and his shoulders looked positively
massive, growth I should have expected, but somehow didn't. In
my mind, he was still the Boston that punched Linc in the face
when he caught us together five years ago.

"Hey, Boston."

There was a beat of awkward silence. Boston was probably
stunned I'd answered his call. He'd tried to reach out quite a bit

the last few years and I'd answer occasionally, but only via text. Kind of hard to call or video chat with a noisy toddler running around that you hadn't even told your brother about.

"I'm so glad I caught you. I meant to call yesterday on Thanksgiving, but I was flying home from Italy, and with the time change and the flight, I missed the holiday."

"Are you back for a visit or shipping off somewhere else? And what's with that hair?"

His handsome face split into a grin. "It's different out there. They don't mind if we grow our hair out, and after spending ten years with a buzz cut, I wanted to give it a try." He chuckled and even as I wanted to be indifferent, the sound still reminded me of our youth, when things were still good in our family. "I'm actually here in the States for good."

I felt Linc come up behind me, his hand on my back and peering over my shoulder at the phone. I stiffened, watching Boston's face morph from a gentle smile to shock to slowly shaking his head.

"Bro, you suck at keeping in contact." Boston didn't seem mad though.

Linc kissed my cheek, almost shoving our relationship in Boston's face, which I didn't think was a good idea considering how things had worked out before.

"Linc," I whispered.

Linc's hand tightened on my waist. "It's okay. I got Boston's permission before I even moved here."

Now I was the one irritated. "Permission?"

Boston held up his hand, his beefy palm almost covering the whole camera. "Hold up. Before we go down that rabbit hole, I called because I wanted to apologize."

My attention turned to my brother, but my irritation was cranking up into angry. "Apologize for what? Punching Linc in the face? Ghosting me for thirteen years?"

Boston winced. "Yeah. For all of that and I'm sure quite a bit more. I, uh, want to come visit, Annabel. Talk through everything."

"No one calls me Annabel." Yes, I could revert to a petulant teen in the blink of an eye.

"I call you Annabel," Boston growled. Then he waved his hand and kept going. "I just wanted to make sure you knew how sorry I was for keeping you and Linc apart. If I'd known y'all would carry these feelings this long, I wouldn't have punched him in the face. Or convinced him to go back into the Army. Or sent back your letter."

I gasped, pain lancing me like an actual blow to the chest. The phone began to shake and Linc had to take it from me to keep it steady.

"Why didn't you tell me, man?" Linc sounded shocked too.

I put my face right in front of the camera. "You did that?"

Boston frowned. "Which part?"

"The letter? Why?" My one effort to reach out to Linc wasn't thwarted because of a mailing error or because Linc didn't care about me as I'd originally thought. My own brother had carelessly set that wheel in motion.

Boston made a slew of faces, looking lost and stubborn at the same time. "Because you're my baby sister, Annabel. I thought Linc was using you and I wasn't going to allow that. I wasn't physically there to protect you when I shipped off to the Army, so I thought I could protect you now. Make up for my absence, I guess. Why do you think I've been calling and texting every month? I want to be involved in your life."

"Mama?" Lucas tugged on my sweater.

I looked down at him, surprised when a tear slipped down my cheek. Brushing it away quickly, I reached down and picked him up, placing him on my hip and hugging him tight. I gave myself a second or two to just breathe in the little-boy smell of him. When Lucas began to fidget and I heard Boston coughing like he'd choked, I let my boy down again.

"Yeah, baby?"

"Can Ellie and me play on the jungle gym?"

I smiled down at the best thing that ever happened to me, tousling his dark hair and watching my new ring sparkle in the winter sunlight. "Sure, baby. Be careful though." He ran off with a shout, a tangle of growing arms and legs.

When I looked up at Linc, I was centered again despite the anger clear on his face. Things had gone horribly wrong and yet they'd worked out in the end. Linc had been right. We were meant for each other and fate had worked to bring us back together.

Didn't mean I was happy with my brother for interfering though.

"Annabel," Boston said, his voice low and broken.

I turned to the screen to see my brother staring at me wide-eyed. I nodded. "Yeah. That's my son, Lucas. Your nephew. That letter, Boston? That letter was to tell Linc I was pregnant."

I stormed off, leaving Linc to deal with the lughead I called my brother. I was too pissed off right now to speak to him without bursting into angry tears. I needed to catch my breath, think it all through, and then maybe I could talk to him again and not simply yell until my voice got hoarse. Boston left me to run off to the Army years ago and he had to pick that exact moment in time to come roaring back into my life to play big brother? Talk about horrible timing.

I marched over to a picnic table at the periphery of the festivities. I could just barely see Lucas from here and there were no other adults present. Perfect. I sat, dropped my head to my hands, and just breathed.

The bench sagged next to me a few minutes later. "Hey." Linc's warm hand landed on my back, rubbing circles. His knees pinned me in as he straddled the picnic bench. He dropped my phone on the table and pulled me in to kiss the top of my head.

"I told him we'd talk to him later. Much later." He kissed my head again and then cupped my face to gently twist me around so he could kiss my lips. "Talk to me, sweetheart. What's going on in that head of yours?"

I shook my head, realizing that all that blame I'd placed at Linc's feet was actually a series of unfortunate events. There was no villain here. No one to point my finger at, exonerating myself from all the blame. I should have tried harder to reach out. Linc should have put me first instead of my brother's wishes. Boston should have kept his nose out of my business.

"I've spent years feeling like people always abandon me. I've used that hurt as a shield, which I can't really be upset about. It held me and Lucas up. That strength to do everything myself got me through these last few years. And then the one time someone does try to stick around and protect me, it backfires." A giggle that wasn't altogether steady bubbled up and out. "I mean, if it wasn't my life we were talking about, it would almost be funny."

Linc grimaced. "I think it's okay to laugh. Okay to cry too. I would guess it's going to take some time for all of us to adjust to this new reality and let the old one go."

I inhaled, feeling a bit lighter now that all my secrets were out in the open. I hadn't realized what a heavy load it was to conceal a little boy from your own family. Maybe Boston and I would never be super close, but at least there weren't secrets between us now. My fingers circled Linc's wrists as he held my face in his palms.

"I certainly love this new reality. You here with me and Lucas."

Linc leaned down and pressed his lips to mine. He backed away too quickly, but when he spoke, it made me feel like everything was right in the world. "This is your forever reality. I love you. I love Lucas. We're a family now. Forever."

I grinned, overwhelmed with love for this man that had come back for me. "I love you."

"Love you too," he said against my lips.

And then his tongue was dancing across my bottom lip,

pushing inside to obliterate all the bad feelings from that conversation. His hand left my face to trail down my side before cupping my breast. I gasped, knowing we were out in the open and anyone could have looked over and seen us, but not actually caring. He paused, and when I didn't push him away, he deepened the kiss. My head was spinning and my finger felt like a thousand pounds with my new ring on it. Linc was mine and I was his.

A heart-stopping shriek had us jumping apart. Several adults ran to one corner of the playground. I jumped up, heart in my throat.

"Lucas!" A mama always knew the sound of her child's voice.

I stumbled getting over the bench and Linc steadied me before we both took off running. Somehow we made it over to the playground, pushing through our friends to see our boy on the ground, crying and holding his arm.

I fell to my knees and put my hands on his precious face. Tears were streaming down his cheeks. "It's okay, baby. Mama's here." I looked down at his arm and saw that it was already swelling as he clutched it to his chest. My perfect baby was hurt. Badly. Nausea bloomed and I had to look away and hold my breath to keep from retching.

"I called 9-1-1."

"Somebody get some ice!"

"Don't move him. What happened?"

I heard Elise crying somewhere beside us, and I wanted to comfort her, but I didn't have the capacity to do anything but try to comfort my own son. I felt Linc at my back and I heard his deep voice calmly talking to my son, but I couldn't look away from the pain telegraphed on Lucas's face. There was nothing I could do to ease Lucas's pain. It felt like forever before the ambulance came and two paramedics came over to examine him. By the time they got a splint on his arm and some ice, he wasn't crying any longer, though I knew I'd hear that cry in my sleep for months to come.

"Wow, Lucas. You get to ride in an ambulance," Linc was explaining to him while I sat there mute, my trembling hands still on Lucas's shoulders. "I've never been in an ambulance."

"Really?" Lucas seemed to find that funny.

"We got room for one parent," the kind paramedic told us, looking between Linc and me.

"You go ahead," Linc said instantly, rubbing his hand on my back. "I'll follow in the car."

"I want Daddy," Lucas said. "He never been in an ambuwance."

Linc looked at me. The decision was mine. I knew that, and yet, I felt like there was an elephant sitting on my chest, preventing me from speaking. Then I looked at Lucas and saw how calm he was around Linc and I knew I had to do what was best for my son. I nodded, and the paramedics helped Lucas up on his feet.

Linc kissed my cheek. "I'll take good care of him. I promise. Meet me at the hospital?"

I nodded again, too overwhelmed to speak. I felt Paisley slip to my side, her arm coming around my back. Then Audrey was on my other side, Marlo right next to her. I watched as Linc reached down and picked up Lucas, climbing onto the ambulance and getting him settled on the gurney inside. They both waved at me as if they were going for a joy ride around town. The doors banged shut and the ambulance was off.

And as for me, my heart was still in a stutter step while my brain was trying to convince me that everything was okay.

"Keva?" Paisley asked, squeezing my waist. "Let's take my truck."

I nodded. Apparently that was the only thing I could do in an emergency. Nod and get in the way. My son had needed me and I was over on the picnic benches making out with a guy like I was a teenager with zero responsibilities.

"He's in good hands, babe. That paramedic was Xavier, my

brother Callan's old partner." Audrey and Marlo were right behind us.

Sadly, her reassurance did nothing to ease the thoughts racing through my brain.

"I'm such a bad mom," I moaned as we scrambled to get to Paisley's truck.

She beeped the remote to unlock the truck, shooting me a frown. "Every kid breaks bones, Keevs."

Not my son. He'd never broken a bone in his four years of life.

Only now when his mother got distracted by a man.

CHAPTER TWENTY-SIX

$\mathscr{L}$incoln

I'D SEEN a lot of blood in my time in the military. It was simply part of the job and something you became adept at handling. But absolutely nothing prepared me for seeing my own son writhing on the ground in pain. If that wasn't bad enough, observing the woman I loved completely fall apart was second on the list of worst things. Keva was pale naturally but seeing her go a shade of white reserved for ghosts pulled me out of the shock of the moment. She wasn't capable of handling the situation, so I would. Anything to help my family.

When Keva nodded her head, giving me permission to go in the ambulance with Lucas, I nearly wept. She finally trusted me. When shit hit the fan with our son, she trusted me to take care of him. A trip to the ER wasn't the way I wanted our first day of being engaged to go, but hell if it wasn't a glorious ending, knowing that Keva fully trusted me.

The paramedics were great. The one riding in the back with

us kept up a steady stream of age-appropriate jokes that had Lucas giggling despite the pain I knew he was in.

"We're here!" the paramedic announced, opening the back doors of the ambulance and jumping down. The sliding glass doors of the county hospital were behind him. "Let's get you inside so they can take pictures of your arm, Lucas. Did you know they have X-ray vision here? We're going to see your bones!"

"Cool!" Lucas barely needed my help to get out of the ambulance, such was his rush to see his bones.

I followed behind, accepting the clipboards from the nurses at the front desk, tucking them under my arm and making sure I kept up with my boy. The attending ER doctor wanted X-rays right away, and somehow, there was no wait time. Perhaps Lucas had chosen the exact right day and time to break a bone.

"We'll need you to wait right outside the room during the X-rays," the lab technician stated kindly.

I squatted down and looked Lucas in the eye. "I'll be right outside this door. You need me, just shout, okay?"

"Okay, Daddy."

His instant trust nearly knocked me over. I wasn't sure what I'd done right in this world to deserve this kid, but I was damn grateful. I ruffled his hair and stepped outside, sitting in the chair in the hallway by the door and filling out the paperwork as quickly as I could. I didn't know his social security number or the family health history on Keva's side, but I did the best I could.

"Where is he?" Keva's shrill voice brought my head up. She was racing down the hallway alone, her face still that sickly pale white. Her huge bag swung behind her.

I stook quickly and put the clipboards on the chair. I caught her arms as she barreled up to me. "Hey, hey. He's okay. Doing great, actually. Just inside there getting X-rays."

"Why aren't you in there? He must be scared out of his mind!" Keva's eyes were wide and panicked. I'd seen that look before, usually when shit was going sideways and shots were being fired.

"He's not scared, Keva. You've raised a brave young man. He's getting some X-rays and we can't be in there. He'll be out any second, I promise."

Keva stared at me, her chest heaving. I wasn't sure if what I'd said calmed her at all, but the door opened behind me. Her gaze darted over my shoulder and then she was ripping her arms away from me.

"Lucas, baby!" She pulled him into her side as he walked out, and addressed the X-ray technician. "How bad is the break?"

The woman smiled kindly. "I'll have the doctor read the X-ray right away, but from what I saw, he should heal nicely."

Keva nodded, latching on to the positivity, which was good. Lucas was already starting to react to her panic, looking back and forth between the adults, eyes widening.

"Let's have you all come back to the exam room and I'll send in the doctor." The technician led us to a room down a long corridor of doors.

The exam room was sterile and held all sort of instruments. Keva picked up Lucas and put him on the examination table, hopping up and sitting right next to him.

"Well, this is a fun trip, huh, buddy?" I said with a smile.

Lucas broke into a grin, but Keva jumped in and dashed that grin. "This is not a fun trip, Linc."

"Okay." I put my hand on her knee but she moved her leg away. My heart sank. Just when I thought we'd gotten beyond the hurdles in our relationship, here we were again, doing the same two-steps-forward-one-step-back dance. Keva was pulling away again.

The door flew open before I could address the tension in the room. A female doctor with dark hair and eyes looked through a chart and then graced us with a professional smile.

"Lucas Mooney?"

"Me!" Lucas answered bravely.

The doctor's smile turned warm. "Well, hello there, big guy. Looks like you got what we call a buckle fracture. Want to see the X-ray?"

Lucas nodded and the doctor put the X-ray up on the wall where a light backlit the film. There was his little arm, two bones cracked between his wrist and his elbow.

"Cool!" Lucas shouted and the doctor laughed.

"It's actually a nice break, all things considered. Easy to heal from because your growth plates were untouched. We'll want you in a brace at all times, except for bathing. Unless you have questions, just sit tight and I'll get a tech in here to fit you for the brace."

I stepped forward when Keva only blinked at the doctor, eyes glassy and unfocused. "Should we ice it? Ibuprofen if he's in pain?"

The doctor nodded. "Ice for the next three days, twenty minutes on, twenty minutes off. Ibuprofen at the dosage for his age, but he shouldn't need much past tonight."

I nodded. "Okay, thank you, Doc."

The doctor turned to the door, then spun back around. "Oh! I almost forgot." She fished around in the pocket of her white coat. "I had the tech make a small one so you can show your friends when you go back to school."

She handed Lucas a wallet-sized picture of his broken arm. Lucas whooped and they shared a smile. Then she nodded at the adults and left the room. Keva stared at the X-ray still on the wall and took deep, measured breaths. Lucas started babbling about how cool his broken arm looked and how Elise was going to be so mad that she didn't have one too.

I put my hand on Keva's shoulder. She flinched but didn't fling my hand off. I leaned in close. "Hey. He's all right."

Keva shook her head, looking over my shoulder, eyes filling with tears.

I opened my mouth again, but the door opened and the next technician entered the room with supplies on a rolling tray. He had a red beard that rivaled Santa's and a belly to match, but he said all the right things to make Lucas smile and giggle. He also had stickers of every kind stuffed in his pockets, which was a sure hit with Lucas.

"How about Mom and Dad go outside and deal with the boring paperwork while we decide on Batman black or Spiderman red for our brace, huh?"

I took Keva's hand and tugged her off the examination table to give the guy more room. She hesitated, but the tech shot her a wink. "I'll take good care of him, ma'am."

She gave him a warning look that had us both freezing in our tracks, but she finally nodded and headed out the door with me. One of the ladies from the check-in desk was there, the clipboards I'd filled out in hand.

"Okay, so just bill this insurance for Lincoln Angelo?"

"Yes, that should be fine."

"Wait. I have my insurance card here somewhere." Keva pulled the strap of her huge bag off her shoulder and rummaged through. "I can't imagine it's very good, but it should cover some of the cost. Dear God, the ambulance ride. That must cost a fortune." Her hands started to shake.

I put my hand over hers. "It's okay. I put him on my insurance already. Whatever it doesn't cover, I'll charge it to a card and pay it off eventually."

Keva's head flew up, her bag forgotten. "You put him on your insurance?"

I smiled patiently. When would this woman learn? "Yeah, the same week I found out about him. I told you I'd take care of you, didn't I?"

I could see the front desk woman's head swiveling back and forth, taking in our private conversation. Keva just stared at me and I tried not to be insulted. Turning to the woman, I asked if there was anything else. She kind of jumped in her shoes and shook her head, rushing off to submit the insurance for our visit.

"Let's have a seat and wait for Lucas to be done." I steered

Keva to a chair outside the exam room and sat down next to her, deflated and not sure when I would have this woman's full trust. We could hear him and the tech laughing and chatting with the door cracked open. The smell of the hospital irritated my nose. I should be feeling relief that our boy was okay, but all I could focus on was the woman beside me. She was pulling back and I wasn't sure there was anything I could do to stop it.

Keva's hand gripped the arm of the chair between us. I peeled her fingers off and laced our hands together. "He's going to be just fine, sweetheart."

She squeezed my hand but then let go, clasping her hands in her lap. The symbolism wasn't lost on me. When she was hurting, she retreated into herself. She'd had to in the past to make it through, but now that I was here, she wasn't ready to learn to do this life as a team. She'd said she was, but when push came to shove, she shoved me away. Hard.

"I know. I know, but it should never have happened."

"Kids break bones all the time on the playground."

Keva shook her head. "That's what everyone keeps saying but he never broke a bone the first four years of his life."

I frowned. Here we go. "What are you inferring?"

Keva inhaled so deeply I thought she might pass out. Then she turned to me and the blood froze in my veins. All the sounds of the hospital around us faded away. "I just think everything between us has been a bit of a distraction."

Anger and hurt, the kind that leaves a mark on a person, surged through me. I loved the woman and was turning my life inside out to show her, and she called it a distraction? "Is that what we are? A distraction?"

Keva nodded. She lifted her nose in the air, buying into her own bullshit. "We've moved pretty fast since you've been back, and I'm not sure that's what's best for Lucas."

I twisted in my seat and leaned in closer, watching the way her gaze danced all over my face but wouldn't look me in the eye. "You mean, what's best for *you*."

Her lips—the same ones I'd kissed this morning when she'd said yes to my marriage proposal—pressed together into a thin line.

Fuck.

I knew defeat when I saw it.

CHAPTER TWENTY-SEVEN

eva

I'D MADE a promise to Lucas two days after he was born. It was our first day at home, and as I rocked him to sleep that night, I looked down at his tiny fist wrapped around my finger. I promised that forever and always he'd be my priority. I'd do whatever I had to in order to give him the life he deserved. And I'd never failed on that promise, not even when I was running on a couple hours of sleep for weeks on end, or working extra hours with him strapped to my chest to afford more diapers, or when I turned down social outings with my friends to take him to the park. For four straight years it had been me and him against the world. And we'd done alright.

Ever since Linc had come back, I'd been distracted. Without even realizing it, I'd adjusted my priority list, putting Linc up there with Lucas. It had worked out, since I had the ring on my finger showing that Linc had made us his priority too, but that had all come crashing down when Lucas fell off the play set. More than just Lucas's arm had broken in that moment.

Linc was staring at me like he wanted to wrap his hands around my neck and squeeze. The beep of machines in exam rooms all around us in the emergency room reminded me that things could have been so much worse. I'd been given a chance to do better.

"It's never been about what's best for me, Linc. My entire adult life has been about doing what's best for that little boy in there." I waved my hand to the exam room where he and the tech were laughing like long-lost friends.

Linc hadn't been there for those years that I'd put myself on hold and given everything to Lucas. He couldn't possibly understand. Before Linc could argue, I held up my hand.

"I'm not saying we can't have a relationship. I think it's good for Lucas to have his parents together. I'm just saying we need to pump the brakes. Keep our focus on him instead of getting swept away."

Linc's jaw pulsed as he ground his teeth. His eyes were flashing and I had to work at holding my spine straight under his angry stare. "What the hell does that mean?"

"Just...put off the wedding plans for right now. Settle into being engaged for a bit." I felt like I was skating on a sheet of ice, just waiting for the second where I lost control and crashed and burned. At least if I had a heart attack from the stress, I was in the right place to get help.

He dropped his arms where they'd been folded over his chest and stepped back. "I have done nothing but supported you and Lucas since I came back. I've jumped into being Lucas's dad with open arms, Keva. I have proven myself over and over again, but it's never going to work, is it? You'll never believe that I could be just as dedicated as you. Only Keva can give everything to that little boy, right?"

Now I was angry. "That's not it at all. You haven't been here to—"

"Exactly!" Linc exploded, cutting me off and drawing stares from the staff. "You missed out on having a partner to help you raise Lucas. I missed out on being there for my son for his first four years." Linc's voice broke but he inhaled sharply and kept going. "We both missed out on a lot, but if you keep pushing me away, we're going to keep missing out for the rest of our lives!"

I reached out for his arm, but he shifted out of the way. I'd never seen him this angry, and quite frankly, I wasn't sure if my heart could take seeing him this way. "I'm not saying we can't be together, Linc."

He shook his head, hurt, anger, and maybe even disgust lining his face. "I can't be with you, giving you everything I have, while you're holding back. It would kill me. Slowly but surely."

My heart was pounding so loudly I was surprised I could still hear him. My fingers began to twist the diamond ring on my finger around and around. Linc's gaze dropped to my hands and then he was finally touching me, his hand dropping on top of mine to still my movements.

"Don't do this. Do not take that fucking ring off, Keva."

Our gazes locked and time stood still. I was angry and exhausted and not entirely sure that he didn't have a very valid point.

"Look at it!" Lucas's excited shout had us both turning to see him running out the door, the tech behind him. Lucas held up his arm, a brand-new green-and-black brace making him look half machine and entirely too old.

My inhale was stuttered, like my throat was no longer working, but I managed a smile. Crouching down, I gave my boy a hug and oohed and aahed over his new brace.

"The coolest brace I've ever seen, buddy," Linc said quietly, putting his hand on Lucas's shoulder and kissing the top of his head.

"I'm going to head out. You got him?"

I looked up to see Linc talking to me, but not really looking at me. I nodded and he spun to exit, leaving me feeling like I was about to burst into tears. I dealt with checking out of the ER and found my friends still waiting in the waiting room for us.

"Look!" Lucas ran for my friends, showing off his brace.

Paisley looked up at me and moved away from my son to whisper, "What happened? Linc marched out of here in a mood. I thought Gannon looked scary when he was pissed..."

I shook my head, trying to staunch the tears that kept stinging my eyes. "I'm not sure, actually."

Paisley stared at me for a few seconds and then must have come to a conclusion. "Hey, Lucas! Want to come over and play with Elise while we feed your mom?"

"Okay!" Lucas held Marlo's hand, and as a group, we walked back out to the parking lot.

"Hang on, mama. We'll chat it out at the house," Paisley whispered before leaving my side to get behind the wheel of her truck.

I watched the familiar town flick by my window, not sure what all I was feeling. Could a human feel every single emotion that existed in the span of one day and not fall apart completely?

I watched in a fog while Paisley got the kids playing in the family room while we headed for the front room. I crashed on the sofa and laid my head on Audrey's shoulder. Marlo rushed in, a pan clutched to her torso.

"They didn't eat the brownies!" She set the pan down on the coffee table and ripped the foil off the top. For someone so thin, that girl could pack in the sugar. It was one of those cruel tricks of nature.

When everyone was seated, Marlo cut up the sheet of brownies and handed everyone a brownie on a napkin. I took my piece and eyed it, sudden nausea making me place it back down on the coffee table. "I think I might have fucked up."

Audrey snorted. "I think we got that from Lincoln's face as he thundered through the ER."

"Audrey!" Marlo snapped.

"What? I've never seen him anything but worshipful looking at Keva, but he didn't look like that today." Audrey let out an exaggerated shiver. "I know he's taken, but damn! That glower was hot."

I closed my eyes and tried to just breathe. "I told him we needed to slow down."

Paisley nearly choked on her bite of brownie. "Didn't you say yes to his proposal just this morning?"

Oh God, I was going to be sick. "Yeah. Shit timing, huh?"

Marlo reached across the table from where she sat on the floor. "Why do you want to slow down? Isn't this what you've always dreamed of?"

I opened my mouth to explain myself but came up empty. What kind of fucking moron is scared of all her dreams literally coming true right before her eyes? This moron, apparently.

"Ah. I see. You're scared," Marlo concluded quietly. "I've seen widows who despised their husbands absolutely fall apart at the funerals. Turns out they don't miss the husband, they're just scared of doing life alone."

I shook my head. "I've been alone for years, Marlo. I'm good alone."

"But are you really?" Paisley asked, swallowing the last of her brownie and sitting forward. "Or have you just gotten used to being so alone that you've become this little island? All to yourself. Unable to compromise and mesh your life with someone you love."

I glared at her. "That makes me sound terrible."

"You're not terrible," Audrey said quickly. "But you do have a tendency to go all martyr-y."

I wrinkled my nose. "That's not a word."

"It is now and it's totally you. You'd rather be miserable on your own than share the load with someone else and have to share the glory."

I gaped at her.

"Remember when we had to spring the baby shower on you?" Paisley added. "You tried to stop us until Lucy had to threaten to fire you."

"And literally all of us went to those birthing classes with you and yet you wouldn't let any of us actually help you during the birth."

I looked around at my friends, the ones who loved me more than I loved myself some days. They were straight shooters and I was feeling the shot for sure. Truth was painful when it hit you in the face.

"Oh God. I really fucked up, didn't I?" I cried, finally crumpling into a crying mess. "I hate crying!" I wailed, burying my face in my hands.

I'd somehow pushed away the man who dropped everything the second he came back home. He'd been having a rough time adjusting to civilian life and yet he'd embraced being a father with everything he had. And I'd just told him I needed to go slower.

It was official. I was a fucking moron.

My friends let me cry it out, soothing me instead of whipping me with truths like I deserved. I was hiccupping by the time I lifted my head. Audrey handed me a handful of tissues to clean my face. Marlo handed me the brownie.

"Ugh," I moaned, putting it back down. "That makes me want to puke."

I wiped my face and blew my nose again. When I looked up, all three of my friends were staring at each other with wide eyes. Oh good Lord, maybe they weren't done slapping me with the truth. I braced myself for more.

"What now?"

Paisley bit her lip but then looked at me sternly. "You couldn't touch a brownie the whole time you were pregnant with Lucas."

Her words hung there like a bomb threat, the meaning finally sinking in.

My swollen eyes went wide and then I was up and running to the bathroom to puke my guts out.

CHAPTER TWENTY-EIGHT

*L*incoln

"Too fuckin' cold out here to be digging ditches, huh?"

I'd heard Gannon coming up behind me for the last ten minutes. The guy wasn't exactly quiet traipsing through the woods on the southern part of the property. I swiped my sleeve across my forehead and rested against the shovel. Wasn't cold once you started working, that was for sure.

"Just clearing some lines in case we need 'em come fire season." The trench would break the fire line, sending any flames down toward the lake on the property next to us.

Gannon squinted, looking out across the trees. "Only YOU can prevent forest fires?" He smirked, delivering the famous line from Smokey the Bear.

I shrugged, realizing my arms were aching. I'd been out here since right before the sun came up, digging the trench line and trying to sort things out in my head. I hadn't come to any conclusions, but maybe I'd prevented a fire from taking out Glamper's Paradise in the future.

"Somethin' like that."

"What's going on, man?" Gannon crossed his arms across his chest, barely able to do it in the thick denim jacket he wore to keep out the lowering temperatures. "The girls were at my place for hours last night, keeping me up. Did you piss her off? Were you a dumbass?"

I let the shovel clang to the forest floor. "I wasn't a dumbass, Gannon."

"Why else would Keva have a diamond ring on her finger, but be at my house crying?"

My head whipped up. "She was crying?"

Fuck. I was mad at her, while also holding out hope we could work this all out in time. But I hated to hear she was crying. My returning here and stepping up once I found out about Lucas was to ease her worries, not pile on top.

"Hey, Gannon? Mind giving us a minute?" Keva's sweet voice came from behind the huge man.

Gannon twirled around, hand on his chest. "Jesus, woman. You nearly gave me a heart attack. How'd you find us?"

Keva lifted her dark eyebrow. "You're not exactly hard to follow. You were talking to every squirrel who crossed your path out here."

Gannon dipped his head, hiding behind the bill of his ball cap. "Yeah, okay. I'm just gonna go...away. Somewhere far. Have fun, you two." He traipsed back through the forest, kicking rocks and snapping twigs with every step.

I wasn't watching him though. My gaze stayed trained on Keva. The way her dark hair blew across her face. Her delicate fingers with red-painted nails pushed the hair behind her ear. The pink tint to her pale cheeks that never failed to mesmerize me. She wasn't wearing that red lipstick I loved, but her lips curved up at the corners ever so slightly, an improvement from the harsh frown of yesterday. Her huge bag was slung on her shoulder, as if she was leaving soon. My heart sunk to the bottom of the ditch I'd been digging.

"How's Lucas?"

Keva smiled then, looking shy. "He's good. Real good. We stayed over at Paisley's last night and he's currently about to inhale a stack of waffles."

"No pain?" It killed me to only ask about my son and not her, but I wasn't sure if turning the focus would be met with another step back. We couldn't take too many more steps back or we wouldn't be in the same state.

"No pain. He's a tough guy, just like his daddy."

I nodded, unsure if that was a compliment or not. My hands physically ached to pull her into me. To feel her warm skin under my palms. To know she was still here with me. It had been my job in the military to make things right for everyone in my squad. I was a fixer. I stepped up and did what needed to be done for the unit to operate cohesively. I desperately wanted to do the same thing here, but I was finding I couldn't force anything as a civilian. Definitely not in a relationship. No one could make Keva trust me except Keva.

She stepped closer, her hands twisting in front of her. My ring was still there, thank God, but I wondered if this was the moment she was going to take it off for good. I braced for it, even while knowing there was nothing I could do to prepare for that kind of pain if she did.

"I, uh, wanted to talk to you about yesterday," she said quietly.

I nodded toward a fallen tree a few feet away. "How about we have a seat?"

If she was going to kick my legs out from under me, I needed to be closer to the ground for the fall. I sat first and then she sat with a few inches between us. I tried not to read into the space.

"I'm so sorry, Linc," she said quickly. "I freaked out seeing Lucas hurt and I reverted to what I do best."

"Which is?" I was still holding my breath.

Keva licked her lips. "Folding in on myself and pushing everyone away. I assume the worst in situations like that. I assume that I'm the only one who can shoulder the responsibilities of life." She shrugged. "Historically, that's been true."

I nodded. She wasn't lying. She'd had to deal with her parents' death, Boston ditching her, and me leaving her to raise Lucas all on her own.

"But—"

She raised her hand, interrupting me. "I know. You're here now. For good. My heart knows this but my head is taking a little longer to get with the program." Keva reached over and squeezed my hand. "Linc. Even though I know you should be pissed off at me, I really need you to forgive me."

"Why?" My heart was pounding, but I needed to hear her say it. I needed to know that this was her, turning a corner and choosing a different life. With me.

Her eyes filled with tears. I had to grind my teeth to keep from pulling her into my arms and telling her everything would be okay.

"Because I love you. Have loved you since the day I met you. I love our family. I want the future you promised me yesterday morning. I want to lean on you and I want you to be able to lean on me. I haven't made life easy for you since you've been back, and I'm going to change that. First, by trusting you with everything I am. Second, with building a life together."

My heart started beating again, hope rising like the tide. "I like the sound of that." I hated myself for needing the reassurance, but my heart couldn't handle another step back. "But how do I know you're truly ready?"

Keva slid off the tree trunk and into the dirt, her leggings surely tearing in the rough sticks. She knelt between my knees, gripping my hands and pleading up at me with her gorgeous eyes. Her huge bag swung off her shoulder and hit me in the leg.

"Assaulting me with that damn bag is your way of apologizing?" I asked wryly. Keva shot me a warning look, but her lips were pulling into a smile.

"No. But this bag holds what you're looking for."

I tilted my head and she let go of my hands to pull the straps off her arms and dig around in the bag. She came back with some white copy paper in her hands. "I'm ready to take the leap, Linc. Here's the form for legally changing Lucas's name. You just have to sign it to get the process started. I'd like him to have your last name. He's ours, not just mine."

Every bit of me that had argued for caution finally relaxed. "Keevs..." I wanted to say more, but my throat was too tight.

"And!" Keva put the papers in my lap and rummaged around in her bag again.

"There's more?"

Keva straightened, something now hidden behind her back. "I'm finding there's always more when it comes to Lincoln Angelo." She smirked, looking so pretty I reached out to get my hands on her, but she lurched back. "I have more!"

I shook my head. "I don't need more. I just need you."

"Oh, you're going to want to hear this. Trust me."

"Say it quick, sweetheart, or I'm going to give you something else to do while you're on your knees."

Her eyes heated but she held strong. "You can trust that I'm ready to marry you and build a life together because I got the second biggest shock of my life last night and I'm still here. I'm done running. Done hiding. Done shouldering everything alone." Her nose tipped in the air and I could have sworn she'd never looked prettier than when true confidence transformed her face.

She pulled her arm out from behind her and held out a white stick. I glanced down at it, my thundering heart stopping in its tracks yet again. I didn't know much about these things, but that looked like a pregnancy test.

"Keva. Is that...?" I breathed, gripping her shaking hand and trying to get a look at the test.

"It's positive. I'm pregnant."

I quit trying to look at the test and instead stared at my fiancée. I didn't know a person could cry and smile so bright they blotted out the sun, but Keva managed it.

"Really?" I asked. Sure, it was a dumb question, but I was having a hard time forming coherent thoughts, let alone sentences.

"We get a do-over, Linc, and I will do everything in my power to do it differently this time. With you." Twin tears ran down Keva's cheeks.

I was suddenly on my feet, pulling Keva out of the dirt and into my arms. I let out a whoop that echoed off the tree trunks. Keva laughed and I couldn't seem to let her go. I was never letting her out of my sight again. Looking down into her face, I knew I was looking at my future. No more steps backward.

"I don't know if it was fate or God or the universe, but something out there wants us together real bad, Lincoln Angelo."

I winked. "Either that or I really do have superhero swimmers."

Keva snorted and I whooped again, lifting her up and spinning her around. I set her back on her feet, a million thoughts running through my head.

"How do you feel about a Christmas wedding?"

Keva gasped. "I can't find a dress in a month!"

My hands slid from her waist to her ass, holding her against me. "I'm just going to rip it off of you at the first available opportunity."

Keva gasped again while my chest rumbled with laughter. Pretty sure I'd never been this happy before.

"I'm kidding. Kind of. But seriously, sweetheart. I'm not wasting anymore time making you mine." Another thought struck me. "We need to buy a house. And another car seat. Holy shit, what if it's a girl? I better ask Gannon if he was serious about making me a partner. I have a whole family to support now."

Keva's hands landed on my cheeks. "Hey! Calm down, Daddy. We've got nine months to sort it all out. I don't care about a big house or fancy clothes or all the gadgets they make for babies. We don't need all that, believe me. I don't care if we're on the back of a scooter or in a fancy SUV. Trailer or house. Two kids or twenty. I just need you by my side."

I leaned down and kissed her, inhaling the scent of her and wondering how I got so lucky. "You got me. Forever."

"Awesome," she said against my mouth. "Now how do you feel about sex in the woods because while I can't even look at a brownie, I get really horny when pregnant."

I pulled back and stared down at her. "You are a literal dream come true."

My baby mama grinned up at me, licking her lips again, suggestively this time. "How about you sit back down on that log, husband-to-be?"

I never sat so quickly in my life. I barely got my zipper down before she had her leggings off and straddled my lap. She took control, wrapping her hand around my cock and guiding me to her opening. She didn't waste a second, just sank right down on me and moaned like she'd been waiting her whole life for me to fill her.

With our foreheads touching and breath mingling in the cold winter morning air, she rode me hard, taking what she needed from me while also taking me along for the ride. When I reached under her sweater to pinch her nipple through her bra, she keened into the quiet air, tipping her head back with the kind of abandon she used to allow herself. Back before life became heavy for her. Then her hands gripped my shoulders so hard her nails surely left dents in my skin and she was squeezing around me, shuddering and shivering.

Her release set off mine, the forest holding our moans and heavy breathing like a happy secret. Keva slumped against my chest and I ignored the sharp scrape of the tree trunk below me. I held her, happy and sated and ecstatic for our future, but my shoulders began to shake with laughter. Keva might have to dig a splinter out of my ass this morning and wasn't that a memorable way to celebrate us getting our life together?

"What's so funny?" Keva gasped, pulling her head off my

shoulder. Her cheeks were bright red and her eyes were still hazy.

Big gulps of laughter escaped me, taking the place of our moans from moments before. "I'm just happy, sweetheart. So damn happy."

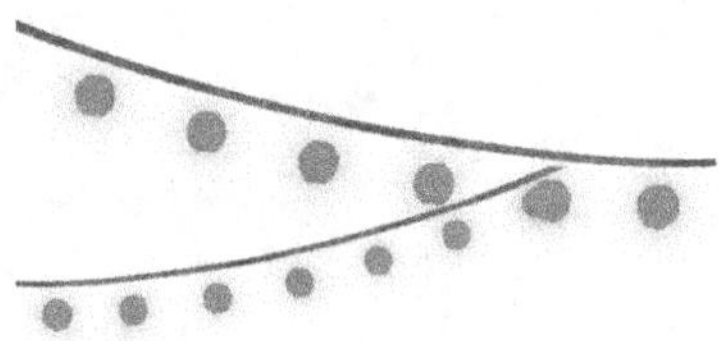

Me: I think that splinter got me good. Hurts to sit down.

Baby Mama x 2: The girls just asked me why my calves are all scraped up.

Me: How about next time we get busy outside, we use blankets and pillows and shit?

Baby Mama x 2: Are you done putting down Lucas?

Me: Just got him to sleep.

Baby Mama x 2: Good. Bring the baby monitor and meet me at your place. I want this trailer rockin' after you come knockin'.

Me: And to think I missed all this last time you were pregnant…

CHAPTER TWENTY-NINE

Keva

"I THINK THIS IS IT."

I turned in a full circle, eyeing the tacky green countertops and the outdated brown carpet. Greenery outside the windows drew my gaze outward and away from what would be a huge project. Glamper's Paradise was only a few miles down the road, easy access for Linc, who was now a full-fledged partner in the business.

Linc came up behind me and put one hand on my shoulder, the other wrapping around my waist to rest his palm on my rapidly growing belly. No one warns you that you start showing way sooner with a second baby. I'd barely told friends and family before everyone in town would have guessed anyway. That and my double-D boobs were a dead giveaway.

"You sure?" Linc nuzzled his face into my neck, making me shiver. "I have no doubt I can make this place beautiful by the time the baby's here, but I want you to love it." He turned me around and looked me in the eye. "I want this to be your home.

Where we can stay for a long while and raise a family. I want our kids to have stability, but I want that for you too. If you want this place, then I'll make it happen."

I smiled, leaning into his chest. There was so much comfort in his touch. I hadn't known what I was missing until I let all my baggage go and trusted him. I'd never been able to fully relax until Lincoln. He was showing me every day and in every way that I could.

"And I want you to love it here. It's not enough for me to want it. I'm done making decisions on my own. It's up to both of us."

Linc leaned down and kissed the tip of my nose. "I don't give a fuck where we live, sweetheart. I could live in a tent with you and be perfectly happy."

I laughed, just envisioning being a mom of two in a damn tent. "Okay, so I know what I said, but a tent's not going to work for me."

"Then let's buy this house and turn it into a home together."

My eyes filled with tears. Damn these pregnancy hormones. I was crying with joy every single day. I even cried the other day with the girls when we were watching a cheesy Christmas movie. Cried at the *commercial*, not even the damn movie. "That sounds perfect."

"This is really touching and all, but if you're going to make an offer, we better do that soon." Audrey interrupted our moment, but she was right. Real estate was hot right now and homes were snatched up fast.

Linc released me enough that I could address my friend and her broker. Audrey had just gotten her real estate license last month and was still shadowing Jason Montaña, Nikki Hellman's new husband. This house was in need of some massive repair and remodel, so the price wasn't as high as most homes in the area, but I hoped it would give Audrey her first commission check.

"We'll take it!"

Audrey squealed and Jason smiled, even as he rolled his eyes.

"We'll be in the kitchen. You kids take your time looking around and we'll get the paperwork rolling."

We went to the primary bedroom first, discussing where we'd put our bed. The view out the window was partially blocked by a huge oak tree, but even so, you could see the rolling green hills beyond that extended all the way to the north of Glamper's Paradise.

"We should put out a squirrel feeder in that tree," Linc said quietly, looking out the same window.

I snorted. "Oh jeez. Gannon's got you talking to the squirrels now too?"

Linc looked offended. "What? They're pretty cute."

I burst out laughing, thinking about these two strong men out there in the woods talking to squirrels in high-pitched voices. Linc growled and picked me up at the waist, pinning me to the wall, right where our headboard would be. My legs went around his hips, still plenty of room even with a growing belly.

I gasped, pretending to be shocked. "Are you about to commit violence against a pregnant woman?"

He growled again, burying his face in my neck and flexing his hips against mine. "I'm about to commit sexual pleasure against a pregnant woman."

I slid my fingers into his hair and practically purred. "I'm definitely okay with that."

Linc groaned, dropping his forehead to mine and squeezing his eyes shut. "Why do you do this to me when we aren't alone?"

I ground my hips against the hard length beneath his jeans. My eyes nearly rolled back in my head. "Pregnancy hormones. Gotta love 'em."

"Guys? We're ready for you to sign on the offer form," Audrey called from somewhere in the house.

Linc groaned again but let me slide down his body until my feet were on the floor. He stood behind me, adjusting the front of his jeans while I snickered. "We're going straight home after this, woman."

"No, we're not! The Christmas Festival is starting." I laughed harder when he continued to groan. "You whine more than Lucas."

"I'm just making up for lost time. We have five years to make up for." Linc slid his arm around my waist and led us out of the room.

I came to an abrupt halt and turned to him, hand on his chest. "Promise me something?"

His eyes were serious, so focused on me at all times. "Anything."

"Promise me when the kids are all grown, you'll get a Harley again and we'll go cruising through Blueball early in the morning, pissing off all the old people. Just like the day we met."

His grin was what I lived for now. "Promise."

We signed our offer papers and Audrey submitted them. She and Jason told us to go to the festival and have fun. They'd call us the minute they heard back from the seller. We swung by the preschool and picked up Lucas first. Today was the last day of school before the Christmas break and the kids were all extra hyper when they got out.

After scoring a parking spot only a few blocks away from downtown, I got Lucas out of the car seat in the back and swung my loaded bag on my shoulder. Linc groaned and I shot him a warning look that ended in a giggle. I wasn't going to be walking around a festival all day without all the items in my bag. Who knew if someone would need a Band-Aid, or an antacid, or a button sewed back on?

Linc hefted Lucas up on his shoulders, a move that made our little boy insanely happy. Linc grabbed my hand and off we went to the festival. It wasn't long before Lucas was begging to get down. All the friends he'd made at preschool were here, racing from one vendor to another before coming back to the petting zoo. His hands were stained rainbow color from the ice cream cart You Got Served had at the festival. I winced as my feet began to ache from all the walking around. My ankles needed almost no provocation to start swelling these days.

"Okay, that's it. Have a seat. I've got him." Linc nearly pushed me down on one of the wood benches outside the fence to the Christmas goats. I wasn't sure how Christmas goats were different than regular goats, but I was happy to finally sit. Linc kissed the top of my head and left in a hurry to run after our son.

"Want a sip?"

I turned to see Muriel sitting on the other side of the bench, a twinkle in her eye and a silver flask held out in my direction.

"Oh, no, thank you." I rubbed my belly. "Got another one coming."

Her face lit up as she tucked the flask away again. "Oh! That's right! I heard about that. Congratulations. I don't blame you. Procreating with that hot piece was definitely the right move."

I bit back a smile. Muriel always said whatever she was thinking. "Definitely."

Hattie, the town librarian, came over. "Just the person I wanted to see." She sat between us, wedging herself in and thankfully shutting down further conversation about procreating. "I wanted to see if you would think about making a Little Free Library at Glamper's Paradise. I could supply you with some of our overstock books?"

I nodded. "That's a great idea. I'm sure I can get Linc to build a little box for it."

My phone vibrated and I fished it out of my bag to see a text from my brother. I put my phone back without looking at the text.

"Awesome! I asked Gannon already and he said to 'put it on the list' which didn't sound like it was ever going to happen. I just think with you all having babies and all the kids that come to glamp for vacation, we should have books available, you know?"

I patted Hattie's knee. "It's a great idea. I'll see if Linc can work on that before the baby's here."

"Time for pampering!" Paisley hollered, pushing her big belly through the crowd, Marlo and Audrey at her side.

I grinned, always happy to see my best friends. "What are you talking about?"

Audrey rushed forward and tugged me off the bench. "Sorry, ladies, but we need to steal Keva. She has an appointment with Andrea Lucky."

"I do?" Andrea owned Lucky Hands, the massage therapy place in town. "Shouldn't Paisley have an appointment? She's the one due any day now."

Marlo flapped her hands, like we were wasting time. "She does. You're right after her. Back and feet massages for you both. Now let's march."

Paisley and I linked elbows and walked to our appointments at the tent at the far end of the festival. I squeezed her tighter, heart nearly bursting with happiness. The first time I was pregnant had felt so lonely. This time was the complete opposite. "I can't tell you how glad I am to be pregnant with my best friend this time around."

Paisley shot me a grin, looking happy and content in her new role as mother and wife. "And I can't tell you how glad I am to see you pregnant with Lincoln by your side this time."

Tears burned my eyes. "Shh, or my eyes will leak."

Paisley laughed and I cried. As usual. But damn, did that massage feel like heaven. When Linc found me with a tired Lucas in his arms an hour later, I could barely walk back to the car. My legs were rubbery and my back felt better than it had since I was a teenager. Linc laughed at me while he handled getting Lucas in his car seat and driving us home.

"I like the look of relaxation on you," he said quietly, taking the curves in the road back to our trailer.

My phone vibrated again. When I didn't reach for it, Linc lifted an eyebrow. "Everything okay?"

I sighed, some of that relaxation seeping away. "Yeah, it's probably just Boston. He's been texting me a lot since Thanksgiving."

Linc nodded, looking out the windshield. The moonlight highlighted the way he clenched his jaw. "Yeah, he's been texting me too, but I keep telling him he has to clear things with you first."

"I don't want you to feel like you can't talk to your best friend."

Linc gave his head a shake. "I know, but you and Lucas and the baby come first. He needs to make things right with you and I can't do that for him."

I sighed. "I know. And I should probably answer his texts at some point. Everything's been so good, I just didn't want to jinx it."

Linc reached over and held my hand. "You don't have to talk to him. In fact, you never have to forgive him if you don't want."

I wrinkled my nose. "Ugh. That sounds like a petty Betty."

Linc chuckled. "Petty Betty, huh?"

"I'll call him tomorrow," I stated firmly, making the decision. "I don't want to raise another baby with strained family relationships."

"Proud of you." Linc squeezed my hand.

I swiveled my head to see Lucas already asleep in his car seat. Turning back to Linc, I waggled my eyebrows. "Wanna show me how proud you are of me tonight once we put Lucas down?"

Linc fought a smile. "Damn, woman. These pregnancy hormones are my new favorite thing."

"Less talking, more action, Sergeant," I shot back.

Linc snorted and shook his head while I shook with silent laughter.

Who would have thought I'd be pregnant again and feeling like life was one big, fun adventure?

EPILOGUE

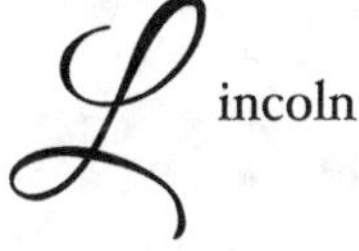incoln

"Thanks, man."

I took the animal from the man's arms and quietly let myself back into our house just as the sun rose in the sky. The floor still creaked but the wood was re-stained and glossy now. Most of the house had been redone since moving in, each project making me curse under my breath but also filling me with pride when I learned a new skill. Gannon came over quite a bit to help me. Boston too, once he and Keva settled things between them. It was nice to have my best friend back.

I crept into our bedroom, scratching the little girl's head. She blinked up at me like she remembered me, but I was probably imagining it. I looked down at Keva, sleeping peacefully on her side with an array of pillows around her. Each month of her pregnancy, new pillows somehow made it into our bed. If it kept her growing belly and aching back comfortable, I'd move onto the couch to give her room for a whole mountain of pillows.

"Hey, sweetheart," I whispered, reaching out to run my fingers through her hair.

She'd been growing it out, a change I wholeheartedly agreed with. I was a sick enough bastard to love how longer hair gave me more to wrap around my fist when we made love. Keva didn't seem to mind either. Once the morning sickness let up, the woman had been insatiable. Pretty sure I'd formed calluses on my dick for how many times she dragged me into the bathroom and locked the door with a wicked gleam in her eyes.

Keva briefly opened her eyes and then she groaned, rolling onto her back like she wanted to go back to sleep. "Is it time?"

"Not yet." Today was our wedding day and I knew she had the girls coming over right after breakfast to help her get ready. "I have your gift though."

Her eyes snapped open. "Gift?"

I shifted the weight under my arm so she could see. Her eyes went wide and then she was flailing her arms to try to sit up. I helped her first and then sat on the edge of the bed next to her, handing her the lump of piglet.

"Is this—?"

I grinned. "Yep. I tracked down Spunky and bought her back."

"Oh my God!" Keva started crying, holding Spunky to her chest. The micro pig squealed and then smashed her snout against her face over and over. "Are you sure she won't miss her family?"

"Her owners were all too happy to accept the money. They had goats and bunnies too. I think they were a little overwhelmed and little Spunky here was getting lost in the mix."

Keva reached over and squeezed my hand. "Thank you, Linc. Best wedding gift ever."

I couldn't help the snort, which Spunky immediately echoed. "Said no one ever...except my beautiful bride."

Keva laughed, standing up with Spunky and dancing her around the room in the little sleep shirt that barely held in her growing breasts. "Wait until Lucas sees you! You're about to be the most spoiled piglet in the whole county!"

I groaned and got busy making breakfast for my family. When Keva's friends came over, I put Spunky in the pen I'd made on the back deck. I made sure she had plenty of food, water, and shade before tossing in a few play toys. Then I kissed my bride and headed over to Gannon's house where the men would get ready.

We were keeping the wedding small. Just a few family and friends in our backyard and then a trip to the courthouse for our date with the judge to change Lucas's last name. By the time I made it back to our house, Lucy and Bain had set up chairs in the back and Shelby, the florist from Auburn Hill, was delivering the flowers. Janice had flown back for a few days to surprise Keva. When she came over last night, I thought Keva might cause some local flooding with all the crying she did.

"Can I have a word?" Lucy grabbed my arm and hauled me to the side by the fence in the backyard I'd fixed just last week. She pinned me with a stare that almost had me standing at attention and saluting. "I was there the day Keva found out she was pregnant with Lucas. I was there when the world fell apart for that girl."

My whole chest wanted to cave in on itself. "Thank you for taking care of her. And him. Before I could."

She smiled then, tears shining in her eyes. "Of course. I'm just glad you're back now. If you leave her again, I'll track your ass down and make you regret the day you took that weapon of destruction out of your pants."

Ice froze my veins. "Yes, ma'am. Love not war."

"Damn right." Then she walked off, stopped, looked over her shoulder and used two fingers to point at her eyeballs and then pointed at me, meaning clear. She was watching my ass and watching Keva's back.

While I didn't like her assumption that I would ever fail my family, I was happy Keva had such strong friends. I was grateful she had a strong community to take care of her and Lucas until I came back. I tugged on my collar and took my place at the front of the chairs. Ken Morgan, the chief of police in this little town and the one who would marry us today, clapped me on the back.

"Ready, son?"

I nodded. "I was ready five years ago, but I think I finally convinced her."

He guffawed. "That's how you know you got a good one. A good woman is hard to pin down."

I would have replied, but at that moment Lucas came running out of the house and bounded down the stairs of the porch. He paused, like he just remembered he wasn't supposed to run. He grinned at me and then he was marching down the aisle, holding out the pillow that contained our wedding bands. He stopped by my side and I crouched down to give him a hug. I was already getting choked up and the ceremony had just begun. Maybe Keva's crying spells were rubbing off on me.

"Well done, son. Come stand by me."

He tucked himself into my side and we turned to watch Keva come out of the house in a white dress gathered above her baby belly. The top was mostly lace, making her look like a delicate angel when I knew she was stronger than most men. Her flat white sandals sunk into the grass, the hem of the dress dusting across her toes. She paused there at the foot of the stairs, inhaling and fixing her gaze on me. My family, along with the friends we'd made here in Blueball, all stood up.

I lost control of my face and attempted a smile that was mostly just trembling of my lips. I'd been lost and only slightly hopeful when I'd zoomed back into Blueball. A little broken and a lot naive. Keva had every reason to hate me forever and yet here she was, walking toward me with a promise in her eyes that brought me to my knees.

She took my hands, the flowers somehow transferred to Paisley while I was lost in a place where only my little family existed. Chief Morgan began the ceremony and I answered when he prompted me, the actual words a jumble in my head. The only thing I heard was Keva repeating "I do." And then I was kissing her, our baby pressed between us and our son whooping it up behind me. I brought her back up to standing and we stood there grinning at each other like lovesick idiots.

Eventually, we remembered to thank our friends and family for coming. My sisters hovered around Keva like they'd just been waiting for yet another sister to join their fold. The entire group split up into various cars, heading over to the courthouse for the second half of today's celebration. Keva would take my last name and now so would Lucas.

When the judge signed off on the paperwork and declared us a family, Keva was already crying and I wasn't far behind her. Lucas threw his healed arm in the air and our family clapped from behind us. There'd been a lot of terrible moments in my adult life that would forever be kept like snapshots in my brain, but today I replaced them with good ones. Snapshots of time that would be at the forefront of my memories, a story to tell my grandkids, and reasons why I loved this woman. Keva had provided everything I'd ever wanted, shouldering the responsibilities of our family until I could come back to her. I'd be forever grateful to the woman who'd accosted me on my scooter, carrying around sperm and a piglet, letting me into her heart and her body that day. That hadn't been our time, but it was now.

And it would be forever.

"Um, guys?" Paisley said loudly. Her voice echoed off the hallway of the courthouse as we all piled outside. "My water just broke."

Everyone spoke at once. While Gannon swung Paisley up in his arms, Keva grabbed Elise. As a very loud unit, we all piled back in our cars to head for the hospital.

Keva held my hand while the two kids chattered in the back seat. She was still in her wedding dress and prettier than any woman I'd ever seen.

"Well, this wasn't how I saw our wedding day panning out," she drawled.

I squeezed her hand and kept my eyes on the road the most I could with her beauty distracting me. "I promised to rip that wedding dress off you first chance I got. Think they have a private bathroom in the hospital waiting room we could visit?"

Keva tossed her head back and laughed. "They better, Sergeant. I'm not wearing any panties."

ALSO BY MARIKA RAY

<u>Steamy RomComs - Blueball Band of Brothers:</u>

Grumpy the Bear - Blueball Band of Brothers #1

S'more Than a Feeling - Blueball Band of Brothers #2

***

<u>All Steamy RomComs Set in Hell:</u>

Grumpy As Hell - Hellman Brothers #1

Bro Code Hell - Hellman Brothers #2

Friend Zone Hell - Hellman Brothers #3

Cougar From Hell - Hellman Brothers #4

Falling First Hell - Hellman Brothers #5

***

Ridin' Solo - Sisters From Hell #1

One Night Bride - Sisters From Hell #2

Smarty Pants - Sisters From Hell #3

Ex Best Thing - Sisters From Hell #4

***

Love Bank - Jobs From Hell #1

Uber Bossy - Jobs From Hell #2

Unfriend Me - Jobs From Hell #3

Side Hustle - Jobs From Hell #4

Man Glitter - Jobs From Hell Novella - Grab it FREE here!

***

Backroom Boy - Standalone

<u>Steamy RomComs:</u>

The Missing Ingredient - Reality of Love #1

Mom-Com - Reality of Love #2

Desperately Seeking Househusbands - Reality of Love #3

***

Happy New You - Standalone

Steamy RomComs with Delancey Stewart:

The Spare and the Single Mom

Sweet RomComs with Delancey Stewart:

Texting With the Enemy - Digital Dating #1

While You Were Texting - Digital Dating #2

Save the Last Text - Digital Dating #3

How to Lose a Girl in 10 Texts - Digital Dating #4

Sweet Romances:

The Marriage Sham - Standalone

***

The Widower's Girlfriend-Faking It #1

Home Run Fiancé - Faking It #2

Guarding the Princess - Faking It #3

***

Lines We Cross - Nickel Bay Brothers #1

Perfectly Imperfect Us - Nickel Bay Brothers #2

Steamy Beach Romance:

1) Sweet Dreams - Beach Squad #1

2) Love on the Defense - Beach Squad #2

3) Barefoot Chaos - Beach Squad #3

* Novella - Handcuffed Hussy

4) Beach Babe Billionaire- Beach Squad #4

5) Brighter Than the Boss - Beach Squad #5

* Novella - Christmas Eve Do-Over

ABOUT THE AUTHOR

Marika Ray is a USA Today bestselling author, writing small town RomCom to make your heart explode and bring a smile to your face. All her books come with a money-back guarantee that you'll laugh at least once with every book.

Marika spends her time behind a computer crafting stories, walking along the beach, and making healthy food for her kids and husband whether they like it or not. Prior to writing novels, Marika held various jobs in the finance industry, with private start-up companies, and then in health & fitness. Cats may have nine lives, but Marika believes everyone should have nine careers to keep things spicy.

If you'd like to know more about Marika or the other novels she's currently writing, please find her in her private <u>Reader Group</u>.

If you want to take your stalking to the next level, here are other legal-ish places you can find Marika:

Join her Newsletter -
http://bit.ly/MarikaRayNews

Amazon - https://www.amazon.com/author/marikaray

Goodreads - https://www.goodreads.com/author/show/16856659.Marika_Ray

Bookbub - https://www.bookbub.com/authors/marika-ray

TikTok - https://vm.tiktok.com/ZMJvnQ2Cv